HER SECRET SONG

Books by Mary Connealy

From Bethany House Publishers

THE KINCAID BRIDES

Out of Control

In Too Deep

Over the Edge

TROUBLE IN TEXAS

Swept Away

Fired Up

Stuck Together

WILD AT HEART

Tried and True

Now and Forever

Fire and Ice

THE CIMARRON LEGACY

No Way Up

Long Time Gone

Too Far Down

HIGH SIERRA SWEETHEARTS

The Accidental Guardian

The Reluctant Warrior

The Unexpected Champion

BRIDES OF HOPE MOUNTAIN

Aiming for Love

Woman of Sunlight

Her Secret Song

*The Boden Birthright:
A CIMARRON LEGACY Novella*

*Meeting Her Match: A MATCH
MADE IN TEXAS Novella*

*Runaway Bride: A KINCAID
BRIDES and TROUBLE IN TEXAS
Novella (WITH THIS RING?
Collection)*

*The Tangled Ties That Bind:
A KINCAID BRIDES Novella
(HEARTS ENTWINED Collection)*

HER
SECRET
SONG

MARY CONNEALY

BETHANY HOUSE
a division of Baker Publishing Group
Minneapolis, Minnesota

© 2020 by Mary Connealy

Published by Bethany House Publishers
11400 Hampshire Avenue South
Bloomington, Minnesota 55438
www.bethanyhouse.com

Bethany House Publishers is a division of
Baker Publishing Group, Grand Rapids, Michigan

Printed in the United States of America

ISBN 978-0-7642-3260-2 (trade paper)
ISBN 978-0-7642-3778-2 (casebound)

Scripture quotations are from the King James Version of the Bible.

This is a work of fiction. Names, characters, incidents, and dialogues are products
of the author's imagination and are not to be construed as real. Any resemblance
to actual events or persons, living or dead, is entirely coincidental.

Cover design by Dan Thornberg, Design Source Creative Services

Author is represented by the Natasha Kern Literary Agency.

20   21   22   23   24   25   26   7   6   5   4   3   2   1

Her Secret Song is dedicated
to my new granddaughter, Adrian Isabelle.
A wonderful, joyful addition to our lives
in a year where the world
has had so much hardship and sickness.

I love you, Adrian, welcome to the family.
Born in 2020, may you always have 2020 vision.

1

March 1874
Hope Mountain
Near Bucksnort, Colorado, Near Grizzly Peak, Colorado

Wax Mosby was living a life that was going to kill him. Probably shot in the back by one of the men he worked with.

If he wanted to live, he had to get away from here, and his time was running out.

But before he could leave, he had to go up.

His honor demanded he face the Wardens. And his gut told him they were at the top of the mountain.

He'd put off the treacherous climb all winter. You could hardly tell it by the remaining snowdrifts, and he'd lost track of what day it was, but the hours of daylight and dark were nearly even. It had to be almost spring.

If he put off his climb any longer, riders would finally get through the snow-packed trail from Bludgeon Pike's ranch. Wax didn't want to be around when they got here.

He had to find Quill Warden—hopefully alive—and learn the truth about Pike's land grab.

He hiked toward the base of the mountain, the snow getting deeper and the trail getting steeper with each step. Looking up, he knew he'd only just begun.

Foolish idea climbing up there. What in the world was he doing?

Finding the Wardens, that was what. And he'd do it, and today was as good a day as he'd get unless he waited until warm weather fully arrived. Wax planned to be long gone by then.

Come fully warm weather, the Wardens, a tough family with some salty cowhands, would pour down off that mountaintop, guns blazing.

And Pike's hands would come pouring onto this ranch, guns blazing.

And here would stand Wax Mosby, who intended to never draw his gun again. He'd be right smack in the middle of a gun battle, with no plans to kill honest folks like the Wardens, no desire to kill evil men like Pike's, and no wish to die.

When the path grew too steep, he had to use tree trunks to grip and drag himself upward. The way got harder. The trees grew straight up, right alongside the mountain slope. Finally, breathing hard, and nearly halfway up the mountain, he realized he was getting close to the ledge where he'd seen the avenging angel.

Last fall, after the Wardens had been run off, Wax had been *with* the man who'd shot a fleeing Quill Warden. Wax had diverted his saddle partner long enough for Quill to get away. But Wax had no way of knowing how badly hurt Quill was. He stuck to his horse, so Wax hoped the man had survived the ugly bullet shot at him from behind by that coward gunman hired by Pike, Smiling Bob.

A few days after the shooting, Wax, along with Smiling Bob and Canada Phelps, had come to look around the cabin. Wax, being an uncommonly watchful man, spotted a man sitting on the ledge Wax was right now climbing for.

To Wax's mind, God had perched an angel up there. Even now, a chill ran up and down Wax's spine that had nothing to do with the cold wind.

That angel had looked down on Wax and judged him for an unrepentant sinner. And that had set Wax on a path to redemption. When Pike had sent Wax over here to live for the winter, he'd spent his time figuring out he had to change his life. No more hiring out his gun. He'd be a different man when he got out of here in the spring.

But first, the Wardens had to be found. Wax felt as if it were a charge straight from God. He had to talk to them before the shooting started. But the mountain still waited between them.

He moved fast, clinging to narrow hand and toe holds, intent on reaching that ledge. He was still a few feet away when he heard hoofbeats below.

Turning, his hold on the mountain unsure, he studied the trails around the ranch yard and saw five riders. Mean looking. Polished looking. No one Wax had seen before, which meant not Bludge Pike's men.

Probably.

The men spread out in a wide circle around the house. They dismounted at the same moment, with the same graceful, economical movements, as if they were five bodies controlled by one mind.

They drew their guns and moved slowly, silently, toward the house.

Come for the Wardens, or come for Wax?

He might have more than his share of enemies, but the ranch was where someone would come if they were hunting the Wardens. They hadn't spread it around town about abandoning their ranch for the top of the mountain.

Wax wasn't about to hike down there and have a visit with this tough-looking crew.

The men riding with him the day he'd seen the avenging angel hadn't noticed a man perched up here. People didn't tend to look up.

But one of the five did.

No shout of warning or greeting. No questions asked. The first man pivoted toward the rock wall and opened fire. Then another did, then all five. It was a terrible angle, shooting so far up. And these men had pistols, which were notoriously hard to aim at this distance.

Wax just stayed still and let them waste their lead.

Then one of the men grabbed his rifle out of the scabbard on his saddle; the rest followed suit. The bullets got closer. Rocks shattered and slit Wax's skin. Another shot broke rocks under his hands. Wax lost his grip and started sliding down, picking up speed. A bullet struck—or something sure did—and his slide turned into plummeting as flying lead sang around him.

This was his end. He'd needed to ride off, change his life, change his name, change his soul. But he'd waited too long.

Hurtling through the air, he dropped into the trees. He hit a tree branch and a shout of pain escaped him. Then he clamped his mouth shut and dropped out of sight of those killers. He landed hard against the trunk of a tree and was pinned between the tree and the mountain . . . and he heard laughter. Cruel, ugly laughter.

One of the men shouted, "That wasn't even him. I know what Pierce looks like. But a little target practice doesn't hurt."

There was laughter and horses walking. Men walking, talking. It took Wax a while to realize they weren't coming to make sure he was dead. They were uninterested in the man they'd just shot to rags.

Wax lay there, feeling the life draining out of him, bleeding and broken. But he stubbornly refused to die. He wasn't sure how long he was pinned there. He might've blacked out for a time, but he couldn't see the sun or judge minutes or hours from his position.

Finally, with terrible pain gnawing his legs—especially his left one—and his back, his head, his side, his arms, and just plain everywhere, he moved. He only moved his head enough to see through the treetops that the five men, saddlebags and bedrolls in hand, were heading into the cabin.

Maybe they'd decided to stay and wait for whoever Pierce was, or just hole up in an abandoned cabin now that the man living in it was dead.

He couldn't go down, and for a long time, he couldn't go up.

Then he found the guts to try.

One arm moved well. The other worked, but it was

murderously painful to use it. His left leg might be broken. It felt like a wolf had sunk its fangs in deep. It was hard to tell if he'd been shot or if he'd landed so hard it just felt like a bullet wound.

He fumbled beneath his heavy coat, drew his knife out of a scabbard he wore across his chest, then cut strips from his shirt. With miserable slowness, he found wounds and did his best to staunch the blood. It seemed that the blood had finally quit flowing, or maybe he was just running out of it.

Lying sideways, caught by a tree trunk at the waist, and wedged against the cliff, he righted himself. His stomach twisted and heaved as he raised his head. His vision narrowed, and a throb like the beat of a drum banged behind his eyes. But it was quit and die, or take the pain with him when he moved. It made him mad to think of those men, now in that comfortable house while he lay here.

They'd *laughed*. They knew they'd shot the wrong man, and instead of trying to find him, trying to make right a terrible wrong, they'd laughed and gone in where it was warm.

Wax Mosby was no quitter. And he wasn't going to die without a fight.

He wanted to live just so he could go down there and kill every man jack of them.

That thought, that powerful, ugly thought, stopped him.

Was that a reason to live? Was that the goal a man wanted to set, when his life hung by a thread?

No.

No, by all the saints, no.

A real man would act differently when he faced insurmountable odds and terrible pain.

A real man would pray.

Gathering every ounce of the knowledge of his sinful life in hand, he gave it all to God. He begged forgiveness.

More important, he accepted that forgiveness, and he believed.

2

S tay up here and lose her mind. Go down and die.

The devil's own choice.

Ursula Nordegren was either finding a deep well of faith and drawing on it with all her might, or committing a terrible sin.

The fact that she wasn't sure tormented her.

Stay up and go mad. Go down and die.

In her head, she'd been back and forth about this for two months. And always, whatever her thoughts were, she sang. She searched for peace, wisdom, and happiness in her songs. She'd done this all her life.

These days her songs were mournful.

At first, when the trail to the north snowed shut, she'd been relieved. And yes, it was frightening to be so alone, so cut off. But she deserved it after abandoning Ilsa. Her littlest sister had gotten sick, was maybe dying, and Ursula ran.

Ilsa had survived, then up and married Mitch Warden. The two of them had gone down the mountain and not come back.

Josephine had come, though, with her new husband, Dave Warden, Mitch's little brother. Jo had brought supplies, and Dave had chopped wood and done repairs on this strange stone house Ursula had found in the high mountain valley. They'd begged her to abandon this ancient place and live with them for the winter. To give up her reclusive life.

But Ursula was so frightened of Dave and his family and his cowhands. The lowlands were full of disease and violence and death. Grandma had said it a thousand times. Grandpa ten thousand. Go to the lowlands and die.

Ursula had rejected all Jo's pleading. Then the high narrow trail between here and where Jo was closed up tight.

For a time, it had felt safe to be cut off up here, but slowly as the months wore on and the bitter cold seeped in, the absolute loneliness had eaten away at her until she felt like she teetered on the edge of madness.

Ursula ran her hand over the small hatchet Jo and Dave had left for her. Dave said it was for splitting kindling, though he'd done the splitting for her and left a mountain of firewood.

At first, she'd ignored the hatchet, not wanting to use anything from the Wardens. Then she realized they wouldn't know if she used it, and if they did find out, they wouldn't care. Frankly, she was so bored nothing mattered much anymore. Not even those invading Wardens who'd gone and married both of her little sisters.

She started throwing the hatchet first just to occupy her idle hands. But as the winter stretched long, she learned to throw it straight and hard with a growing fierceness.

Jo had her bow and arrow. Ilsa was fast with her knife.

Ursula could hit what she aimed at with a bow, but she wasn't nearly as skilled as Jo. And she was handy with a knife. She could skin a rabbit with a few swift, sure strokes and hit a tree dead center. But both her sisters were better than Ursula with their weapons.

Now Ursula had one of her own.

The hatchet had a small ax-head, maybe five inches long and four wide, with a blade that she sharpened until it could split a hair. The handle was just a bit longer than the head and slipped easily into a leather belt she'd made specifically to hold it. It made her feel safe and strong to go around with her handy ax, and soon she never went anywhere without it.

She spent hours flinging it at the same tree she used to aim her arrows. She mostly practiced overhand, which seemed best. But she alternated throwing underhand, too. She practiced slipping it out of her belt quickly. Turning and throwing in a single motion. She stood close up, then stepped far away. If she needed to hunt, she needed to be as swift as the wild creatures, and if she needed to fight, she wanted to be ready.

Reading, singing, walking, and throwing her hatchet filled her days, but still the silence closed in and echoed in her head, her heart, her soul.

So she continued to practice, often for so long the cold finally drove her inside. And by the time the winter weather began to fade, she had a true talent. She didn't count singing in this case, since that wouldn't put food on the table.

Still the winter wouldn't end. Still she was alone, and the day finally came when even hours of hatchet throwing weren't enough. She began to think constantly of the other way down. A treacherous cliff, but it could be scaled. Mitch had come up that cliff to find his family after the regular trail to the lowlands snowed shut.

She had to go down that cliff or lose her mind. Those honestly seemed like her only choices.

She'd spent weeks considering she might climb down, but a renewed cold snap gave her a good excuse not to go. Then the weather had turned mild enough to have melted the snow that would be clinging to the sides of the cliff. She'd packed supplies and walked every day to the place Mitch had climbed up.

She had been tempted and frightened, lured and repelled. She'd stand up there, staring down, tormented with the longing to hear someone else's voice.

But each time, she'd hear Grandma and Grandpa's dire warnings and turn away in fear.

But today she had to do it. She had to go down.

She'd come prepared as always, with a satchel of food and a canteen full of water. Her bow and quiver were strapped on. She carried a wickedly sharp knife and knew how to use it. And, of course, her hatchet.

She stood for a long stretch of time at the top. She could see for miles. It was beautiful. That was part of the lure. Hints of spring were coming at the bottom of Hope Mountain. The trees that climbed halfway up the cliff were starting to bud, and patches of lush green grass were peeking through the snow. And best of all, she heard birds singing. They did that up here, too, but not spring birds. Not robins and larks. Not yet. But down below, they were nesting and thriving.

Today it was impossible to turn away. She wanted to see it, be part of it, to make her move, climb over the edge, and force herself to climb down. Each step was a victory over fear—or was it a step into perdition?

Move one foot. Move one hand.

She prayed and she feared. She goaded herself and hated herself.

Jo and Ilsa had chosen to risk death rather than remain isolated. Her little sisters had reached out to strangers and found gunshot wounds and sickness. But they hadn't turned their back on that danger. Instead, they'd faced it and then tried to draw Ursula into it with them.

And she'd left them. Even still, Jo and Dave had come and brought food and other supplies. They'd worked hard to make the ancient relic of a home livable for Ursula. Cut wood, built a sturdy door, and brought warm clothes, books, and a goodly amount of food.

The books had shocked her because only recently had all the Nordegren girls realized they didn't know how to read. Ursula thought she had been reading all her life. But only since the Warden family had come up the mountain had she realized she only repeated words she had memorized. They only had two books. The Bibles. And Ursula had known both of them by heart. Well, except for some stretches of the bigger Bible Grandma had told them to skip.

Now Ursula wanted to read both Bibles for herself, for real. Jo had brought her a McGuffey Reader and spent time teaching her the basics, but the visits had stopped when the snow had made the trail in impassable. And so Ursula spent the winter alone. Until today.

Today she was climbing down this mountain. Down. Down to death. Or maybe down to life.

Was God whispering in her ear to find the courage to stop cutting herself off? Or was it Satan tempting her to enter a sinful world?

Was climbing down an act of faith or a terrible sin?

Her thoughts circled and twisted. She steadied herself against the cold rock of the cliffside and took a moment to be glad she wore her leather britches and hadn't succumbed to the lowland temptation of wearing the dress Dave's ma had given her. The britches made climbing possible. She'd take one more step, just one more.

She took it. Then another.

Her steps led her downward, perhaps to eternal fire.

And then she came upon someone who was worse off than a woman climbing down into hell.

Wax was dead.

He'd been shot.

He'd fallen a long way off a mountain. He was battered and bleeding and broken. But through the agony, he'd gathered himself enough to realize that none of it had killed him.

Shifting between the tree trunk and the cliff, Wax bound the rest of his wounds. And because he couldn't go down—that's where the men who'd shot at him were— he climbed up. It was a terrible climb even when a man was feeling well. Wax was a long way from well. He had reached a ledge wide enough to lie down on and let himself rest when a shadow passed over him.

And that's when he knew he was, in fact, dead.

He smelled his own blood. He heard his breath going in and out. Which made it seem like he was alive—but he must be dead. That was the only possible answer to why he was seeing an angel.

She fluttered down beside him, then gasped and knelt beside his sprawled body and took his hand.

An angel with long white hair that curled and bounced in the mountain breeze. She wore a black woolen bonnet but still the curls escaped.

It struck him that angels shouldn't need warm bonnets. They shouldn't be bothered by the cold. But who knew more about what angels needed than God?

She had blue eyes that looked on him as if she cared. She crouched there on the mountainside and brushed back his hair. It was as if she floated. How else had she gotten up here . . . or down here?

Surely, she came from up.

He'd died, and he realized with a lifted heart that she'd come to take him to heaven. Surely God didn't send angels when a man wasn't going to be taken through the pearly gates.

Quite a different type showed up in that case.

But here was an angel, and Wax felt a blissful joy. Before today, he'd feared his afterlife because he hadn't lived a life that would earn a man heaven. Now here he was— dead—with proof that faith, belief, was enough.

Except . . .

Did angels wear britches?

That gave him pause.

He lifted his head from where it lay on the cold stone.

He must have been dead awhile because the sun was setting and the ugliness of being shot had happened early in the day. Or maybe it was yesterday, and it had taken him that long to die.

Except . . .

Did the sun set in heaven?

"Can I help you? Can you move? I can't carry you."

And shouldn't an angel, even a slender angel, be able to carry anyone?

Wax really needed to read his Bible more carefully because this britches-wearing angel who made a man carry his own weight, well, that wasn't from any part he remembered.

Of course, it *had* been a while.

"It's too far to go down the mountain and find shelter like this." The angel had a beautiful voice. Like music. Yes, surely he was in heaven.

He raised his head again, and the pain almost knocked him over. Heaven shouldn't be this painful.

"But if you can help me, I'll take you to my home." The angel pulled a canteen out of a bag she wore slung over her neck and under one arm. She opened it and helped him sit up.

He sipped, and the cold, wet drink bathed his deadly dry throat. He took a long pull, then another.

She withdrew the canteen, and he grabbed at it. He needed to drink it all down to soothe the bone-dry insides of his mouth and throat.

"Have more then, but we've got a bit of a climb. We don't want to drain all our water."

He drank deeply. Then he realized he was trying to gulp it all down in fear she'd take it away.

An angel wouldn't do a thing like that.

Releasing the canteen, through blurred vision, he saw blood and dirt under his torn fingernails. His shirtsleeve was covered in blood dried black. How long ago had he been shot?

"Will you heal my wounds, or does God do that?"

He realized that was the first time he'd spoken. If he said the wrong thing, was there still time for God to change His mind?

The angel arched a brow and tilted her head. She looked like she might wonder if he was really meant to make it into heaven. That wasn't very nice. If God sent her, she shouldn't question it.

"Can you move?"

Proving it could cost him, but if an angel asked you to move, you moved.

"Let's get you to the top. I wanted to go back anyway."

"Well, of course you did. Who wants to leave heaven?"

Another arched brow, her head tilted a bit further. "Um . . . I can see why I was compelled to come down. God wanted me to find you and save you."

"Sounds like something an angel would say." His throat barely worked. He wanted more water.

Then as he fully sat up, his stomach twisted, and for a few seconds, he fought the need to cast up everything in his belly.

He won the battle, but possibly only because his throat was too dry to work properly.

23

He concentrated on hanging on tight to the angel. They moved.

It was agony.

After all Wax had heard about how nice it was after death—if things went well—God had some explaining to do.

3

Ursula was so glad she had a reason to climb back up that she didn't even mind the dirty, bleeding, heavy man. Much.

God had sent her down. God had sent her to save someone's life.

Her heart soared. In fact, it felt so light, so full, she was surprised it didn't just lift her right up to the mountaintop.

Unfortunately, she still had to climb. But finding the man gave her ridiculous joy.

"What is that song?"

Startled, she looked at the man. His face was so bruised and covered with scratches and blood, she couldn't even guess what he looked like. He had a strange almost pointy beard and a droopy moustache. His blue eyes were dazed, and the swelling was so bad she could barely see the color. She wondered at his ability to speak.

And yet he'd asked her about the singing.

Smiling, she said, "I'm sorry. I didn't even realize I was doing it. I live alone on the mountaintop, and I find myself singing."

"Talk . . . helps me keep going."

"Um . . ." Ursula had been alone all winter. Hadn't talked to anyone in months. On the other hand, he wasn't likely to complain if she had little of interest to say. And that made her realize she had plenty to say. But just plain talking to a stranger? It didn't come easy. She hesitated, then forged on. "The song is one I made up. I think of Bible verses, and they come to me with music. The story of the 'Good Samaritan' swept through me when I found you and began to help you. And my thoughts became a song."

A certain man went down from Jerusalem to Jericho, and fell among thieves, which stripped him of his raiment, and wounded him, and departed, leaving him half dead.

Ursula's voice flowed over him like soothing balm.

"That does sound like me," Wax said, gathering the strength to take a step up. "You have the v-voice of . . . of an angel. But of course you do."

He moved both hands. His poor battered face contorted in pain. She saw the blood under his broken fingernails. A gasp of pain escaped as he raised one arm to reach up. When she saw his back, she swallowed hard, shocked by the large circle of dried blood. He had torn a strip off the bottom of his shirt to cover a wound low on his side. Whatever he'd hit there had hurt him, and he'd bled heavily.

There was another large circle of dried blood near his collar. He'd pressed a thick bandage there and secured it with his neckerchief. One pant leg was black from bleeding and a bandage wrapped there just below his knee. Besides that, he was battered and cut up in so many places, his face perhaps worst of all, that she couldn't begin to count all his injuries.

For all that, he kept moving. She wondered at the core of pure stone that could hold together at such a beating.

"Keep singing please." Then he clamped his mouth shut, and no more sounds escaped. The man grasped a ledge, then pushed up with his feet and knees.

How could she deny such a strong man a simple request, especially when singing came almost without thought to her. To *stop* singing was the difficult part.

She continued to set the "Good Samaritan" to music. As he climbed, she found words of encouragement from Scripture that turned into song. The Scripture she had stored in her memory, but the music came as if given to her by God himself.

The injured man used one arm well, but the other seemed too stiff to move. When he crawled forward up the steep slope, she saw his bleeding leg had swelled enough that she wondered if his boot might cut off the circulation.

A broken leg maybe or a terrible sprain. Grandpa had sprained his ankle once when Ilsa was just barely old enough to help care for him, and Ursula had done a lot of the tending. He'd been laid up awhile, which reminded Ursula of a cane. This man might need one. Maybe once they reached the top, she'd hunt for a bit in the forest near where they'd climb and use her hatchet to build a cane.

The next time he stopped to rest she said, "I want to loosen this bandage on your knee. I'm afraid it's so tight it might make the injury to your leg worse. When Grandpa sprained his ankle, he said not to wrap it too tight."

"Do as you think best." The words were faint, as if he had no energy for more.

"Do you think your leg is broken?"

"I think I was hit with a—" The man coughed, and the effort of that exhausted him until she couldn't bear to question him more. When the coughing fit ended, he lay flat on his face on the mountainside. She'd picked a spot that wasn't quite straight up and down so he could rest.

He turned his head so his eyes met hers. There was something there. Ursula didn't know just what—a sadness maybe? Something hard, something more than just the pain he was in and the brutal strain of this climb. As if he carried a weight beyond himself.

She loosened the bandage, looked at the odd slit in his skin just above his boot. It created an ugly furrow that had mostly stopped bleeding due to the tight bandage. It didn't start up bleeding fast again, but it oozed blood slowly. He must've fallen. One of the branches or maybe a jagged rock left this gash.

She wished she hadn't undone the bandage. It might have been better to leave it. She bound it again, only a bit less tight.

"Have another drink."

He rolled to his side with a stifled groan and managed to lean against a boulder so he could take a drink.

He gulped down water as if he was desperately thirsty. She let him have all he wanted because she knew where a spring was at the top of this mountain.

"Can you go again?" She had no idea what she'd do if he said no.

The briefest of wordless nods told her he was saving every ounce of his strength for the climb.

He inched on, dragging himself on his belly when the mountain was too steep, sometimes on his hands and knees when a slope allowed. Every inch of progress he made seemed to use the last of his strength. Then he found more.

For a stretch, the climbing got very rugged, nearly vertical. A section she'd climbed down with caution became a nightmare with his wounds.

A sudden tremor from his hands loosened his grip. She grabbed his arm and pressed it against the inch-wide ledge he held. Then she started sliding. Ursula whipped out her hatchet and rammed it into a narrow cleft in the rock, right above her head. She stopped sliding, but he didn't.

"Hang on! Hang on! Find a handhold," Ursula shouted as, for a stomach-twisting moment, the only thing that held him from falling to his death was her meager strength. She couldn't hold him for long.

With a roar like a furious animal, he clawed with his almost useless left hand and stopped himself. They held the position. Both breathing hard. Ursula fighting panic, thinking of the treacherous climb yet to come.

Finally, he said, "You saved me. Again. You and your incredible strength and that hatchet."

"It does come in handy." She managed a smile as her fear eased. "Let's go on."

He nodded wordlessly. After long minutes, they got past the worst of the climb.

Pain etched his face. But he kept moving. He glanced

at her and said, "I suppose the saying had to come from somewhere."

"What saying?" She only realized she was singing when she stopped.

The man was delirious. He muttered, "The voice of an angel."

She thought of her little sister Ilsa's doctoring skills. Grandpa had called her his little medicine woman. He'd called Jo his little huntress. He hadn't had a name like that for Ursula, but he had liked her singing.

Well, Little Medicine Woman Ilsa was far away. She'd spent the winter in the lowlands. Jo had said Ilsa and Mitch might have gone to New York City. She also said it took a long half a day to ride to Bucksnort, the nearest town, which had one hundred people—too many to fathom. And New York City was farther away and even bigger.

Mitch claimed New York City had nearly a million people. And apparently that was a lot more than one hundred.

Grandma had only taught them to count to one hundred. It seemed unlikely they'd ever have more than one hundred of anything, so Grandma thought going higher was a waste of time.

A groan from the man broke her thoughts free. The man needed her. She hadn't the strength to carry him up a mountainside, but she should pay attention and help any way she could.

God had sent her to save him, so God would give her the strength. Ursula caught his hand and brought it to a solid place. When he pulled forward, she guided his foot to a small rough ledge.

He needed more help with every passing moment. She

couldn't lift him, but she could add her strength to his, and that was enough to keep them going.

"Talk to me, please. Or sing."

She sang again, and they inched onward. When he collapsed, she let him rest, sitting beside him, and while he gathered himself enough to go again, she'd give him a drink. Once she brought out her venison jerky. He chewed as if he were starving, then started to choke on it. More water got the food down.

"It's too tough."

She got out bread and tore the crust off part of one small loaf. She fed him bits of the tender white center and ate the crust herself.

He managed to get that down, then nodded. "Thanks."

After that long stop, she saw him gather himself.

"Let's go again," he said.

And on they went, up toward the top. The mountain had never seemed so huge.

Ursula talked, then sang, barely realizing when she switched from one to the other. Thinking of mountains and climbing, she sang about Jacob's ladder. She sang from the bigger of the two Bibles mostly.

Many times, they paused for another drink, then moved on. The sun sank past the western mountains and cast them into shadows.

She sang about shadows. The valley of the shadow of death to be specific.

Then thoughts of shadows led her to Job, and considering all this man was going through, she could have sung that whole book.

"We're nearing the top." A notion crossed Ursula's mind

that almost made her blush. She really wasn't used to people. "My name is Ursula."

The man was busy climbing, gritting his teeth. Ursula let him ignore the obvious opportunity to tell her his name.

"I didn't expect death to hurt quite this much." His lips moved, but he focused strictly on climbing. "Dying, sure. But heaven? Heaven should be nicer. Warmer too."

She had no idea what he was talking about. But at least he was talking. He wasn't dying on her. Ursula knelt beside him. The top was near, but he needed another break.

She asked, "Do you want more water?"

His eyes popped open—as wide as they were able. They were a darker blue than hers. Hers were a faded, washed-out shade of blue that were the equal of her grandmother. Of course, she only knew what she'd been told of her appearance and from rippling reflections in a stream.

"Water. Yes. Please." He rolled to his back with such effort that Ursula hoped he could get back to his belly to continue crawling.

"And more bread?" Ursula slid one arm beneath his shoulders, and he heaved himself forward to prop up on his elbows.

"No. Can't eat now."

She guided the canteen to his mouth, and he sipped, then said, "Wait, let the water soak in."

A few seconds passed. Ursula thought of songs about living water and drinking from a well that never runs dry.

She sang, "'As the hart panteth after the water brooks, so panteth my soul after thee, O God.'"

The man gestured for the canteen again and drank deeply. When he paused, Ursula realized just how thirsty she was and took a small sip. The canteen was running low. But they had enough to make it to the spring, so she took another.

She looked down at the man with the strange pointy beard and a face so bruised and swollen she couldn't imagine what he really looked like. "What's your name?"

The man swallowed so hard that Ursula offered him another drink, and he took it. After far too long of a pause, he said, "Wax Mosby."

He gave Ursula a strange look. It reminded her of the look he'd given her when she'd mentioned the odd furrowed cut in his leg.

He was so battered she wasn't sure, but he looked almost fearful. She had no idea why.

"You've never heard that name?"

"I live up here. I don't go to the lowlands and meet other people." She didn't go into details about how alone she was, but she couldn't feel a bit of danger from him. That thought startled her. From the moment she'd found him so injured, it had never crossed her mind to fear him. Rather, she'd felt certain God had sent her to him.

It seemed foolish now that she hadn't been more cautious. But it was hard to look at the man and consider him dangerous.

"Real name's Jacob, but folks call me Wax." He dropped flat onto his back and whispered through swollen lips, "Just a few minutes rest."

Unless he started running a fever or broke out in a rash, Wax was the most harmless man who ever lived.

4

He was a killer. But she didn't know that, and he wasn't about to tell her. "You're singing again."

The singing stopped. Wax wanted to smile. His head had cleared some since she'd found him, although *cleared* might not be the right word because he was seeing two or three of everything. But he did realize he wasn't dead after all. Exhausted, shot, and beaten to a pulp by his fall, but not dead.

Heaven couldn't possibly hurt this much.

"Please, sing. It helps me."

And her beautiful voice resumed.

He gathered himself for the final stretch of the climb. He dragged himself over stones, his face nearly buried in the pebbles and ice-cold dust of the mountainside. The tips of his fingers were scraped and bleeding. He hurt all over, but his left shoulder tore at him each time he moved it. He ached bone-deep everywhere.

He sorely feared if the angel, or no, the pretty woman with the angelic voice, hadn't been here, he'd've fallen asleep and no doubt rolled all the way back down the mountain.

The way was too steep to stand up and walk to the top, but not too hard to climb . . . if a man was at full strength.

At Wax's strength, it was torture. But there was no quit in him. He went on up, pain or not. To distract himself from what he must do, he listened to the woman.

He didn't remember exactly what he'd said to her, but all her strange looks made more sense now that he knew he wasn't dead.

She was no angel.

But she was wonderfully close.

Wax dragged himself around a pile of boulders, then reached a wider ledge and realized it wasn't a ledge—he'd made it. The top of the mountain.

He'd gotten away from the men who'd shot him. They'd laughed, not interested in his death. Not caring if they had left him wounded and dying by inches. But he had made it.

He rolled onto his back. He was so exhausted he was barely aware that she rested a hand on his right shoulder and another on his face.

"I live a long hike from here," the woman said. He remembered that she had told him her name was Ursula.

And he'd told her his. And she had no idea of his reputation, didn't fear him. That was so different from how people usually acted around him. That alone felt like heaven.

"Let me rest a few minutes, then I'll get up and we'll walk." He wondered if he was able. "Night is coming on, and we need to get under shelter."

Then he remembered wondering if his leg was broken. With a sigh of relief, he knew it couldn't be. He'd used it enough on the climb to be sure. But it hurt like it was being gnawed on by a rabid badger. Maybe shot, maybe hit by flying rocks or injured in the long fall, maybe all three. But not broken, and that gave him a small surge of energy.

She guided the canteen to his lips.

After a long drink, he said, "I feel like it's soaking into my mouth and throat, and there's none left to get to my belly."

She smiled. The kindest smile he'd seen since his ma.

"You have the prettiest blue eyes. And to listen to you sing." He fumbled for words and noticed his speech was slurred. "It's a great honor. Beautiful voice."

Shrugging, Ursula offered him the canteen again. "Have all you want. We'll soon walk right past a spring."

He drank his fill.

When he was done, she slung the canteen over her neck, under her arm, and asked, "Do you think you can walk?"

"I think . . . I have to." He tried to smile but doubted his lips curved.

"I think I could find a tree branch to use as a cane, but I don't want to leave you here alone to search. I'll keep my eyes open for the right thing while we walk. Until then, lean on me."

She slid an arm behind his back. He gathered himself and shoved to his feet.

Nearly choking on the cry of pain, he buckled. His left leg wouldn't hold him. He quickly shifted his weight so he stood on his right foot only.

He fought to stay silent. Whining and complaining didn't help anything. When he was steady, he realized his weight was nearly crushing her.

She staggered but somehow remained upright. She was a tall woman, sturdy. Slender but not skinny. Her arm across his back was near to holding him on his feet—foot. His own strength might have been enough, but it was a close thing.

"We will get you home by remembering the Bible story of 'The Crow and the Pitcher of Water.'"

Wax's brow furrowed as he looked at her. "I don't remember that story."

"The crow's beak was too short to reach the water in the pitcher, so he dropped pebbles into it until the water rose to a depth the crow could reach. It teaches us that being wise will save you."

"My ma read the Bible to me and my brothers and sisters every night. I'm sure she never read the story of 'The Crow and the Pitcher of Water.'"

"Your ma read to only her children? Or did she read to your pa, too?"

"Pa died when I was really young."

Quietly, she said, "Both of my parents died when I was young, too. They left to go to town, and we never saw them again. My grandparents had the care of us."

He slid an arm across her shoulders. "Let's begin walking. We may need to rest often, but we will make it."

He looked at the sun, low on the horizon. He doubted he could go on for long. But for right now, he'd take a step, one at a time.

"Tell me more about the crow and the pitcher. Bearing

so much of my weight will exhaust you soon enough. While you have the strength to talk, tell me a story."

She'd gone and pulled a heretic up the mountain, but Ursula didn't have the heart to try and save his soul just now.

Hearing about his father had touched something deep in her heart. She felt a wave of compassion for him. A wave of shared pain.

Wax was close to collapsing and a talking-to about believing in the Bibles was more than he could probably bear for the time being. He was moving with pure grit and strength no normal person could have, so she had every hope he'd survive to be preached at later.

Not that Ursula knew many normal people. She most certainly didn't count herself as one. She asked God to spare his soul and save his life and to use her in both pursuits however He wished.

Wax stumbled and caught himself by using his injured leg. A gasp of pain slipped past his taut jaw. Her iron grip on his gun belt held but just barely. His left leg was so swollen and painful that she hoped she knew enough healing to help it mend.

She knew this high canyon as well as she knew her own hands and feet. She remembered her grandma saying she knew something as well as she knew her own face, but Ursula didn't own a mirror—only had vague memories of such a thing, and had little idea what her face looked like, so hands and feet would have to do.

And along with knowing the canyon, she knew Wax

couldn't make it to her stone house tonight. Just ahead, thirty or forty paces, they would reach the western edge of the canyon. Then they had a long walk along that edge, heading north to the stone house. It was only a couple of hours when Ursula walked at a brisk pace, less if she ran, and she liked to run.

With Wax, at the speed they were limping along, he would never stay on his feet that long.

Right where they turned, there was a shallow cave near a spring. And there they'd stay for the night. She'd let him drink his fill of water.

And she'd let him rest. She'd give him some tough venison jerky and hope he had the strength to gnaw on it, but she could tell the effort of eating earlier had exhausted him, and his face was so terribly bruised that every movement must hurt.

She had supplies in her pack, including a blanket, her hatchet to fetch kindling, a small pot, and matches to start a fire. All things she'd been given by Jo's new family, the Wardens.

She should be too proud to use things given by people she didn't trust. She should be too ashamed to use things given by the family she betrayed.

"Just a few more steps."

He lifted his head. "We're home?"

"We're to a shelter that is closer than my house." She never thought of the stone house as a home. She was an intruder there, and the place had something ancient and nearly haunted about it, though she didn't believe there were such things as haunting spirits.

Still, the place wasn't her home and never would be, even if she lived there the rest of her life.

There was a large boulder near the entrance of the cave that was reasonably flat on top, a little over knee high.

As if God had provided Wax with a chair.

"Sit here." She guided him down, and he didn't resist. In fact, he sat, then lay backward, flat on the boulder.

Studying him, she wondered if he might just go ahead and sleep on that hard rock.

She hadn't dared lead him into the cave yet. She needed to check it for hibernating grizzlies and other less deadly varmints who might object to sharing their winter den.

It wasn't much of a cave, not very deep, so she hoped no animal found it a fit place for a long winter. She held her hatchet firmly in her right hand and stepped in.

There was no critter to fight, thank heavens. She tucked her hatchet back into her belt.

Emerging, she frowned down at Wax. The man hadn't moved. Was he asleep or unconscious? Whichever it was, she needed to get him out of the cold and next to a warm fire.

She collected sticks and chopped up kindling. She thought how odd it was that she'd become so attached to the hatchet, and now it was such a blessing to have it along.

The cave was about ten feet deep with a wide-open entrance, so the wind would whistle in when it gusted. But the night was mostly still, so she could make it habitable. She started the fire between the entrance and the back wall. She'd get Wax to sleep between the fire and the wall, and heat would reflect back and forth, warming him from all sides.

The fire also lit the farthest corners of the cave so she could be doubly sure they were alone.

A nice stand of trees nearby was littered with long dead branches, and even with no light but the moon and the stars, she went back several times to build up a supply of kindling to last the night.

Her patient slept on. He'd said folks called him Wax, which was very odd. He'd been nicknamed after a . . . candle? Each time she went by with an armload of kindling, she glanced at him utterly still on that rock. She gave serious thought to just leaving him there. He seemed comfortable.

Looking up, she watched snow sift down. It really was spring. Or close anyway, judging by the length of the days. But it still snowed at least lightly most every day.

She couldn't let the poor man sleep in the snow.

But what could she do if he *had* passed out?

Nothing. She left him to heat up some water and make a broth.

Fortunately her supplies were extensive because she'd packed with the intention of climbing all the way down the mountain and might have been gone for days.

Maybe forever.

Now she just had to get through one night, and she'd be back home so they could eat well.

Soup with a thin broth and bits of venison bubbled over the crackling fire within minutes.

She left the soup to simmer, hoping the venison would get tender enough for Wax to eat, then she went back to study him. The fire was behind her but close enough some of the heat reached them.

Wondering what to do, she saw him stir. His eyes popped open.

"A fire." His words slurred.

He groaned, coming all the way out of his slumber, and shoved himself inch by inch to a sitting position. "Heat feels so good."

He staggered to his feet . . . foot . . . and, using the rock wall for balance, hopped into the cave. Quickly Ursula spread her blanket on the ground between the fire and the back wall of the cave.

"Sit here, rest or sleep if you want. I have a small pot, so I made a hot soup. I brought a few things with me in case I went to the bottom of the mountain and just kept walking."

Wax made it to the blanket and dropped to one knee, protecting the injured leg, then fell over flat on his face.

Ursula let him go.

Maybe the smell of broth would wake him. If not, she'd eat her fill, then bathe his wounds as best she could, and if that didn't wake him, she'd let him sleep.

5

The first day she'd let him rest out of compassion. The second, a sudden chill wind swept through in such a way the cave caught every bit of it. And a storm was brewing.

It could be rain or snow. Rain would blow right into the cave just like the wind. Snow, if it was heavy—and this storm did look threatening—could make it nearly impossible to get home, maybe for days.

Fear drove Ursula to a different kind of compassion. If he wanted to survive, she had to get him out of here.

She shook Wax gently but relentlessly until his eyes popped open.

The swelling on his face had reduced just a bit, but the bruising was nearly black and terrible to look at. He had a gash on his face all along the left side that had bled. It was the worst of many such cuts. She could imagine him falling into the tops of trees, getting raked by hundreds of stiffened branches.

She had tried to doctor his injuries. But she was afraid she wouldn't be able to get his boot back on his swollen foot if she once got it off, and she'd found the bandages he'd fashioned stuck to the wounds because of dried blood. She didn't have the supplies she needed to uncover his cuts and scrapes without hurting him terribly, so she just left his wounds alone.

After two days he had no fever, so she hoped he wouldn't get one.

Hoped and prayed.

"We have to get out of here," she insisted. "There are clouds coming from the west. If we don't go now, we might be stuck in this cold cave for a week and our food won't last that long."

"I want all of you out of here."

Ursula blinked as she tried to figure out what that meant. "If you can't make it, I'll hike home and get more supplies, blankets, things like that. But this cave is a miserable little place. And I can't tend your wounds much with no bandages, and I have none of the healing herbs I've collected."

He responded by snoring.

Gently, she shook his shoulder. It gained her nothing. Shaking harder, he blinked, then his eyes fell shut, but he breathed deeply. The look on his battered face told her he was gathering his strength.

With an effort that seemed to come from some inner core, he rolled to his side, shoved at the ground until he sat up, and said, "I can make it."

With serious doubts, Ursula gave him a deep drink of broth, then a second cup with her dried bread soaked in it. It seemed to wake him fully.

He shoved against the cave floor with his one good hand. Ursula, by now used to the ways she could help, got behind him and pushed. With a terrible effort, and all Ursula's strength, he stood. She slid her arm across his back and helped him hop out of the cave.

"Let me s-sit on—" Wax pointed a shaking finger at the boulder at the cave entrance.

"The one you sat on when we got here?"

He blinked his bruised, puffy eyes at her. "I don't remember much." Then his voice lowered. "Except you. I remember . . . you found me. Sang to me. Saved me."

Those kind words echoed in Ursula's ears. She'd been so lonely. And now finally there was someone to talk to. Someone kind.

He sank onto the stone and braced his right arm behind him to keep him from toppling over. His left arm and leg were the worst injured. And his face. And the back of his head. Oh, it was hard to list them in order of seriousness.

"I'll roll up the blanket, and we'll go." There were a few more things to gather, but she made short work of it because she'd done as much as she could before she woke him. She came back out to find him still upright, eyes closed, lines of pain etched into his face.

Shaking her head, Ursula looked toward the west and saw those threatening clouds. The sun was just barely up, and they had a long trek ahead of them. She was right about needing to go, but it was a terrible thing to ask of him. She drank the last of the broth with bread soaked in it. Then she let him drink deeply of water, refilled the canteen, and packed it away.

She picked up all her things she'd set aside, then slid her arm along Wax's back. That opened his eyes.

"There aren't two of you, are there?"

Shaking her head, she said, "No. I wish there were so we could bear more of your weight. I considered making you a cane, but your injured arm isn't strong enough to make use of it. Maybe when you're better. For now, we have to get home and out of this weather. And it's a fair distance."

Nodding, he didn't speak, as if he wanted to save every ounce of energy.

She was already wondering again if she should have raced home, gathered supplies, and come back to ride out the storm here. In his condition, they'd be all day getting home.

But they set out, his good arm slid across her shoulders, while Ursula did the work of his leg, somewhat.

He managed one step, then two, then ten, and they kept going.

She marveled at his strength and felt a strange trembling deep inside from touching another human being. Speaking to another human being. Though she did most of the speaking, but knowing there were listening ears was like breath in her body.

She found a song about touch. All the times Jesus had touched someone to heal them, or He'd been touched by those around Him. She sang, and though it might be fanciful, she thought Wax walked more steadily when there was music.

Whether it was true or not, they kept going. Him on one foot, then leaning on her as if she were his other foot. He'd hop forward leaning, then take another step.

They found a steady rhythm. When they'd gone half-way and were still setting a slow but steady pace, she knew

48

they'd win the race. They were the tortoise in this race, not the hare. No hare to be seen anywhere.

And it wouldn't be all day. The storm clouds darkened and crept toward them, but there was time.

Just barely enough time.

"What is this place?" Wax heard the wonder in his voice. He had no energy to do anything but get inside and pass out. But carved stones were shocking.

"Dave Warden and his family have talked of other ruins like this. They can be found all over the mountains, but I've never seen any others. In fact, I've lived on this mountain all my life with my sisters, and Jo—that's Josephine, one of my two little sisters—discovered this only last fall. When she got married to Dave, they moved into the house I shared with Jo and Ilsa. And I came up here."

"A house already built. That's . . ." Wax's words faded. "Got to lie down."

Ursula led him into the first of what must have once been a room, but the walls were tumbled down, and there was no roof. She made several turns, walking deeper into the maze of walls.

Wax was dizzy anyway, and the turns and walls made it worse.

Then they reached a door. A sturdy door built of split saplings that were barely weathered.

She swung the door open, and they entered a very civilized house . . . not counting the stone walls. There was a cold fireplace stacked neatly with kindling ready to light. He saw a table and two chairs—then he saw a third chair against the wall. Then, mercifully, he saw a bed. She took him straight to it and eased him down.

He sat, then he tipped sideways. Fighting to stay conscious, he blinked eyelids that suddenly had the weight of those stones.

"Thank you, Ursula."

"Go to sleep. The walk was so hard on you. I'll get some food going and wake you after a bit. You need to put something in your belly."

"Yep, starving." Those were the last words he could force past his lips. A buzzing in his head made him want to shoo away a swarm of bees.

No stings though. Good thing because, after a day of constant moving, it hurt too much to even swat.

Forcing his eyes open he looked up at the concerned woman who had nearly broken her back hauling his worthless hide to this comfortable place.

He watched her rush to the fireplace and get a fire crackling. Warmth hadn't reached him but neither did the cold in his dizzy exhaustion.

And then the heat did get to him but not from the fire. Instead, the warmth was too intense and seemed to come from his bones.

Ursula came back and leaned over him, looking so worried.

"I should do a better job of bathing and bandaging you. I need to get that boot off and see what I can do for your leg. I need to wash and mend your clothes and—"

The buzzing in his ears was louder than her voice, though he could see that her lips kept moving. He watched her and her twin sister. She'd said something about a sister.

Now both of them stood before him, then three Ursulas. This room was getting crowded. He saw a black frame form around her. A circular frame that was like looking through a train tunnel.

The tunnel tightened, narrowed, he saw two Ursulas, then one. Then it closed on complete blackness.

She was lucky she'd gotten him inside and on the bed.

He'd been running on pure grit for the whole day, and once he could let go, he was unconscious within seconds. She'd been running on grit, too. Being a crutch for a one-legged man for hours had been a weight she could hardly bear.

If he had the strength to do it, in his condition, then for her to fail would make her a pure weakling. She'd found a toughness in herself that surprised her. But she was worn clean out.

Now she had a man in her room. And no ability to help him that she could figure out.

Approaching him, she studied his wounds. His facial bruises had taken on a blackish-purple hue. The swelling covered most of the upper half of his face. He was bleeding from at least one head wound.

Then she remembered his leg. Getting his boot off was something she could do, and as much pain as he'd shown the few times he'd used it, she was glad he'd sleep through the tugging.

Going to the end of the bed, she decided to start with the good leg. She'd never taken a man's boot off, and she should probably practice before tackling the injured leg.

The first boot slid off without much trouble. He wore a woolen sock, and it pulled off with the boot.

Now the other foot.

Gritting her teeth, she reached for the heel and toe just as she had before. Dreading how much this might hurt him, she tugged slowly but steadily. This boot didn't give as easily, probably because his ankle was so swollen.

With all her strength, she got the boot to move, fighting for each inch. Wax groaned, and without waking up, tried to pull his foot away from the pain. It helped, and she got the boot free. She dropped it with a thud to the floor beside the other one.

The sock was still on, but she was able to ease it off without disturbing him enough to make any sound. Then she unwound the bandage around his injured leg.

It seemed straight. Very swollen, badly bruised, especially around that odd slit in his skin. It was probably just another slashing cut from some tree branch. It wasn't swollen in the same way Grandpa's had been. Neither broken nor sprained, just terribly cut and bruised.

Wax had roughly bandaged most of his wounds. She needed to unwrap and bathe them, then tie them up with clean bandages, but before that, she came to his side and knelt by the bed.

And prayed.

As she did, she pushed up the sleeve of his right arm, the one least injured, and rested her fingers on him. A slow, strong pulse bumped against her fingers.

Even unconscious, she felt the coiled muscles in his forearm. An iron-hard man with an iron will.

A man who fought for life as Wax had, by climbing

that mountain and walking so far to get here, would live. She felt that steely determination in his pulse and corded muscles.

There was much to do, and she had no idea if her untutored nursing would help. Most likely the man would rest his fill, then wake up and hop on out of here.

She saw no rush to tend him and maybe disturb him when he was so soundly asleep. Though if removing his boot hadn't stirred him, she could've probably done anything.

She took a blanket and covered Wax, though the stone house was warming nicely. From the other blankets left by Jo and Dave, she made a pallet on the floor closer to the fire so she could get up and stoke it.

There was plenty to do, and she should do it right now. She should get a baking of bread rising. She should start a hearty soup so she could feed Wax when he awoke. She should at least make something and eat it herself to restore her strength. But she was used up, and the warmth of the fire eased into her bones and lured her into sweet sleep.

Her last thoughts were good ones.

She wasn't alone anymore.

Ursula woke up in the night to the sound of Wax muttering. She went to his side, not sure what to do. Try to wake him, assuming he was asleep and not unconscious? Let whatever churned in his mind go on, a nightmare that would pass?

None of his words made sense, then he cried out, "Ma, no. Not Ma."

He reached out and almost smacked Ursula in the head.

She ducked in time and watched him claw at the air, tossing and turning.

"I'll kill you." His voice rang with intent. Furious, murderous, as determined as if he were swearing an oath.

The thrashing went on until she feared he might fall out of bed or reopen his wounds. But to shake him awake, she'd have to dodge his flailing hands. She stayed low and shook his right upper arm—that kept her mostly out of reach. But before she'd touched him more than a few moments she realized why he was so unsettled.

He was burning up with fever. She snatched her hand away.

Fever. All Grandma and Grandpa's dire warnings hit hard. All death came from the lowlands. Violence and disease were everywhere.

Stay on top of the mountain where it's safe.

Like a fool, she'd helped a man who now had a fever. The price for ignoring the knowledge that had been trained into her since her earliest memory.

And when Ilsa, the closest she'd ever have to a daughter, had a fever, Ursula had chosen to abandon her. Ursula had betrayed her little sister, which was why she lived up here alone. She didn't deserve to have a family.

If she wouldn't stay by Ilsa's side, then how dare she stay with this man?

She stared, frozen by fear, at the injured man, then she leapt to her feet and ran.

"We made the ride from Bucksnort to the train in a single day last time." Ilsa Warden was riding along in Mitch's fancy private railroad car, heading home.

Mitch Warden looked at his wife and felt his heart lift or expand. Whatever was going on in his chest, it felt great. "We'll have to ride horseback all the way from the Kansas-Colorado state line this time. Taking the southern route of the train meant we had less chance of having to dig ourselves out of a blizzard, like we did heading to Chicago. We won't ride straight through like before. We'll stop each night. It's not safe for you to ride for such long hours. Not in your condition."

A private smile curved Ilsa's pretty pink lips. Her hand went to her not-quite-flat stomach, and his eyes followed the gesture.

Such wonder had come into his life. Chicago had been hard, but they'd cleared up his troubles. The man who had hired gunmen to kill Mitch was dead, and his daughter, who also happened to be Mitch's old girlfriend, was arrested. Before her wealthy, ruthless father died, she'd killed her husband for going bankrupt. Then she'd made plans to come for Mitch and Ilsa because she knew Mitch would never stop hunting for the man behind the hired murder attempts.

By the time that was done, it had been too cold and snowy to take the long train ride back to Colorado—even on the southern route. And no matter which route they took, they would have had to leave the train and ride for brutally cold hours across harsh territory. No railroad tracks led to Bucksnort. So Mitch had convinced Ilsa to wait out the winter in Chicago.

It was still too early to make the trip in Mitch's opinion, but Ilsa had pushed to go home. Now that they were on their way, Mitch was looking forward to going home himself. But early March wasn't spring on the top of Hope Mountain, not by a long shot.

Mitch was a wealthy man, and as he rode in the luxurious car, he juggled ideas in his head of building the tracks to Bucksnort himself. Though lots of men had gone bankrupt building railroads, and he wasn't eager to join them.

And Bucksnort was so remote there wasn't even a clear trail broken. He wouldn't be selling a lot of tickets on his train, although towns tended to crop up along railroad lines. But the trip from Bucksnort to any good-sized city was so hard no one would ever travel unless circumstances demanded it—as Mitch's had. And he liked the idea of traveling now and then, so he didn't completely give up the idea of building a train track to Bucksnort. Better idea: find a way to get someone else to pay for it.

The sun was warm, and once they got to the end of the railroad line, the going would be easy for a while. They'd lead two packhorses, and Mitch had included a sturdy tent of the kind he'd learned to use during his years in the Civil War. They'd be warm and reasonably comfortable once they were riding. The weather could be nasty in early March, but they had a chance of some decent travel days. It was only in the highlands that deep snow lingered. And Hope Mountain was as high as the highlands got.

"Soon we'll be home." Ilsa smiled. Her blue eyes flashed, and a few black curls sprang free from the knot she wore it in.

"Yes, soon. I'm sure our families are still stuck on the mountaintop and planning to come down in a blaze of fury and fire to drive Bludgeon Pike and his men off the Circle Dash Ranch. I'd like to be there before there's any gunfire." Mitch hoped he'd found a way to settle Pike's land grab without any shooting.

"I'll see Jo again." Ilsa's smile dimmed. "And Ursula if she'll allow it."

Mitch didn't comment on that. He'd said his piece concerning Ilsa's half-wit big sister. He didn't mention how Ursula had run when confronted with Ilsa coming down with a rash and fever. She'd run when Mitch got sick, but Mitch's ma had sent all the Nordegren sisters away. Ursula just headed out faster than the rest.

But when Ilsa got sick, Mitch thought with grim anger, Ursula should have stayed. Ilsa had cried out for Ursula while she burned up with fever. Ursula, only seven years older than Ilsa, had stepped in when their grandma died and cared for Ilsa. Ursula was only eleven, and that was a mighty young mother. But she was the closest thing to a mother Ilsa had.

When Ursula abandoned her sick little sister, her cowardice had been a torment to Ilsa.

Jo had stayed by Ilsa's side. Mitch's ma had done her best to tend to Ilsa in Ursula's place, and in her fevered confusion, Ilsa would be comforted. Then later she would cry out for Ursula again.

Mitch didn't like the anger he harbored in his heart for Ursula. He fought it down many times and didn't speak of Ursula's betrayal. Ilsa knew all too well her sister had run. He'd warned Ilsa often enough her big sister might not want to rejoin the family.

But forgiving someone, quelling your anger toward someone, wasn't the same as trusting them. More correctly, it wasn't the same as *knowing* them. Mitch knew

Ursula had, when things were hardest, failed everyone. She'd run to save herself from terrors that were more imagined than real.

When Ma sent the Nordegren sisters away from Mitch, she'd feared his rash and fever might be smallpox. But it was a far less serious sickness Ma had heard called chicken pox. Ursula knew that, and she'd run anyway.

He'd forgive her. Welcome her back to the family. Be kind and encouraging. But trust? That she'd have to prove she deserved.

Ilsa loved her. But Ursula had some things to prove to Mitch before he'd trust her again. Hurting the woman he loved made it mighty easy to distrust.

6

For a time, misery was the only thing Wax was conscious of. Hot misery.

Had the devil claimed his soul after all? It broke his heart because he had some vague memory of an angel taking him to heaven.

And could God change His mind like that? And was there still a chance he'd go back up out of the flames of the underworld?

When would this be settled? And how?

Deep in the back of his mind, only hot misery invaded.

But then, so quiet it barely penetrated, there was something else. Beneath all the misery was a song. A private song for him alone, almost like the angel had followed him into hell.

That single secret song kept him from dropping so far down into the hot black misery he'd never be able to get back up.

That delicate but unbreakable silken thread of quiet, soothing music was all he clung to. It held him to life.

The music called to him. Lured him up out of the black.

He awoke in his hot misery once and found himself in a dark blurry room that seemed to be a stone cave. They'd buried Jesus in a cave, hadn't they?

Was Wax buried then?

He surfaced enough, and hurt enough, that he was forced to admit he was alive.

At least for now. And where was that secret song?

Before he could find it, he sank back into the hot black misery.

Ursula had run from the fever, then found she couldn't leave him.

It seemed a terrible sin to care for him when she'd abandoned Ilsa. But Jo had been there for Ilsa, along with Dave and Mrs. Warden.

There was no one for this man but her. And he'd said she was sent by God to save him.

It had taken all her courage, but she'd returned within minutes of running out. It wasn't as if she could catch what he had.

This fever wasn't a sickness. He was reacting to his injuries.

She bathed his fevered brow and coaxed a bit of water down him, but little more than a sip at a time.

She didn't talk to him much beyond the coaxing. She had no idea what to say. But he'd liked it when she sang, so she put all her hopes and fears into songs. Songs sent to her, it seemed, by God. Songs of comfort and healing, pleas for help from almighty God to heal this terribly battered man.

It struck her as she sang her prayers that this was more important than being isolated. Not cutting yourself off to be safe, but turning to God for protection.

Jo had said those beautiful words to her once, "To live is Christ. To die is gain."

Why could a person fear so much, choose to be so alone, if the worst that could happen—death—was gain? It was a question she had time to consider as she fought for this wounded man's life.

The singing came again and lifted him out of the depths. Those tones, so pure and clear, were the only things in Wax's world that didn't hurt.

Time passed. Or he thought it passed.

Things cleared for longer each time he surfaced. The pain was on the surface, so it took all his will to reach upward. But maybe that's what God asked of man. To reach upward even when it was hard.

Once, he felt a cool cloth on his forehead along with the music. He fought back the pain that came when his head cleared, lured by that beautiful song. Would the song end if he didn't wake up? He felt as if she . . . yes, it was a woman singing . . . she wanted him to come fully awake. But when he did, wolves gnawed on him. His head, his shoulder, his gut, his legs. Everywhere was pain and hot misery.

But he had to keep her near, the singer that kept him anchored to life.

Facing the gnawing pain, he forced his eyes open. And saw two beautiful women. His vision wavered, and there were three, then one.

"Angel . . . s-singing." Those words, spoken aloud, made his head throb and his stomach whirl. Afraid he'd be sick, he closed his eyes. She bathed his aching head and spoke words he couldn't understand. He hoped it was enough. He hoped she'd accept that one bleak look, those halting words, and stay.

Then she sang again as if promising she wouldn't leave him. The song followed him into the black.

His eyes flickered open. They were glazed with pain, but he was fully awake for the first time in days.

"Wax!" For one short moment, he looked at her. Ursula thought there was real consciousness in that look. He hadn't opened his eyes like this since the fever began. Or rather, when he did open his eyes, he blinked a few times and didn't seem to focus on much.

Ursula leaned close. "You're running a fever, but if we can beat that, I think you'll be all right. None of the wounds are suppurating."

She'd found him nearly a week ago now. Since the fever had come up, he'd been barely able to sip water. He was thinner, his cheeks hollow. The swelling around his eyes was less, but the bruising was worse, an awful purple-black. She wondered at his strange beard, but it was the least of her worries.

This was the first she'd seen him even close to conscious.

She heard him whisper, "Angel singing."

She took that to mean her song brought him comfort, so she kept on.

That was all he said as he passed out again.

Wax's pain began to separate.

His head was the worst. But at least he could separate the pain in his head from the all-over agony.

He tried to move his arms, and one shoulder was nearly on fire.

His leg. He thought he'd taken a bullet there, and his side. He had to have cracked or broken ribs because every breath hurt.

But overwhelming all the general pain was his head. He'd hit it hard, and the fever on top of it muddled his thoughts, making any understanding of where he was and how badly he was hurt distant and blurry.

But there was that song. Always a beautiful song.

The next time Wax opened his eyes, he heard singing from somewhere nearby. He lay silent. Gathered himself to get up. Bracing himself against the pain, he turned his head to see that woman at the table.

Singing as she mixed something with flour. Maybe biscuits. He saw a fireplace with a pot hanging from it. He wasn't sure what food—soup or stew maybe—but something smelled delicious.

"H-hello?"

Her head came up with a snap. Her eyes flashed with . . . happiness. She was happy he was here. He wasn't sure when that had ever happened to him before. Maybe not since his ma.

"Wax." She rose from the table with such womanly grace her movements matched the music.

"Do you want water?" When she said it, she lifted a tin cup from the table beside him, slid a strong but gentle arm behind his shoulders, and lifted. He couldn't believe she was strong enough to do it, and he was no help because every move hurt. He had to concentrate to keep from crying out. As he was lifted, his vision faded and blurred. But he fought off unconsciousness and sipped the water.

She pulled the cup back after what seemed only drops. The water barely coated his dry-as-dead-bones mouth. It soaked in until it didn't even reach his throat.

"You're still feverish. But your wounds look to be healing."

He thought she'd said this before, maybe several times. It sounded familiar.

"M-more water."

She gave him a bit more, very stingy. He tried to grab the cup, but lifting his arms hurt until he was at her mercy.

Then she gave him more, then a long drink. She eased the cup away and her smile was so full of worry and caring and happiness he could have wept.

"Can you drink more?"

"Yes please. And what smells so wonderful?"

"It's rabbit stew. I made it with a very thin broth so you can drink it. Would you like some?" She let him drink his fill of water, which didn't take long.

His stomach was suddenly stretched to the point of pain.

"I want some, but maybe I'll just rest awhile first."

Ursula watched him pass out again. Or maybe sleep. It wasn't quite a natural sleep. And she wouldn't want to see if she could wake him. But it was more sleep than what he'd been doing before.

To wake him, she'd probably have to shake him, and she could tell every movement was agony. As if she had a choice, she decided to let him sleep.

She should have offered the broth first. Gotten something more nourishing than water into him. She'd remember that next time.

She watched over him. Watched his chest rise and fall. Wondered at his kindness and the way he spoke of her singing. It lifted her heart, filled all the lonely places.

After far too long, she stepped away and went back to her biscuits, her prayers, and her songs.

7

There's just no way through, honey." Dave caught up with her and fished her out of the snowdrift.

Jo turned to Dave, her jaw clenched tight. She was a living snowball, and she was sure she looked like a fool.

He got her free of the drift that filled the narrow gap into the high canyon. Then waited. She'd probably scared him into not saying anything for fear she'd start yelling at him. It wasn't the first time she'd tried to get through this stupid drift.

"Why can't we climb it?" It was a cry of frustration, not a real question. She knew exactly why she couldn't climb it. It was unclimbable. "I've climbed up snowdrifts before."

Jo stomped and swatted at snow.

Dave stood well back so she wouldn't coat him with snow even more than she already had.

"Ursula has been alone in there for too long." Jo dragged the bonnet off her head and whacked it against her legs. "I have to see if she made it through the winter alive."

"Now, Jo. We gave her all she needed. That room in the

stone house was as comfortable as our cabin. We left food, firewood, and lots of supplies. And your sister knows how to get more of both if she runs low. She's lived up here in cold country all her life."

"But not alone. She always had me and Ilsa." Jo gave up on her snow removal. Her shoulders drooped. She came to Dave and flung her arms around his waist and buried her face in his chest.

Dave's arms tightened around her. One of his big hands cradled the nape of her neck. He was a full head taller than she was, so her face rested comfortably on his chest, his chin on the top of her head, and she could hear the beating of his strong, kind, loving heart.

"I'm imagining her hungry and cold, but truthfully, the real worry is that she'll go mad."

There was too long a hesitation before Dave said cautiously, "She already is a little crazy, you know that, right?"

Jo punched him in the back, but she didn't hit hard. He was right, and they both knew it.

Dave kissed the top of her head. "This snow is too fluffy."

"I know what snow is like up here. I've lived here longer than you have." They both knew that, too. But it was Jo who was kicking against the simple truth.

"The sun is shining stronger every day. We don't have to wait long for the snow level to drop."

They both turned their heads to look at the trail that led through a tight canyon pass that was currently filled high over their heads with snow. It might not fully melt until summer.

"A few more days and it'll form a crust on top of the snow."

"Days or weeks or months," Jo muttered.

"Then we'll walk right over top of the drift." Dave was so upbeat and hopeful she wanted to clobber him. "Until then all we'll do is sink and flounder."

She was living proof of that. Because here she stood, coated in snow in warm weather. Well, warm compared to winter anyway.

She and Dave lived in the cabin Jo and her sisters had lived in all their lives. First Jo had lived with her parents and grandparents. Then Jo's parents had gone to the lowlands and never came back.

All of Grandma's fears exploded when her only son—only living son, she'd lost other children to sickness—failed to return. After that, she was relentless in her demand that the girls never go down.

There was a high valley beyond Jo's cabin where they'd found another, smaller cabin. It answered a lot of questions Jo had never thought to ask. Grandpa was gone a lot. He was a fur trapper, and he wandered far and stayed away for weeks.

But that cabin wasn't far from their home. Since she'd found it, she remembered Grandma scolding him, loading him down with her disapproval when he continued to go to town to trade.

Looking at their marriage with the eyes of a happily married adult woman, Jo knew her grandparents hadn't liked each other much.

Grandpa had built that cabin in a higher valley, and when things weren't happy at home, he'd gone away for a stretch.

Jo had never seen Grandpa's other cabin until last fall.

Nor had she ever seen the ancient stone house she'd found while exploring after Mitch had come.

And when Ilsa had come down with Mitch's sickness, Ursula, who had all of Grandma and Grandpa's worst fears, had run for that house and refused to come back to live with them. Instead, she hid up there with all of her grandparents' warnings and forebodings ringing in her ears.

"She'll lose her mind being alone for so long." Jo was losing her mind worrying about her. But at least she had Dave to hang on to.

"It's what she wanted."

Shaking her head, Jo thought of Ursula and all her fears. "Ursula worked at Grandma's side day and night. The cooking and cleaning, gathering eggs, milking the cows, tending the garden. And while they did it, they sang. Grandma loved to sing. They both had the most beautiful singing voices, and she gave that love to Ursula. Their music was a bond between them, and with that bond came Grandma's dread of leaving the mountain." She sighed. "But Ursula thinks like Grandma in some very good ways, too."

"Besides the crazy ways?" Dave asked.

Jo nodded her head, feeling glum.

Dave turned her away from the trail. Side by side, they left behind any chance of finding a way in, and as they walked back to their horses, Jo tried to explain Ursula's anxiety—to Dave but also to herself.

"Grandpa was closer to Ilsa and me. We spent time with him, hunting and exploring outside. Until Grandma died, he never shared her fears overly. Even so, Ilsa and I were never as deeply terrified of the dangers of the lowlands as

Ursula. It's not her fault that she ran when people came too close and disease and gunfire erupted. She was trained to be deeply afraid."

Sliding her hand up and down Dave's back, she leaned close. "I'm so glad I met you. And I'm so angry with Ursula for being such a coward. But I love her, and if I can't get through that trail soon, I'm going to rip that mountain down one rock at a time."

Dave squeezed her a bit, and she turned to look at him. He smiled down at her. "You could do it. I never doubt that you're up to anything you set your mind to."

With his left arm slung around her, he reached with his right and laid it over her slightly rounded belly. "But I'd as soon you didn't tear a mountain down in your condition. We're just going to have to wait until we can get in. It'll happen soon. A rainstorm will harden the snow, or a long day of bright sun will crust it over. We will get in. And Ursula will not be crazy."

Jo tipped her head from side to side. "No more than she was last fall."

He chuckled softly. "What she'll be is so lonely she'll set aside her fears and come down and join our family. We'll get her to do it somehow. Maybe being an aunt will be the thing that brings her back to us."

Jo slowed, then looked back over her shoulder. "She's been alone for so long. How could anyone survive such isolation?"

Jo reluctantly turned away. She hoped Dave was right, but she didn't like it. Poor Ursula, so utterly alone.

Whispering, more to heaven than to Dave, she said, "God save her from her reclusive ways."

Ursula was so busy taking care of her company—that's how she'd come to think of Wax—she barely had time to eat.

She'd never had company before. Not willingly. She was enjoying it.

That her guest was mostly unconscious was a small twinge in the back of her thoughts. He didn't exactly count as company. Though it did help her to tend to the terribly personal parts of caring for him that he wasn't aware of much.

She also admitted that she didn't have to be much of a hostess to take good care of a man who thought she was an angel.

He did have one strong mark against him as a guest. There was always the possibility he might die.

She stood beside him, or sometimes knelt, a few times even sat on the bed beside him. And while she bathed his face with cool water, she discovered how fascinating a man was.

The strength of his arms. The warmth from when he'd leaned against her on their journey home. All that touching. She rarely touched even her sisters. They weren't a hugging family.

Now she realized how nice it was. How she longed for touch of any kind. And how strange it was that it was this man she really didn't know who helped her understand the loveliness of touch.

She spent long moments resting her hands on the steady pulse on his wrist, or laying her open hand over his heart.

And while she touched, she prayed and sang. For her the two were mostly the same.

Finally, the fever broke for good, and the day came when he asked to be left alone to deal with private things by himself. It was a relief, but at the same time, she worried that he'd fall and worsen his injuries.

He'd lost weight. His cheeks were hollow, and his eyes nearly sunken from being so sick, but he had survived. The worst was past. Sitting up slowly on the bed, he swung his legs over the edge and sat. Just sat.

"Don't try and stand up suddenly."

"Good advice." Wax dragged both hands down his face. "I'd end up face-first on the floor."

She watched him run his hands over his head and flinch. He still had cuts and bruises all over, and egg-sized lumps here and there on his scalp explained a lot of his unsteadiness.

"Here's some broth," Ursula offered. "This is only beef broth, I strained out anything solid. But once your head clears, I think you should eat something solid. I've made a baking of sourdough bread."

"I've been smelling it since I woke up. I am really hungry for the first time since I was hurt." He sipped the broth. "This is really good." He finished it and handed the tin cup back. When she took it from him, their hands brushed.

Their eyes met. With a rueful smile he said, "There are still two of you. And they're both blurry."

"I'll try to believe I have another woman here for company."

He nodded silently. "I think I might be able to manage

a bit more broth and maybe some beef along with it and some of that bread."

"It's a good day to try and manage a few little things. There's a wild spring storm outside. Rain with thunder and lightning in the night, then snow this morning that's still falling. You wouldn't want to be out there anyway."

Wax paused and seemed to look through the thick stone walls. "It's storming right now? I can't hear anything."

"The noise is over. Now a thick snow is coming down. Probably at least a foot of it. Last night the storm was wild. But I only knew about it because I went out last night in the rain and again this morning in the snow. This room we're in is more cave than building. I think that's why the roof hasn't collapsed in this area. There are several rooms still standing that are built into this rock overhang."

"When will spring finally come?" He sounded tired, like a man glad to have survived another winter. Most everyone felt that way by springtime.

"It's always a battle between seasons. Spring breaks in for a while, then winter takes over, then they push and shove until spring finally wins. Soon the cold will fade and we'll get some really warm weather. I don't even know what day it is, but it must be March. The night and day seem near the same length. Winter lasts a long time up here, but we've survived the worst of it."

"The thought of warm weather puts heart into a man."

"A meal will do more of that. I'll dish up the soup and bread and bring it over to you."

"No, I think I'd like to get out of bed. Sit in a chair."

"Are you sure? Are you ready for that? What about your leg?"

"Can I lean on you like I did walking here?"

"Yes, we can get you to the table that way. But I wondered . . . well, I've been working on a cane. I'm a fair hand with carving wood." She touched the hatchet she always wore.

He looked at her, right in the eye. She was so thrilled to have someone here. To listen when she spoke. Act as if they appreciated her. It was like balm to a wounded soul.

"Ursula, you saved my life. And now you think to my care and comfort. You're a wonderful woman."

"I feel like God sent you to me. I was so lonely. I hate to think God let you fall off a mountain in order for me to have company, though."

A wry smile curved Wax's lips. "Let's don't blame God for the bad but thank Him for the good."

Ursula nodded. "That sounds nice. I'll get the cane." She hurried out and was right back with it.

He reached for the head of the bed and slowly rose. He didn't try to walk. He just stood.

"My vision's going black. Give me a minute."

Ursula stood near but not too near. How did a woman know how near was the right distance?

"It's best to be close to the bed in case you have to sit down suddenly." Ursula felt herself smile. She'd done so little smiling since she'd isolated herself in here.

His vision must have cleared because he reached for the cane. He slowly moved the few paces in the small room to the table. His legs looked wobbly, and the cane was awkward, but he made it. All five steps.

He sat down to his first real meal since she'd known him. And she'd known him quite a while.

"Did you know you have terrible bruises on your face?"

Wax's head jerked as he looked at her. "Really?" He ran his hands over his face again. "I'm not surprised, as far as I fell, but no, I didn't know it."

"Your eyes were nearly swollen shut, but the swelling has gone down some. Now it's mainly dark purple bruises. It's worst under your eyes, and across the left side of your face."

Wax ran two fingers over his moustache, then on one side, he pulled the long corner of the whiskers to a point and twisted. His eyes narrowed as if he'd thought of something unpleasant.

"Can I heat water and shave, do you think? I'm scruffy all over. I think I'll get rid of this beard and moustache. I have my skinning knife with me." He patted a pouch that hung on a leather thong under his shirt. "If you've got a strop or a whetstone, I should be able to clean up."

"I'll get things set up for you, then leave you to it. I've set up a pallet in another room." Ursula pointed to the door. "It's right on the other side of that wall, so we share the fireplace. This section seems to be the only part of this old building that's fully intact."

Wax's eyes narrowed as he looked around. "What is this place?"

"I have no idea. From the way the outer walls are tumbled down, I think it has to be ancient."

"Who built it? Who lived here?"

Ursula shook her head. "I don't know. There have never been people up here that I know of. And my grandparents didn't like anyone nearby, so I don't think they even knew about this place, and they sure as certain never saw anyone living here."

They talked about the strange house while they ate.

"I've ridden far and wide in my life." Wax chewed on the tender elk meat in the soup and looked to be enjoying every bite. "I've seen a few old places like this."

Ursula sat up straight, shocked. "Really, with people living in them?"

Wax took a bite of sourdough bread and chewed slowly. His eyes were unfocused, as if he were watching a memory unroll in his head. At last he said, "No, they were all old and deserted. Lots of them collapsed. No one I ever talked to knew who'd lived here. Even the Indians didn't know."

Ursula had heard of Indians.

"And a lot of Indian tribes have very ancient stories of their own people. But none included knowledge of who'd built these old houses. I've heard some Indians who won't go into them. They treat them as sacred places, holy ground. To enter them would be a sin. Some native folks think their gods built them before time began and lived here while they created the world."

"Gods? More than one god?" Ursula felt a terrible dread of such a notion.

Wax shrugged one shoulder. "We know there's but one God, but different folks have their own beliefs. It's interesting to listen to their stories. There are many old buildings like this one scattered around in the mountains. I suspect you're the first person to find this one and live in it for . . . probably thousands of years. I like the idea of walking where long ago, other people walked."

Every word he uttered caught Ursula's imagination. To think there were more places like this. To think people knew about them and discussed them and the mystery of who built them and where those people went.

"Maybe I'm the only person in the world who's lived in this lost, secret place for—how many is a thousand? It's more than a hundred, I suppose."

Wax nodded. "I didn't have much schooling, only what Ma taught me, but a thousand is one hundred ten times."

Ursula blinked as she tried to imagine such a huge number of years. "I didn't have much schooling, either. I've spent most of the winter reading, trying to get better at that. I haven't given much thought to counting. Grandma taught us to count to one hundred. She said we'd most likely never have more than one hundred of anything so she didn't see a point to going higher."

"A big number like that doesn't come up often, mostly just in talking about things that don't have much to do with real life. But I've needed to get higher than one hundred a few times. Big herds of cattle can number over one hundred, even over one thousand. So counting higher comes in handy. You should learn it. You'd be surprised at how much use you'll get from big numbers."

Ursula bobbed her head and finished her meal as he finished his. "I've got water hot by the fire. I'll leave you to shave and tend your wounds as you see fit. I'm within shouting distance, but I won't come back until you ask, so if you want to wash up, even bathe, there's a basin." She nodded toward it. "Your clothing is tattered from your fall. I had a lot of fabric and plenty of time, so I did my best to make an outfit of clothing for you. I did some sewing for my grandpa, so I remember how to make an outfit for a man, somewhat." She gestured at her own trouser-clad legs. "Sewing britches is something I'm familiar with. My sisters and I wear britches, too. Or at least we all used to. I might be the only one now."

She reached for the stack of clothes she'd made and left lying on Grandpa's chest of drawers that Jo and Dave had brought to her. "I hope I've made a size that will fit you." She set the clothes on the table, wanting him to have them within reach. "I'll mend and wash your things, if you can drop them outside the door. They are torn near to shreds and bloodstained, but I can make them wearable, I hope. There's more soup and bread on the table if you're still hungry or get hungry again later. I won't need to join you until you're ready."

"Thank you, Ursula. Can you . . . I'm sorry, I'm still so shaky . . . you've done so much, but can I ask you to pour a basin full of water before you leave? Then I'll get on with cleaning up and seeing how I'm healing."

She swiftly poured the water, glad he'd asked for help. She laid the strop on the table, then picked up the dirty dishes. She'd take them with her into the next room. She had it set up so she could stay there from now on. Now that he was awake, she couldn't stay in this room with him.

"You don't have a mirror, do you?"

She blinked at him. She had a vague notion about what a mirror was, but she most certainly didn't have one. "No."

"It's fine. Don't worry about it. Sometimes if a mirror is handy, I look in it while I shave."

Ursula had seen herself in a stream before. "Maybe the basin of water will make a likely mirror."

"Thank you. I'll let you go now." He stood unsteadily,

and Ursula didn't leave, afraid he might topple over. He walked, using the cane, to the basin she'd just filled, and that brought him close to her. He rested one hand on her shoulder.

It was startling, the strength and warmth she felt in that touch. He'd been asleep most of the time since she'd met him, including being more asleep than awake while he climbed the mountain and walked across the valley.

"You saved my life, Ursula."

The deep sincerity in his words touched her as nothing ever had. She wanted to lean into the strength of his hand.

"You saved me," he said again. "Thank you."

For a moment they stood close, him touching her. Her feeling the wonder of saving a life. Of God putting her in the right place and using her hands in such a miraculous way.

"I didn't do it alone. God was there. And you were strong from the first moment I found you lying on that ledge on the side of the mountain. Even battered as you were, even when you were stricken with fever, I never doubted for a moment that you'd live. I'm glad I was able to help."

It struck her that she'd never thought of life this way. His toughness, his ability to survive. She'd always considered life fragile. But maybe it wasn't quite so easily lost as she'd been raised to believe. Maybe she had some toughness of her own.

With a nod, she left him. Yes, she was very glad she'd been able to help this man survive.

⸺◦◯◦⸺

Wax realized just how much Ursula had taken care of him as he stripped out of his clothes. He set his tattered clothes on the floor outside his door as she'd asked him.

Every move hurt. Every bend, every breath. He probably had cracked or broken ribs. He had to sit down often to catch his breath, then it was all he could do to get on with cleaning up.

As he got ready to bathe, he inspected his wounds. Ursula had replaced his own rough bandaging and kept the wounds clean. He had only vague memories of her helping him to a chamber pot.

Considering how shy she seemed, he knew it had taken all her strength and courage to tend him.

He found a furrow just a few inches below the knee of his left leg that had to've been carved by a bullet. It'd missed the bone, but the pain was terrible and made walking of any kind a struggle.

He had a bullet hole in his side, though the way those men had been shooting, it could be a gouge from shattered rock. His whole left side was nearly covered with bruises. He remembered falling. He'd landed wedged between the mountainside and a tree, one of hundreds that grew up that slope.

The sound of those men laughing crept into his thoughts. He hadn't done much thinking since he'd found himself pinned to the mountain. He'd known he couldn't go down, so he'd gone up. Reaching out, one move, one inch of progress, at a time.

In some ways, he'd been doing the same thing ever since. His thoughts weren't even now fully clear after days of depending on Ursula through the journey here and while he was feverish.

It came back to him now, the sound of that laughter, the mocking words they'd said about knowing he wasn't Pierce. Who in the world was Pierce?

He felt the wild surge of hate. The desire to kill.

He'd lived by his guns for a long time now, and his first instinct was to draw, aim, shoot.

Wax wasn't a man to shoot blind, and he remembered every man in that group. Every face, every horse. And he was a top tracker. He'd find them and kill every one of them.

Then he caught himself.

No, he would not kill every one of them. That was the thinking that had driven him to chase down the men who'd killed Ma and his little sisters. That had set his course for years. And he wanted to change course. Change his life.

He'd fight if he had to, to save his own life. To save Ursula or anyone who was in danger. But he wouldn't seek revenge. He wouldn't chase those men down with the blood lust that had gripped him when he'd found his family dead.

No.

He fought down the hate, and it wasn't easy. But he won the battle, one furious thought at a time. He felt Satan pushing him, stirring his anger, feeding his hate. Turning his thoughts to God, he prayed for a peaceful heart.

What does a man do when someone tries to kill him? A normal man? They talk to the law. Wax had always been inclined to fight shy of the law, because there were some who might take exception to the way he made his living.

But not this time. This time he'd tell the sheriff what had happened and leave justice to the law and to God.

When he'd finally, one agonizing wound at a time, dealt with his injuries, he bathed all over, then dressed in Ursula's newly sewn clothes. They fit mighty well.

He found enough strength to eat another bowl of beef soup and drink as much water as he could hold. Then, feeling more alive than he had in a long time, he made his way to the bed and sat down, exhausted from his efforts. He had no energy to shave, and anyway his vision was still so blurred he wasn't sure he could trust himself with a razor.

Without planning to do it, he slid sideways. Good food, clean clothes, healing wounds. The next thing he needed was rest. He fell into a sound sleep.

8

Wax woke up starving, and he wasn't seeing two of everything. Every day for, well, he wasn't sure how long, he'd slept and ate whatever Ursula put in front of him. He'd had no notion of daylight or darkness, though he remembered waking up fully several times and knew he'd stumbled around with a fog in his head more times than that.

But today he woke up and knew he was on the mend.

With slow, painful moves—his leg the worst of all, though his ribs were killing him—he heated more water and filled the basin, not making Ursula do it this time.

He strained to see his reflection in the water.

Then he wished he hadn't.

He was stunned at how awful he looked. No swelling, Ursula had mentioned it had gone down. His bruises were a sickening yellow tint, though he still had solidly black eyes and the left side of his face was badly scabbed.

Boiled down, he could just admit he looked terrible.

He decided while he ate Ursula's delicious soup for breakfast, the time had come to shave his beard and moustache. He could work around the scraped-up face. Most of the scab was ready to come off anyway. The wax was long gone from his facial hair, and he'd grown a good amount of scruff in the time he'd been here. That alone told him it'd been quite a while, but he couldn't guess how long.

Today he'd be done with the beard, along with his past. He wished now he hadn't given Ursula the name Wax. It wasn't his real name after all, Jake Mosby was. But he'd said the name, and there was no turning back from that.

He carefully shaved around his scrapes. Running his hands over his bare face made his fingers itch. He'd favored that sharply waxed beard and moustache for a long time.

Missing the beard wasn't enough to make him regret the shave. He'd done the right thing. And it didn't matter that Ursula knew him as Wax because he had to go confront the Wardens with the full truth of what Pike was doing. That truth would include Wax's part in it. And his name would come out.

He felt steady for the first time since he'd fallen off the mountain. He bathed and stretched awhile, testing his wounds. Then he lingered over rebandaging himself and putting on the tidy clothes Ursula had made for him. He reached for his gun belt, hanging on the bedpost, then stayed his hand. He hadn't given a thought to strapping his guns on in all this time.

This morning it had been a reflex.

He left them where they were, then made slow work of pulling on his boots. It was a while before he realized he was avoiding calling Ursula in.

Just because he wanted her in here so bad.

Wax had gotten used to wanting nothing, and it bothered him that this want ached like a sore tooth.

He could hear her singing in the next room, and the beauty of her voice soothed something in Wax that he hadn't known was savage. But he delayed inviting her back. He was planning to change his whole life, starting right now, and he wasn't sure how to begin. With his head clear at last, he could think.

There was no need to tell Ursula much. Anyone would know Wax was a nickname. No sane mother would name their child that. But he had to find the Wardens, and Ursula had said they were up here.

He dreaded facing them and wanted to put it off. He knew Quill Warden, the owner of the Circle Dash Ranch, had been shot. He might well be dead, and if so, Wax would face Warden's wife and son. Wax hadn't done the shooting, one of the low-down men he rode with had, but the Wardens might not be too particular in who was held responsible.

For now, until he had the strength to go searching for them, Wax didn't want to end this small stretch of time with an innocent woman who didn't recognize his name. He couldn't remember a time when he'd been near a woman who didn't know his reputation. That he was considered a dangerous man wasn't enough to scare off a certain type of woman. In fact, some were drawn to the danger. But a truly fine, innocent, good-hearted woman had never looked at him with such trust.

He should warn her of the kind of man he was, then he thought of that hatchet she always carried, strapped to her side like a gun, and decided she wasn't completely innocent.

Her trust was like a long, soft rain in an arid desert. It was precious, and he couldn't bear to destroy her naïve belief that he was a good man. She'd have to know eventually, but right now, he couldn't stand the thought of putting suspicion and fear in her eyes.

Ursula had a lot to learn about the world, but she also had a sharp intelligence. She wasn't stupid, just sheltered. When he told the Wardens who he was, she'd understand and turn against him. He saw no reason to hasten that day.

A knock at his door turned him so quickly he staggered from the sharp pain. He was surprised at his eagerness as he grabbed his cane and limped to let Ursula in.

She held out a bundle in her arms. "You look like you're feeling better. Here are the clothes you had on when you first came here. I cleaned and mended them as best I could."

He enjoyed looking at her shy smile . . . and he got lost in it for too long. Her smile faltered. She thrust the clothes into his hands and took a step back, but Wax juggled the clothes into one arm and reached out to catch her hand, drawing her forward.

"Don't go. I was just about to see if you'd like to join me for a meal. I'm still hurting, but I feel more myself this morning than I have since you found me."

"Thank heavens. It's been a long three weeks."

That almost sent Wax staggering backward. "Three weeks? I've been up here that long?"

Smiling sadly, Ursula squeezed his hand and came in. "I was afraid you weren't even fully aware much of the time. You spent most of the first week with a fever. And since then you've mostly slept. I couldn't be sure what you understood. But it doesn't surprise me much of it is lost to you."

"I've been moving slow this morning, but at least I'm only seeing one of everything."

The smile returned to her pretty face as she looked at his ill-fitting pants and shirt. "I've made a stew from strips of dried elk. I had a few Indian potatoes and some onions left, so I was able to give it some flavor. There are biscuits, too. I'll get the food and be right back."

She slipped free of his grasp and was soon back with a heavy black pot and a plate covered by a red-checkered napkin. It was early for a noon meal, but Wax's appetite was finally roaring to life.

"Can we eat right now?" Wax inhaled the meaty scent. "I just realized I'm starving. I had the last of your soup from yesterday for breakfast."

Nodding, Ursula said, "It's hot from the fire. And the biscuits are just newly finished baking. Let's eat while it's warm."

Wax dug into his meal, enjoying Ursula's presence across from him. They talked of Wax's healing, and Ursula told him a few things he'd forgotten about their trek home and the time since. She talked of her sisters and their new husbands. He told her about his ma and little sisters dying.

"The sun is strong today," she commented. "Water is gushing out of the snowdrifts."

"Spring had almost reached the bottom of the mountain when I left." As he chewed the tough elk, he thought on all Ursula had told him about being trapped up here—away from the Wardens—by a trail impassable in the winter-time. He wouldn't have to wait much longer to face them.

Ursula made coffee, and they lingered over the meal. He'd never been so happy to be alone with anyone in his life.

She poured a second cup. Some impulse made Wax reach out as she sat, and he rested his hand on hers. She was across the table, but closer in his heart than Wax had ever been to a woman.

Her startled eyes went to his big hand resting on top of hers. Then those beautiful blue eyes lifted.

Silence stretched between them as they gazed into each other's eyes.

9

Ursula, since you found me, all you've done is give. You're a beautiful, wise, strong woman."

"I-I am?"

He smiled. "I thought when I first saw you, I'd died and you were the angel of mercy come to escort me to heaven. And I still believe God sent you, how else is it possible you came along while I lay on that mountain ledge?"

Ursula's hand turned under his. He hadn't expected her to shake off his touch, and the hurt surprised him. If she pulled away from him, he'd lose something precious. He'd lose a piece of his own heart. Then she shifted so the back of her hand was against the table. Their palms together. Her fingers folded so they held his wrist. He clasped her hand the same way.

"You supported me when I leaned on you to get here. You tended my wounds. You pressed cool cloths to my face when I had a fever. Some of it I don't remember. But I will always remember your touch. What's more, is that was all for necessity and doctoring. Now you touch me by choice. And it's a fine feeling."

"God did send me." Her hand tightened as she smiled. "I chose to live up here alone when my sisters married. Then the trail snowed shut, and my choices were taken away. Once I was cut off, it felt as if the loneliness would drive me mad. But despite the terrible loneliness, fear always turned me back. Until that day. Though nothing had changed, I found the courage to climb down. It felt like it would be a sin not to. You are right. I was used by God for the purpose of saving a life."

Wax brushed his thumb along her wrist. "God was compelling you. His voice was whispering in your ear, even if you didn't quite understand that. You only knew it was time to go down on the day I needed you to save me."

She nodded, and Wax saw the absolute wonder in her gaze.

"It's the most joyful feeling. I saved you, but you saved me, too, Wax. You saved me from my loneliness and helped me see how foolish I was to live like a hermit. I thank you for that."

The silence fell again, but this time there was so much between them. So much understanding. The evidence of being guided together by God was so powerful that Wax could see it as he'd see a stone bridge stretching across a mountain gap. That bridge made a way for them to meet in the middle and be together. A gunman like him, a fine woman like her.

He rose slowly, drawing her to her feet, then pulled her forward until her head tilted up. He lowered his head and touched his mouth to those pretty pink lips.

She gasped and turned her head away. Wax waited,

watched, hoped. But it had to be her choice. *Oh, please God, let her choose me.*

She turned back.

Their gazes met and locked. She reached up and touched her lips to his and slipped one strong, gentle hand to the back of his head.

His arms wrapped around her waist. His head tilted, and the kiss deepened. Her other arm crept up until both were wrapped tightly around his neck.

The beauty of the moment was as precious as diamonds. . . . No, far more than that, it was as precious as a prayer.

They lingered over the kiss. It warmed Wax's lonely heart. "Even though I haven't lived like a hermit, I've been a lonely man for a long time. In my own way, I've cut myself off from other people. But I don't want to be apart from you, Ursula."

She searched his eyes. Then reached up to kiss him again.

The kiss was warm and full of the feelings Wax had always kept to himself, knowing he wasn't worthy of the right kind of woman. But with Ursula, he dared to hope.

The door slammed open.

Ursula jumped backward. Wax moved sideways, just as fast. His eyes went to his guns. He coiled his muscles to jump for the weapons.

In the heartbeat between his need to defend and actually doing it, a pretty little dark-haired woman rushed in. Her eyes sought out Ursula. Then she threw her arms wide, screamed, and ran straight for Ursula. Ursula did the same, and the two collided.

"Ilsa!" A scream of pure happiness came from Ursula as they hugged and rocked.

Wax heaved a sigh of relief.

Someone else stepped in.

He'd breathed too soon. He should have gone for the guns after all.

The avenging angel.

A man Wax had seen twice before. Once, with this little brunette in Bucksnort, though he only recognized her when he saw the man. And before that, on the rocks Wax had climbed. He was perched high on the mountainside, watching Wax and two of Pike's hired guns walking into a stolen ranch house.

The man's eyes went straight to Wax.

With Wax's bruised face and his beard and moustache shaved, there was no recognition in the man's eyes.

But there was cold suspicion.

"Ursula." Ilsa hugged her so tight it hurt. And it was the best feeling in the world. Her heart lit with joy that Ilsa would be so happy to see her.

"Oh, Ilsa. You're here." Questions bombarded Ursula's head so fast none of them could escape. All she could do was drink in the love Ilsa was pouring on her. She tightened her grip on the little sister who'd brought out the mother in Ursula. The little sister she'd betrayed.

Then her mind whirled back to what had happened between her and Wax.

What *had* happened?

She had no time to even think of it because Ilsa was here.

With Mitch.

Ursula's joy faded. Having Mitch in the family was going to take some getting used to.

"Who are you?" Mitch's voice cut through Ilsa's joyful noise. She turned to her husband, the smile wiped from her face, then her eyes followed his to Wax. Ilsa hadn't even noticed him.

"Ursula, you got . . . married?" Ilsa sounded shocked and hopeful and doubtful.

"No, of course not." The harsh denial sounded so rude. What would Wax think after she'd kissed him so thoroughly? A man might be badly insulted by a woman willing to kiss him, then sounding so horrified about the very thought of marriage.

"Is he one of Pa Warden's hired hands?" Ilsa looked to Wax, then Mitch.

"I'm Jake," Wax said, to Ursula's surprise. She'd almost forgotten *Wax* was a nickname.

"Mitch Warden." Mitch said with a coldly level tone Ursula didn't like much. "You look like you've been rode hard, partner."

Wax's hand went to his face. "I forget I'm so battered. I fell climbing up the mountain. Ursula found me part way up and helped me get on up here and to her cabin. Along with the cuts and bruises, I hit my head hard enough that I've been more asleep than awake and seeing two of everything since I got here. This is only the second morning that my head has been clear and I've been able to move around much. And even at that, I'm moving mighty slow."

Mitch had a wary expression. He studied Wax until Ursula thought his eyes would fall out of his head.

"Can we share a meal with you, Ursula?" Ilsa looked back at her sister as if she couldn't keep her eyes on anything else. Except maybe the food. "It smells delicious, and we've been living rough for a stretch."

Ursula stepped away from the table. She had three chairs. Jo and Dave had brought one for Ursula and one for each of them, though Ursula had never let Dave sit down at the table. She hadn't liked having him settle in.

Mitch dropped the heavy pack he wore on his back, then helped Ilsa take off a smaller one. As he did, Ursula noticed that Ilsa wore what Mrs. Warden called a riding skirt, and a bright blue top with sprigs of pink flowers showed at the open collar of her heavy coat. At least Mitch was taking care of her little sister. She wore a bonnet that matched the coat, but the bonnet had dropped off her head and hung down her back from the tied strings. Her hair was wild, the black curls escaping a bun at the nape of her neck so little ringlets danced around her face.

Mitch grabbed a chair that had been shoved to one side, against the wall.

"Sit down and tell me about yourself, Jake." He didn't say it as if Wax had any choice in the matter. "What brings you here?"

Ursula's lips tightened with annoyance. Mitch had no need to treat her guest unkindly.

"No," Ursula said, interrupting what looked to be a hard line of questions. "Let's talk about your trip. Jo wasn't sure how far you'd travel. Ilsa, what all have you seen and done?"

Rather than obediently sit in the chair Mitch wanted him in, Wax stepped over to the bed and sank down.

Ursula heard the faintest gasp of discomfort as he shifted himself around so he could lean his back against the wall. She knew every move caused him pain, but except for that one faint noise, he kept silent.

"We spent the winter in Chicago." Ilsa started in talking about wonders that Ursula couldn't even imagine.

Apparently, Chicago was the name of a town. Like this town of Bucksnort Ursula had been told of.

Trains. The idea of it was too odd to get a picture of it in her head. And a building that was ten rooms stacked on top of each other. Stores that sold clothing already made. And places you could go eat a meal someone else prepared and set before you.

"What did you just say? A water closet? What in the world is that?" Ursula served them while Ilsa chattered. Mitch chimed in now and then.

Mitch angled his chair so he could keep an eye on Wax, but when food was set in front of him, he eased up his watching and ate with a good appetite.

They finished the meal with Ursula's mind spinning with all Ilsa had to say. But Ursula had also seen the way Ilsa kept looking to Mitch for everything while she talked. Ilsa had been such a free spirit. So independent she was almost one of the wild creatures of the forest. Marriage had changed her.

And yet she sat here, vital and lively, her eyes sparking as they always had. Ilsa had been off the mountain all winter, and here she was, alive and well. Better than well.

A faint snore came from the bed. Wax had slid down until he was lying flat and was now sound asleep.

"Who is he, Ursula?" Mitch asked.

Ursula's voice dropped to a whisper. "Come into the next room. I'm only in here to bring him a meal. I'm living in another room. We can let him sleep while I tell you about him."

That seemed to ease Mitch's suspicion a bit. As if he liked that there was some separation between them.

Well, of course there was. Ursula could hardly be in here when he was changing his clothes, now could she? But she had been with him a lot since she'd found him. Including helping him with some terribly personal things, because she'd had no choice.

She saw no reason Mitch needed to know that. Ilsa's husband certainly had no say over Ursula's life.

Quietly, Ilsa and Ursula washed and dried the dishes Mitch brought to them. They quickly set the room to rights and turned to leave just as the door slammed open . . . again.

"Ursula!" With a shriek, Jo screamed even louder, "Ilsa, how did you get here?"

Jo charged and flung her arms around them both.

The reunion was cut off by the click of a cocking gun.

Ursula spun around. Her sisters turned with her to see Dave pointing the gun right at Wax's sleeping form. Except Wax wasn't sleeping anymore. The screaming had no doubt awakened him.

Or the metallic crack of the gun.

"Dave, what are you doing?" Ursula wanted to throw all of these people out. Almost as much as she was thrilled to see them.

"The man sleeping in your bed is Wax Mosby."

Ursula didn't respond. That was the name he'd given

her right at the beginning. But it didn't matter how she responded, no one was looking at her anyway.

Mitch turned. "This is Mosby?"

"Yes. This is the man who shot our pa."

Mitch's gun was out and leveled.

10

Wax hadn't slept much, maybe drowsed a bit as Ursula and her family ate.

He'd rested his eyes and let the newcomers ask their questions of Ursula. They'd do it anyway, but he stayed out of it.

Now, still flat on his back, he slowly raised his hands. He couldn't resist taking a quick look at Ursula, hating that what had been—for one shining moment—the finest day of his life was well and truly ruined.

Ursula stared at him, wide-eyed. But was it because he'd just been accused of shooting a man? Or was she horrified that she'd let him kiss her? It didn't really matter which, neither boded well for him.

He had to tear his gaze away from her to deal with the guns aimed at his heart.

"I don't have a gun on me." He didn't look to the foot of the bed where his holstered guns hung, loaded and ready. He always wore two six-shooters tied down. And the leather thong he used to hook them to his holsters was why they'd survived his fall.

Ursula must have taken them off him. He remembered how he'd reached for them this morning out of habit. He didn't feel dressed without them. But he'd stopped himself from belting them on. He was glad of it, and he'd be gladder still if he didn't get a belly full of lead in the next few minutes.

Even though Wax didn't give the guns a single glance, Mitch noticed them hanging there and swiftly moved to unhook them from the bedpost and put them far out of Wax's reach.

"I didn't shoot your pa."

Neither Dave's nor Mitch's guns wavered for an instant.

Dave, taller, with dark hair and cool blue eyes, was a whipcord lean, tough cowboy. A man who used a gun as a tool and was comfortable with it in his hand.

Mitch was shorter, stocky, and had dark blond hair and brown eyes that could've frozen Wax solid. Now that he thought of it, Wax realized Mitch had the look of Quill Warden. But he'd only heard of one son. Clearly, they missed one.

Well, that explained what Mitch was doing climbing up that mountainside back in the fall. Not an avenging angel but an avenging son, which might be worse.

Mitch held that gun like he'd used it a few times, and not just on a rabid wolf like maybe Dave had. He had the cold eyes of a warrior, and Wax knew a lot of young men had gone off to fight in the Civil War a decade ago. Had he just come home last fall? That would explain his absence, and why there'd been no mention of him.

"I ride for Pike," Wax said. "I was at your place to *talk* to you that day when one of the fools with me started shoot-

ing. It wasn't me who shot your pa. I climbed up here—"
He took one quick glance at Ursula. He knew she'd have
to find out, but he'd convinced himself it wouldn't be so
soon. When the avenging angel didn't recognize him, he
thought he might be able to put this off even longer.

His time had run out.

"You came up here to finish what you started?" Dave
asked.

Wax had met Dave a few times, a very few times. They'd
both been in Bucksnort at the same time twice in the year
Wax had been a hand for Pike. No shave, no bruising, was
enough to fool Dave.

"Not if by 'what I started' you mean shooting anyone.
Pike told us your pa was a nester. But one look at his
well-established ranch, and I wasn't taking Pike's word
for anything. I found that Quill Warden had been in this
country over twenty years. He was one of the first set-
tlers, and he owned clear title to his land. I came up here
to tell your pa I had no part in what Pike was up to, and I
knew we were in the wrong. Did your pa survive, then?"

"He lived, no thanks to you."

That was a weight off Wax's mind. He eased himself to
a sitting position. Not easy with his hands raised and every
bone in his body aching.

"And the reason I'm beat up this way is because five
men rode onto your place when I was halfway up the
mountain. They saw me and started shooting. Between a
couple of bullets, ricocheted rocks, and a long fall down
into the tree line, I'm lucky to be alive."

"You were shot?" Ursula looked horrified. Another thing
Wax hadn't told her.

He looked at her, at the concern on her face. He wished every one of these people would get out and never come back. As long as he was making stuff up to want, he wished they'd never come.

Finally, he managed to stand despite the pain. He'd prefer to take his bullets standing up.

"I came around enough after my fall to know I'd have no chance if I climbed down, so I headed up. Ursula found me lying on a ledge on that mountainside." Wax's eyes shifted to Mitch. "I think it was the ledge I saw you sitting on once. You looked right at me."

Nodding his head, Mitch said, "I remember. That time I was too far away. I didn't get a good look at your face. I could make out the waxed beard and moustache, but without them, and with all the bruises, I didn't recognize you."

"Five men?" Dave asked. "There are five men at Pa's house right now?"

"There are," Mitch confirmed. "Ilsa and I saw them and skirted around the place to climb up here. I figured them for Pike's men."

"They aren't from Bludge's crew, unless Bludge sent them to kill me," Wax said. "But I don't think so. I heard them talking after they saw me fall off the mountain, figuring me for dead. One of them said, 'That wasn't even Pierce. I know what Pierce looks like.'"

Mitch flinched, and Dave took his eyes off Wax. "Pierce, that's the name you go by back east. Those men are gunning for you."

"It can't be. We put a stop to that."

It was the first time they'd taken their eyes off Wax. He took it as a good sign.

"Unless," Ilsa said, "Denham Lewis paid out money one more time. Since he gave half of the money when he hired a killer and half when the killing was done, if he'd paid out the first half before he died, his hired gunmen wouldn't know they can't collect the rest. They'd keep coming."

"You're who they are hunting?" Wax lowered his hands, slowly, no sudden moves. And his guns were well and truly out of his reach.

Mitch's jaw tightened into a hard line. "We had two gunmen ride up here last fall before the trail snowed shut. They were after me. Lewis had figured out where I was and sent men out here to kill me."

"I saw those two. They came to your pa's ranch. I slipped back into the woods. I saw one of them in a pine box in Bucksnort, the same day I saw you and"—Wax nodded at Ilsa—"your wife, riding out of town, saying you were headed out here. I never knew either of your names, and I never saw you again. Until now."

"They found the trail up." Mitch's jaw clenched until his cheek twitched. His eyes flicked to Ilsa. "That's when Pa and Dave and Jo rode down to Bucksnort. They left a clear trail, and those two followed it up Hope Mountain."

"I knew there had to be another way up here, but I could never find it with all the snow."

"I have a way up that cattle can pass," Dave said.

"Those two were hunting me, and now it sounds like there are five more." Mitch's eyes took on a chill Wax had seen in his own mirror. The Warden brothers were a pair of dangerous men.

"Lewis, an enemy from back east, hired killers as a way to make my old partner richer. Then before they managed to kill me, my partner went bankrupt. Lewis hired my partner's murder and made another attempt to kill me." Mitch said it in a way that told Wax there was a lot more to the story, but Mitch didn't look inclined to spin a yarn.

"I want to talk to your pa." Wax drew all eyes back to him. "Keep hold of my guns. I don't have any intent to harm him or anyone. When I climbed up here, I didn't know this was some high valley cut off from where you Wardens had set up. I just came this way because I saw you sitting on a ledge on a cliff, Mitch. I knew it was a way up. I wasn't interested in trailing you up here."

"Why now, then? What changed?"

Wax shrugged one shoulder and managed to make a few muscles ache. "I spent the winter shut into your cabin. Bludge wanted me to stay over here to keep an eye on it, and I wanted to get away from the scum he was hiring. By the time I'd had the winter to really think, I knew I was living a life I wasn't proud of. A life that was making me fit for only eternal flames when I died. I'm up here to set things right. I want out of this fight. I want a life that doesn't make me draw my gun for money. And I want to tell that to your pa and tell him I was sorry to be a part of what happened to him last fall."

Wax paused to take a deep, painful breath. "I do know this. Bludge is waiting for spring. He's planning on your coming back, and he's ready to fight to hang on to your land. Arrogant as he is, he's not such a fool as to think he can drive you off that ranch and not pay a hard price for it."

"Pike has more crimes than even you know of," Mitch said.

Wax wasn't sure what he meant by that. "What other crimes?"

"We'll leave that for later. Right now, let's go. You want to face Pa, we do it right now."

Wax gave a single firm jerk of his chin—which hurt. "I'll stand before your pa over what's been done. I'll hope he believes I didn't shoot him, but I was with men who did, and I'm willing to name them to the law."

"You've got a reputation as a bad man, Mosby. Some say you're related to Colonel John Mosby, the Gray Ghost."

"I'm no relation to Mosby, leastways I've never heard of any connection. My real name is Jake Mosby, and no, I'm not a bad man," Wax said, stubborn in the face of two aimed guns. "I'm a dangerous man, I'll admit to that. But I've always fought for the side of right. Pike lied to me to get me to hire on. Anything else you've heard is just fireside talk that builds to tall tales. But when I signed on to work for Pike, I made a mistake, and I aim to make it right. You hold on to my guns and keep them well away from me, Mitch. I won't make a grab for them or fight you. Let's go see your pa."

A short while later, they reached the horses Dave and Jo had brought through the trail. Fortunately, they'd included a packhorse full of supplies for Ursula, and it was saddled.

"We came prepared to take you back with us, if you were willing, Ursula." Jo slid an arm across her sister's back. Then she squeezed her tightly. "You will come with us, won't you?"

Ursula looked from Jo to the three horses and to Wax.

She hesitated a long time, but finally she nodded tightly. Of course, she would. She couldn't bear to stay alone. But now that the moment had come to ride away from this stone house, she was terrified of all the people surrounding the Wardens.

"How are we going to do this?" Mitch asked, taking charge.

Ursula had noticed the man was prone to do that.

Dave unloaded his packhorse. "We'll come back for these supplies later. We need the space."

When the horse was ready to ride, Dave said, "Jo can ride with me. Ilsa can ride with Mitch and Ursula can—can . . . no. Um. Jo can ride with me. Ursula can ride with Ilsa and Wax can ride with Mitch."

"That's too heavy a load for one horse." Mitch frowned. "And I don't want to ride with Wax Mosby. I'll ride with Ilsa. Jo can ride with Ursula and Dave, you can ride with—"

"Stop being half-wits," Wax snapped. "It won't hurt Ursula to ride with me."

"That's if you *didn't* shoot my pa," Dave snapped.

"I didn't. I give you my word."

"The word of a would-be killer isn't worth much."

"Maybe I should just stay up here." Ursula was so lonely that the thought of staying, of being left alone again, was near torture. On the other hand, she'd seen a few people now, and she was remembering that she didn't like most of them. Mitch and Dave for example. She touched her hatchet and was glad for its hefty weight.

Mitch glared at her, then he shifted his eyes to Wax. "The night you saw me sitting on that mountainside, I'd ridden into Bucksnort. As I stood outside the window, I overheard men in a saloon talking about Pa being shot. One said Wax Mosby shot him, and another man said someone else claimed to have done it." He crossed his arms. "Who do *you* say shot him?"

"I was there, and I know Smilin' Bob did it. I saw him shoot your pa right in the back."

Nodding, Mitch said, "That's the name I heard."

"I know who Smilin' Bob is," Dave said. "He rides for Pike."

"All right." Mitch turned to his horse. "Ursula can ride with you. But when the trail gets narrow and we string out, Dave rides ahead, and I follow behind."

Wax nodded then walked to Ursula's side.

She wondered if he would sprout fangs and a tail with rattles. "You lied to me."

"I didn't tell you some things I should have, but I never told a lie."

"You lied with every breath you took."

"I only fully woke up yesterday. Before that I wasn't thinking real clear."

She had to admit there was some truth in that. He'd spent three weeks addled and feverish off and on. Mostly sleeping.

But Ursula expected the worst. "It's the Bible story of 'The Scorpion and the Frog.' I help you, and you sting me."

Mitch slapped himself in the face, then rubbed it as if he were scrubbing with soap and water.

Well, Ursula knew of his heretical beliefs. No surprise there.

Ilsa caught his arm, whispered something to him, and dragged his attention to the horse. They mounted up.

"I haven't stung you, have I?" Wax asked.

"Not yet. But if you shot Quill Warden, then you sure enough have done some stinging."

"Well, I didn't. Let's ride."

Dave led the unloaded packhorse over to them. Wax tossed Ursula up so she straddled the horse. She was grateful she wore britches and suddenly saw the good sense of the strange skirt split into two wide legs that Ilsa wore. Ursula had only been on a horse once in the years since Grandpa had died. She'd ridden some when Grandpa was alive. Now, perched on top of that tall, restless critter, she clung to the saddle horn.

Wax swung up behind her and reached around to pick up the reins. His strength and warmth felt familiar after they'd been together for so long. It was confusing and enticing. All she'd learned about him danced around in her mind. A gunman. Dangerous . . . he admitted to that.

All the lies. All the kindness.

The way he'd spoken of her voice, and thanked her for helping him, saving him. It spun in her head until she was dizzy. Good thing she had a tight grip on the saddle horn.

Wax kicked the horse, and they moved out, three abreast. She looked to her left at Jo, who was looking up behind her, talking and smiling at Dave while she held the reins.

To her right, Ilsa was dressed in those beautiful, warm clothes. Mitch guided the horse with his right hand on the reins and his left circling her waist and holding her much closer than necessary.

Ursula faced forward. She already had three new people near her. And now she was going out to see even more.

She'd met the Wardens last fall. All their cowhands had invaded Hope Mountain like a horde.

And everyone here, except Mitch and Ilsa, had been isolated through the winter months. Well, Wax for only three weeks, but that was long enough.

So no sickness . . . assuming Mitch wasn't carrying some awful plague.

But to feel safe was beyond her. All she could do was ride on. Go because she felt near madness at the thought of not going.

Her heart pounded.

She prayed silently, frantically, as they rode toward the narrow trail that led up and out of this canyon.

Wax's warmth lured her, tempted her to relax into his strength, but she stayed stiff, her backbone straight as the trunk of an oak, refusing to lean on him even though she was sitting right against him. She distracted herself from the coming danger by trying to save Wax's soul.

"Oh, I was going to tell you the story of 'The Scorpion and the Frog.'"

"I'd like that," Wax said nearly into her ear, and she shivered with a confusing kind of pleasure. "I've never heard of that one before, and I'd've said I knew my Bible well as a youngster. Where is that parable?"

Ursula saw Mitch scrubbing his face again.

"It's in the smaller of the two Bibles."

Silence hung heavy over the group for long moments. Ursula waited for one of these heathens to deny the Bible.

And which heathen went first? Wax.

"There's only one Bible," Wax said quietly, almost whispering, as if he didn't want the others to know he said it.

"I had hoped once you were fully awake and feeling

better there would be time to talk of faith. You need to believe if you're to make it into heaven."

"I do believe."

"I can only hope and pray you don't die in your sins before you come to understand the Holy Scriptures."

Mitch scrubbed. Dave whispered to Jo.

Ilsa gave Ursula a worried look, but Ursula couldn't figure out if the look was for Wax not knowing about the two Bibles or for Ursula.

Had both of her sisters fallen away so quickly?

As they rode, Ilsa said, "I found a copy of *Aesop's Fables* in a bookstore in Chicago. It's written in English, not Danish like the book we had, Ursula. Mitch bought one for each of us, and we bought our own Bible, too."

Ilsa paused. Then almost as if she were plunging into something, she said in a rush, "The smaller of our two Bibles is *Aesop's Fables*, Ursula. I've been reading all winter, and if you could see that bookstore, with the Bibles right up front and displayed in an important way, and *Aesop's Fables* in the back along with all the other books, you'd know it's not a second Bible."

Ursula glanced at Jo, who, with a frown of regret, nodded. "It's not a second Bible. You need to trust us, Ursula."

Ursula didn't answer. How could she when her heart was breaking? Her sisters had lost their faith.

Praying for them, for the whole pack of heretics, almost distracted her from the coming terror.

11

The group climbed the side of the canyon to the snow-packed trail. Water ran from it like a river, and a path had been broken through by Jo and Dave. But it was tough going.

Wax figured Jo and Dave must've wanted in here bad.

"You got through that?" Mitch asked. He didn't sound as if he doubted them—the tracks were clear to see. But the tracks showed that the horses had sunk until they were probably shoulder deep in snow part of the time.

"We'll have to wade through for a while, but it's better on the downhill side. The snow is crusted there. We figured the snow was crusted the whole way, but once we reached this side, we sank like it was water. But Jo was frantic to get in to see Ursula. I thought we might bury ourselves, but we made it through, and we'll make it back the same way."

Dave plunged into the snow and helped break out the trail a little more. Following behind, Wax tightened his grip on Ursula. He felt every move and enjoyed holding her close.

They reached the top of a narrow peak, and sure enough, they walked right out on top of the snow.

They rode on down into another valley full of longhorn cattle.

"Is this where you lived through the winter?" Wax pointed at the little cabin. Smoke poured out of the chimney. The cattle grazed on grass Wax couldn't see because it was so new and short. There was a good-sized corral with a dozen horses in it.

"Nope, this is an old cabin Jo, Ursula, and Ilsa's grandfather built. We're using it as a line shack," Dave said.

Ursula, still sitting in front of Wax, whispered to him, "Grandma and Grandpa got along better if Grandpa had a place to go from time to time."

Jo and Ilsa heard, and both turned to Ursula.

"Do you remember that?" Jo asked. "I figured it out since we found this cabin and really gave thought to how much Grandpa was gone. And we talked of it some while we were living in there while Mitch was sick. But do you remember how it was between them?"

"And . . . are your grandparents dead?" Wax asked, trying to figure out just what he'd gotten into.

"Yes, I'd say Grandpa died about ten years ago and Grandma some years before that."

"And you've been up here—just the three of you—for all these years, alone?"

Ursula looked back at him as if she didn't understand the question. "Of course alone. The Wardens only invaded our mountain last fall."

Invaded was a strange word to choose. Wax looked at her a long moment, blinked, then said, "And both of your sisters married the Warden brothers . . . already?"

Ursula frowned. "It's even faster than you think of it

because they both got married last fall, before winter completely closed the mountain. They only knew the men they'd married for—"

"I knew Dave for a while," Jo interrupted.

"The time it took for Mitch to show up," Ursula continued, "which he did almost immediately after Dave. And then for Mitch to get sick, get well, and Ilsa to get sick and well. Was it a month?"

Wax saw Jo's cheeks turn pink and not from the cold weather.

"It *was* quite fast for a woman who'd never been around anyone." She gave her husband a very friendly smile. "But I'm glad I did it."

Dave smiled back.

"And Mitch and Ilsa got married after one or the other of them had been sick most of the time they were getting to know each other?" Wax asked.

Ilsa waved a hand as if she wanted to wipe away the question.

"We were caught in a somewhat—" Mitch cleared his throat—"compromising um . . . well, that is, we, we married in haste, you could say."

"Great haste," Dave said dryly. "That describes it pretty well."

"But it's working out nicely," Ilsa said.

"How much older than Jo are you?" Wax asked her. They looked about the same age to him. Ilsa, too, come to that. But he was no judge of such things. They were all adult women. But it sounded like Ursula must be the oldest.

"I may remember things you don't, Jo." Which was Ursula admitting she was some older.

They reached another trail with sides soaring overhead. It, too, was snow-packed but not as deep as the other.

"We have to walk through this one." Dave swung down and assisted Jo down. Ilsa leapt from the horse like a little cat, agile and fast.

"Be careful," Mitch cautioned.

Ilsa arched a brow as if she didn't understand what the words *be careful* meant.

Wax slid off the back of the horse and went to help Ursula down.

Ursula slid sideways as if she had no notion how to get off a horse.

He reached up to catch Ursula before she fell all the way to the ground. Just as he got his hands on her waist, Dave shoved him sideways.

"Keep your hands off her."

"She's been riding in front of me all the way here." Wax backed off. He wasn't a man with much backup in him, but he wasn't going to show one speck of resistance to the Warden brothers.

With Dave shoving and Wax backing, Ursula fell. Luckily, she was clinging so tight to the saddle horn she managed to stay upright.

Ignoring the shoving men, Ursula said in a tone that Wax hadn't heard before—hostile and seemingly aimed at Mitch, who hadn't been involved in letting her fall off her horse—"Ilsa just climbed a mountainside, and now you tell her to be careful?"

Wax couldn't help but enjoy that. Apparently Ursula didn't like either of the men who'd married her sisters.

"She's . . . she's . . ." Mitch glanced at his wife and grinned.

Pink bloomed on Ilsa's cheeks. "We have a little one on the way."

Jo gasped so loud it was almost a scream on indrawn breath. "I'm having one, too!"

The two sisters rushed forward and threw their arms around each other. After enough squealing to humble a herd of hogs, they drew apart and turned to look at Ursula, who was standing aside and watching with a worried expression on her face.

The two sisters dragged Ursula into the hug. Ursula's arms came around both of them, and they whispered and giggled, and Wax thought one of them was crying.

"Mine is due in the fall. September, the doctor told me," Ilsa said. "When is yours coming?"

"You went to the doctor?" Jo gasped. "Are you sick?"

"No, Mitch made me."

Wax noticed all three women exchange a confused look.

"Ma thinks mine is later than that," Jo said. "October."

The chattering went on a long time before Ursula pulled away. "How can either of you forgive me for what I did last fall? I abandoned you both. I was too afraid to do what was right."

Jo just reached out and dragged her back into the hug.

Ilsa whispered, "I love you, Ursula. I know how hard Grandma was on you, just because you spent so much more time with her. It was Jo and me who broke all the rules we were raised with. Can you forgive us for just doing as we wished without minding all we were taught?"

"There's nothing to forgive. I hope you'll let me come and live closer to you. I don't want to be cut off like I have been. I can't bear any more loneliness." Ursula hugged them tight.

Dave and Mitch watched the women with affectionate eyes. It took Wax a bit to realize he might have the same daft expression on his face. As if this involved him in any way.

Then he remembered kissing Ursula. Oh yes, he remembered it well. He could still feel those strong, slender arms twined around his neck.

Just maybe this did involve him.

A hard swat to the back of the head drew his eyes around.

Dave stood there glowering. With quiet menace, he said, "You stay away from Ursula."

It was quiet enough not to draw the women's attention, but Mitch was there by his brother's side, arms crossed, eyes narrowed in anger.

"I've heard plenty of your reputation," Mitch said. "You're not fit company for any decent woman. And most certainly not someone as fragile as Ursula."

"Fragile?" Whatever Wax had expected, it wasn't these two men thinking Ursula was fragile, and yet here they both stood, clearly thinking just that.

"She hauled me halfway up a mountain. Bore my weight when I had a bullet crease in one leg and a hole in my side. Then we walked for the better part of two days with me leaning heavily on her. She fed me and cared for me through a fever and a whack on the head that left me addled for weeks. She's the strongest woman I've ever known, and my ma was mighty strong."

His voice must've risen because the women quit hugging and chattering and turned to look at him.

"You think I'm strong?" There was something in Ursula's eyes Wax couldn't quite explain. He tried to look deeper and figure it out. Before he could, Dave whacked him on the back of the head hard enough he stumbled forward. Wax was glad they'd taken his guns away. Much as he was determined to change his ways and take whatever punishment Quill Warden handed out, he wasn't all that fond of taking it from the Warden sons.

Then his eyes went to Ursula again. "I'd be dead if not for the iron in your spine and the pure grit and determination you showed. And besides strong, you were thinking, planning, prepared. You were smart as well as strong. And kindhearted about all the burdens I landed smack on top of you. I don't *think* you're strong. *Thinking* makes it sound like there's an opinion involved. I've never imagined a woman so strong."

Ursula took a step toward him.

Jo caught her and said, "Let's get through this trail."

"Yep, let's get on. We're burning daylight." Mitch stepped between Ursula and her melting eyes, and Wax and his deep gratitude and respect for her.

Wax might be dead by the time this was over. It was just as well to set aside any notions he had about the most beautiful of the three women. Not that setting such notions aside was easy. In fact, he set them aside, then picked them right up again. He couldn't seem to stop thinking about her and her strength, how she smiled, how she wielded that hatchet. Her beautiful singing voice. What a woman of contrasts.

At least he'd face Quill Warden and have his say. If he couldn't persuade Quill to trust him, he'd die knowing being shot by an angry Quill Warden was a better way to die than being ambushed by one of Pike's dry-gulching gunhands.

In the end, he was just as dead, but there was such a thing as death with honor. He preferred that.

Dave took his horse's reins and waded into the snow. It was slippery with solid ice under the snow and some mud along the edges. Wax could see why it wasn't wise to ride the horses through it. Though walking was no great idea, either. Jo, Ursula, and Ilsa walked behind Dave, strung out single file. Wax came next with that hothead Mitch Warden at his back.

Ahead of him he heard Ilsa ask, "Why are you carrying that hatchet?"

Wax couldn't hear Ursula's answer, and he'd've liked to.

"Is that trail open yet?" Bludgeon Pike sat behind his desk and looked at the new hand he'd hired. Clip Norton was a skilled gunman willing to shoot anywhere his boss said to aim, as long as the money was good, but not a man to take charge, lead others.

And Bludge needed someone to lead. He preferred to hire that done.

Wax Mosby had been good at it, but he had a code, and Pike had learned early on not to send Wax out on the wrong job. Wax asked questions. He didn't shoot first.

And as a natural leader, he didn't take orders well.

Bludge regretted not firing Wax and sending him down the road once he'd learned Wax had that stubborn code. But by then Wax was almost running the ranch, and Bludge didn't want to do it himself. Instead, he sent Wax to hold the Warden place. But Pike hadn't lived through a Colorado mountain winter before. He'd had no idea the snow would pile up this deep and refuse to melt. It was still deep in places, and the trail between his ranch and the Warden place was a mean one. So Bludge didn't have a way to get over there and fire the man until the snow cleared.

He had a faint hope that Quill Warden, who seemed too stubborn to die most likely, might come storming back to take his ranch, and the two could shoot it out. That'd solve Bludge's Warden problem and his Mosby problem in one go.

Warden was the only other big rancher in the area. By the end of this summer, Bludge would control every acre of land outside of Bucksnort.

He'd rule like a king and enjoy every minute of it. He wanted to rub his hands together and count his money like in those melodramas that were so popular back east. He'd found the perfect place out here. New York City had too much law and order. Out here it was strength that ruled, and Bludge, not a man to throw a punch or draw a gun, had a knack for hiring strength.

Such strength stood before him. But Clip was a loner. And he wasn't above back-shooting and dry-gulching. Anyone with sense stayed clear of him and his famously quick temper. He was a man who held a grudge and didn't let himself be slighted.

"Nope, not yet," answered Clip, bringing Pike's thoughts back to the present. "Reckon a few more days and a man could fight his way through the trail, but we couldn't slip in and set up for an ambush. Too many tracks."

"We need to get someone in to see how Wax made it through the winter." If he survived.

Bludge again thought of how effortlessly Wax took command and wished he could keep him on. The steely-eyed youngster wasn't afraid of anyone—including Pike. That steel went all through the gunman, and men tended to fall in with him and take his orders. But he was too honest. Bludge couldn't trust him. Or rather he *could* trust him not to fight against the Wardens.

"How much longer?" The wait gnawed at Bludge. He wanted this over, and he was paying plenty to finish it.

"'Nother couple weeks or so." The tone Clip used wasn't exactly insolent, though sometimes Bludge wondered. More like . . . lazy. A whip-fast gunman who was lazy. Bludge couldn't quite make those go together. A lazy gunman was usually a dead one. But this man, who had killed ten men known to have a fast draw, might be the exception.

"Keep an eye out. As soon as we can go, we're moving in and running our cattle on that land." It was an order, but maybe Bludge shouldn't have snapped it out quite so hard at such a man as Clip Norton. Bludge liked having him on the payroll, but at the same time, he watched every word he spoke.

With cool amusement, Clip nodded. "Sure 'nuff, boss."

He left Bludge with a chill rushing up and down his spine. These were a different type of enforcers than he'd had in New York City, and Bludge thought again about strength—the kind you hired and the kind you had for yourself. The kind Quill Warden was known to have.

Bludge would be happy when Quill Warden was confirmed dead.

12

Ursula felt her jaw drop in amazement as they rode out of the forest where she could see where the Wardens had set up.

This had been a beautiful stretch of wilderness all her life. It was a vast open grassland studded here and there with bunches of trees, bordered on one end with a gushing stream and surrounded by forest. They came into the valley from the east. Ursula knew that on the far south end was the trail Grandpa had gone down when he went trading. It was the trail her parents had taken and never returned.

It was at the top of that trail, hidden by forest, that eight-year-old Ursula had stood and watched for her parents. Many times she'd escaped Grandma's watchful eye and gone to that trailhead. Many days she'd waited and prayed and feared.

She'd begged Grandpa to take her with him and let her help with the search. But he'd always said no. So she'd waited alone. The trail seemed to grow into a threat until she couldn't imagine taking it down. That trail led to death. It helped nurture her fear of going down and her determination to avoid strangers.

Now the valley held a big cabin. Behind it stood another building, long and low with three chimneys, each one puffing out smoke. Dave was talking with Mitch, who was full of questions after being gone all winter. Ursula heard the long, low building called a bunkhouse. There was a barn built of heavy logs, like every other structure. Corrals with a herd of horses, grazing on something, grass she couldn't see, she guessed.

A chicken coop with a flock of brown chickens and so many baby chicks darting around Ursula couldn't begin to count them all.

And cattle were everywhere. Longhorn cattle, red, tan, black, brown, speckled, and spotted, and all calmly spread across the meadow. None of this had existed last summer.

How had they changed it so much over a single winter? She'd known they were building a cabin last fall, but she hadn't imagined this. All she'd seen was the Wardens invading her cabin that she'd lived in all her life.

Quill and Isabelle Warden had moved into the cabin Ursula and her sisters lived in. Quill had come up here with a bullet wound and needed a warm place to heal.

Yes, they'd told her they were building a cabin, but she'd pictured one small cabin. This looked like a small town. Of course, Ursula had never seen a small town, so that was just a guess.

"You built all this since you came up last fall?" Wax asked.

That was exactly what Ursula had wanted to ask.

"You've got a lot done, Dave," Mitch said. "I'm impressed."

"We had the cabin and bunkhouse mostly up before the snow got too heavy to work. We had a corral built because the horses were harassing the cattle and the coop to keep the chickens from being coyote food. Then we spent the winter on finishing work. Laying floors, building inside doors, cupboards, furniture, and such. We built the barn this spring. Good weather's been here awhile. Even though the trail up to Ursula's stone house was still snowed shut. This will be where we live, Jo and me, once my folks get their cabin back."

He shared a look with Jo. Ursula felt the love and connection between the two. And a baby. One for Jo, another for Ilsa. She felt as if she'd truly and forever lost her sisters.

Wax, who rode behind her, dismounted and lifted her to the ground. She barely noticed it through her confusion and sense of being abandoned.

Ilsa came up beside her and slid an arm across her back. "Little nieces and nephews for you to love, Ursula. You can sing to them and tell them stories of our grandparents and even parents. We never talk about Ma and Pa. But what you said earlier made me realize you remember them better than Jo, and I have no memory of them at all. I'd love to hear about them."

"They went to the lowlands and died." Ursula knew that fact for sure.

"No, not that. I heard that from Grandma and Grandpa a hundred times." Ilsa quirked a smile.

"What's funny about that?"

"Grandma only taught us to count to a hundred, saying

we'd probably never have more than a hundred of anything so why bother counting higher? But Grandma said those words to us far more than a hundred times. So right there was one thing we needed a higher number for."

Shaking her head, Ilsa said, "Anyway, I don't want to hear that story. I have always been told I look like Ma with my dark hair. Do you remember what she looked like? Where was she from? We might have other grandparents somewhere, Ursula. Other family. Her name, before she married Pa, is in the family Bible, but where did she come from? How did they meet if Pa didn't go down the mountain? I'd like to know all about that. And what was she like? Did she laugh a lot? D-do you remember—" Ilsa's voice broke. She steadied her quivering chin, then went on. "What it was like when they left? Was she sad to leave us behind? Did they want to take us? Can you . . . can you remember her holding me or rocking me ever? Did she kiss us goodbye?"

Ursula turned from the buildings that had grown up like weeds in a formerly bare meadow and looked hard at Ilsa.

For a long second, she hesitated. "The memories are from so long ago. I need to think for a while. I can't quite see Ma anymore. Can't picture her face." Ursula felt her eyes burn. She wanted to cry from the sadness of forgetting her beloved mother. Father too. What had he looked like?

"Grandma didn't keep those memories alive for us." Jo came up beside them.

Ursula watched the men put up the horses. They'd go in soon and talk to Quill Warden. Was it possible Wax would be shot?

Forcing herself to think of anything else, Ursula said to her sisters, "I remember Pa arguing with Grandma. He said Ma wanted to go to town. She refused to live up here in isolation all her life. Grandma was furious."

"Grandma was always furious," Jo said quietly.

"That's not true. Only when we talked of the land beyond our mountain. Otherwise she was a hardworking woman. A fine cook and seamstress. She tended the chickens and cows. Grandpa wasn't around much, so those jobs fell to her, and she taught them to us."

"She was cranky," Jo said flatly. "Forget that if you must to convince yourself that all her dire warnings were reasonable, but Grandma wasn't thinking straight toward the end."

Ursula turned on Jo. "I won't listen to you speak ill of her."

Jo took a step back.

Dave came up beside Jo, stopping Ursula from continuing her scolding.

Jo didn't stop though. "I think that's why Grandpa was gone so much. He wanted to find a peaceful life for himself, and I think he knew she was mostly upset with him for daring to go down the mountain. For a while I thought he just wanted to get away from her for himself. But now I think he hoped she would be a kinder woman to us without him around."

Mitch swung open the cabin door. "Ma, Pa, I'm home again."

Mitch had been gone for near ten years before he came home last fall. Then, when killers came after him, he had to go to Chicago to clear up the threat that he'd brought to his family's door. He'd married Ilsa and taken her with him.

His ma rushed to the door and flung her arms around him. He spoke so quietly Ursula couldn't hear him, but a smile bloomed on Isabelle Warden's face that told Ursula exactly what news had been shared. Mrs. Warden rushed at Ilsa and hugged her. Jo came up and Mrs. Warden pulled her into a hug that included all three women.

It was a circle Ursula had no wish to be in, but still it stung. There were no more Warden sons, so even if Ursula were so inclined, and she most certainly wasn't, Mrs. Warden could never be Ma Warden to her.

Quill Warden emerged, spoke two words to Mitch, then his eyes snapped to Wax with a stare as cold and dead as the nails on a casket.

He strode forward.

Wax stood his ground.

Quill was breathing hard by the time he was face-to-face with Wax. And it wasn't because he'd been shot. Quill was all the way healed up.

"I didn't shoot you." Wax figured he should get that information out in the open and do it fast. "I admit I was with the men who did, and I witnessed Smilin' Bob shoot you in the back. I'm willing to go to the sheriff and tell him all I know."

Quill's eyes narrowed, but he was listening.

"Pike told us you were nesters. I'd been at your ranch for all of two seconds when I knew Pike lied. Since last fall, I've been to the land office, seen your homestead claim, seen that you proved up on it years ago. I saw legal proof of the other parcels of land you bought and paid for. I know you were here before anyone else except the native folks." Wax was surprised Quill was letting him talk, and his respect for the man rose with every word.

"I'm up here to see you, face you alone, because I want the truth. I don't shoot first and find out who I'm shooting at after my bullets have landed. I don't hire out my gun-hand to the highest bidder with no interest in who's paying me. I'm a man who fights for the brand, but only when the man behind the brand is honest, and Bludgeon Pike isn't.

"I'm sorry you were shot," Wax continued. "I wanted to go after you to make sure you were all right. But Bob was coming fast, and I knew he had his blood up for a kill. I had to pick between going after you and stopping Bob. I headed off Bob and Canada by claiming I saw you ride a different direction, a path through the woods where the snow hadn't sifted in. They hared off in the wrong way into the trees. The snow was falling fast, and by the time it was safe for me to slip away from Bob, your trail was gone."

Wax fell silent. It was Quill's turn.

Just riding with Smiling Bob that day was enough to earn Wax a fist in the face, and that's if Quill didn't shoot him down like a mangy, lying coyote.

Mrs. Warden came up beside Quill, and Wax shifted his eyes to her.

He nodded his head. "Name's Jake Mosby, ma'am. Folks call me Wax after my fancy beard and moustache. But they're in my past. My life as Wax Mosby is one I've been planning to put behind me just as soon as I cleared things up with you Wardens."

Still silence.

Wax was starting to wonder if the Wardens were right in the head.

"I'm not satisfied." Mitch came up beside his pa, and the two were a picture. As alike as father and son could be. "Maybe you didn't shoot Pa, but you weren't just riding with men that did. You were on Bludge's payroll, and it sounds to me as if you still are. An honest man would've refused Pike's filthy money after you found out the kind of low-down varmint he is."

Wax had to admit that would've been right. "I saw the winter stretch long in front of me. If I'd've had to stay at the Pike ranch, I'd've asked for my time and gone down the trail. But I was sent to your ranch house alone, to use it as a line shack. And Pike didn't get told there was hardly an animal left on the place. It was the kind of bad news his hired men didn't want to pass on. If he'd've known, he probably wouldn't've sent me, except maybe he thought I'd be guarding it against your return. The way I figured it, I could get a winter's pay without having to do any harm, and while I've been there, I've tended your cabin and cared for the bit of livestock you had to abandon. I needed a stake for the road, and I figured Bludge Pike might as well provide it for me."

"And what about the men who are in our cabin right now?" Mitch asked.

"More of Pike's men are there?" Quill asked, his face turning red, his fists clenched. "I thought you said you were there alone."

"I was. I was away from the house, climbing up the same mountain slope Mitch and Ilsa used, coming up here to see if you'd lived through the attack. I figured your family and the cowhands would be up here. I wanted to tell you what went on and confess my part in it. I didn't want to stand against you, and I figured to face up to the trouble."

"He was climbing the cliff when five men rode up to your cabin, Pa," Dave said. "They shot Wax off that cliff."

Quill's eyes skimmed Wax's bruised face and the scabs left from the slash on his cheek.

"They mentioned Mitch Pierce while they laughed about shooting me. I'd say that's more about you than me, Mitch. I didn't set those men there."

Ursula asked quietly, "Could we all just stay up here and leave those five men to fight with the men you think are coming from Pike?"

Quill snapped his head around to look at Ursula. "That's not a bad idea."

Wax turned too. "I'd say it's mighty bloodthirsty, Miss Ursula, to let them thin each other out, then we swoop in to finish off whoever's left standing. But it may come to that."

"We?" Dave asked.

That froze Wax on the spot because of course he needed to do more than apologize and ride off. He stepped back so he could see all four Wardens, who now stood in a line. Mitch, Quill, Mrs. Warden, and Dave. All standing as if they were ready for a shootout at high noon.

Wax nodded. He hated it because he wanted to hang up his guns and change his ways, and he wanted to do it now, but he said, "Yes, we. I'll fight with you. If you'll trust me, and I don't blame you for not doing that, I'll fight with you against the men Pike has hired. He had twenty men last fall: ten cowhands and ten more, including me, who are quick with a firearm. And I know he sent out word that he wanted more. But the cowhands aren't happy doing all the work while the gunmen earn fighting wages and loaf around, so it wouldn't surprise me if Pike's cowhands don't throw in with his gunmen to face you down, so expect ten or more bad characters."

Quill shoved his hands in the front pockets of his blue denim pants, frowning over what lay ahead. "We've got twelve hands, good with a gun and loyal men willing to fight, but I hate asking them to fight to save my land. It ain't right that they should die in a war fought for me."

"And I don't want my husband and sons in a shootout, either." Mrs. Warden looked more like Dave. She was tall, though not quite as tall as Quill, with dark hair and blue eyes.

"It don't matter what we want, Ma. That trail down the mountain will open in another couple of weeks. If we don't go down and face them, they'll find their way up here. There's no avoiding it," Dave said.

"I'm not going to hide up here while they hunt me," Quill said. "I ran last fall because half my cowhands were up here with Dave, and I knew I couldn't stand against the crew I heard Pike was sending. But I won't run like a scared rabbit again. I'm going to do the hunting. As soon as I can get down that trail, I'm driving those vermin off my land, and I won't stop until Pike is dead or in jail."

"You don't trust me now, and I don't blame you." Wax knew they'd have to trust him enough to give him back his guns. He wondered if they'd ever get there. "But maybe after a few days up here you'll be willing to let me side with you."

"It will be like nurturing a viper in our bosom," Mitch said.

"Is that a Bible story, too?" Wax looked nervously at Ursula.

"No, that's Shakespeare." Mitch scrubbed his face. "His writings get confused with the Bible from time to time, too." Then he added, "I've got an idea, and it might mean no shots fired from Warden guns."

Everyone turned to Mitch.

"Let's hear it." Quill Warden pointed to the cabin. "I've got a table built big enough there's a chair for everyone. Even you, Mosby."

They walked in, and before they got settled, Ma was pouring coffee.

Mitch took a long sip, then said, "First I have to explain to you what extortion is."

13

Ursula braced herself to listen to a lot of confusing talk. But most talk was confusing when it came from these folks from the lowlands. Why should now be any different?

"Extortion," Mitch said, "is when a group comes to your store and says, 'If you'll pay us every week, we will protect your business from crime.'"

"That seems very nice of them," Ursula said with a smile. Maybe this was a Bible story.

"It sounds like it, but this group makes it very clear that the ones you need protection from are them. Pay us every week, and *we* won't come in here and burn down your store."

Not so nice, Ursula decided.

"The legal term is *extortion*, but some people call it a protection racket. A gang of criminals take a few dollars from every store in a neighborhood, every week. And they make sure those store owners are afraid not to pay. They teach them that lesson by hurting anyone who won't pay. The first time someone won't pay he gets a beating."

All the Nordegren women gasped. Ilsa drew her knife.

"The next time he or someone he loves gets a leg broken."

Jo pulled the bow off her shoulders. She always carried it and a quiver of arrows slung over her neck and under her arm. Ursula noticed she didn't get out an arrow and notch it, so she must be feeling safe.

"By this time most people are paying. But if there's someone tough enough to defy them, their business catches fire and burns to the ground."

Ursula filled her hand with her hatchet, furious that someone would be hurt that way. She'd like to be there to fight for them.

Mitch's cold brown eyes slid from one person to the next. "You can see why everyone either pays or leaves to start up a business in a neighborhood not controlled by extortion gangs."

"An awful business, Mitch," Quill said. "What's the point of telling us this?"

"Because a man named Morris Canton ran one of the biggest protection rackets in New York City, and he got very rich doing it."

Ursula couldn't figure out what in the world this had to do with them.

Mitch's expression was grim. "He tried to extort money from a little dress shop owned by the wife of a man who worked for me. I decided Canton had to be brought down. By the time I was done with him, he grabbed all his money and ran one step in front of the law. He took his cash and came out west and set up business again. This time as a rancher named Bludgeon Pike."

Stunned silence fell over the group, then as if a dam burst, questions flooded the room.

"How do you know this?" Mrs. Warden asked.

"He can't bring his ways west with him and expect to get away with it." Quill pounded the table.

"Is he doing this because he hates you?" That was Dave. He seemed to love Mitch and, at the same time, have a little problem with him. Ursula could understand that. She tightened her grip on her hatchet.

Ilsa checked the edge of her knife. "We have to stop him."

Jo drew an arrow. "We will stop him."

"Yes, we have to and we will," Mitch said. "And here's how we're going to do it."

With Mitch's plan firmly in place and most everyone equally unhappy with it, the family quit their plotting. The men went out to see what work needed doing among the livestock and to show Mitch all they'd built over the winter.

"I think we'll have fried chicken for dinner. I'll butcher, pluck, and gut the chickens. You girls stay here and have a good visit." Mrs. Warden pulled on her coat and left the cabin.

Ursula sensed that just maybe Mrs. Warden thought they should help, but if that was so, she should have asked.

Ursula was alone with her two sisters. The life she'd always loved. She felt a coil of tension begin to relax. Not completely because there were strangers too close by. But it was better.

But it wouldn't last because part of the plan was for her to leave this mountain.

"I'll get us some coffee." Jo got up and went to the fireplace.

Ursula was amazed at the confident way her sister moved with all the strange things to be found in this new house. The cabin had a fireplace, and a hook held a pot of coffee over the low flames. There was a strange open chamber built into the fireplace that Jo called some kind of oven. Mrs. Warden had pulled a loaf of bread out of it.

Ursula and Ilsa moved to sit on either side of Jo as she got up and poured them all a cup of coffee.

"I think I'll go sleep at our cabin tonight." Ursula looked at Jo. "Are you and Dave staying there? Or do you stay here with Dave's folks?"

"We stayed in our—" Jo grinned and pointed at Ursula, Ilsa, and herself. "I mean *our*—the Nordegren women's— cabin all winter. But since spring work has begun, we've started staying over here most of the time. This is supposed to be our house after all. I told Ma and Pa Warden they could have our old cabin. No one was using it. But they were content to stay with us. And soon they'll be going down the mountain to reclaim their own house."

"Ursula," Ilsa said as she sipped her coffee, "I want to ask you some questions about our parents."

Jo sat up straight, eager to hear what Ilsa would say.

"What is it?" Ursula warmed her hands on the cup even though the fire crackled and the day was fairly mild.

"I've got a thousand questions," Ilsa said. "But the first one is, what do you think happened to them? I was so young I don't even remember any fuss about them not coming back. They were never a part of my life, and yet I feel like I miss them terribly. That can't be true, can it?"

"I've wondered what you might remember that I don't, too." Jo pushed her cup back and rested her elbows on the table and her chin on both fists. "Some things make no sense."

Ursula sipped, thinking back. Wondering what she could tell Ilsa that would help her. Thinking of losing her parents made her stomach roil. She set her cup aside. She couldn't swallow even one more sip.

"You were a baby, Ilsa. Not even one year old. They should have never left you when you were so young. You cried a lot after they left, and you could already say *mama* and *papa*. You cried those words a lot." Ursula fell silent, unsure what her sister really wanted.

"Do you remember why they left?" Ilsa asked. "We never talked much about them, but Ma wanted to live in the lowlands, right? When they didn't come back, Grandpa searched and searched?"

"Grandpa searched for them, it seemed like forever. I was eight. Old enough to remember how upset Grandma was when they didn't come back." Ursula's eyes narrowed as she remembered Grandma's rages. And tears.

"She begged Grandpa to go find them when they were a day late. They'd promised to be back in two weeks. Grandma went on about it before they left and the whole two weeks they were gone. But when they were late she was frantic."

Frowning, Ursula remembered more. "Grandma and Ma were always bickering. Ma wouldn't take all Grandma's fears seriously. And I remember Ma and Pa going down the mountain a few times. That time there was a terrible fight. Ma said they were leaving for good.

"Grandma kicked up such a fuss they agreed to leave us with her until they knew where they'd move to. They'd go down the mountain and find a place, a job for Pa, then they'd come back for us."

Ursula raised her hands to shoulder height as if she were surrendering. "They never did. On the fifteenth day, Grandma raged around until Grandpa agreed to go search for them. Then—"

Ursula rubbed her forehead as if she could dig out the memories. "I'd forgotten this, but there was some kind of trouble with the trail. Grandpa couldn't get down it. He came back, really upset."

"Dave told me he thinks there was an avalanche," Jo said. "He said when he and Mitch were young, climbing around the mountain, they would follow a trail up a ways, then it stopped. He had to do a lot of digging to get his horses and cows up here."

Ursula frowned. "We had cows and horses up here."

"I think the trail Grandpa found, the one he used to get his livestock up here and go up and down on his way to town, collapsed somehow."

"Do you think Ma and Pa died in the avalanche?" Ilsa's bottom lip trembled.

Ursula jerked her head back. "I've never considered such a thing. I hadn't thought of that trail for years. But it must've happened, the avalanche, right then. They went down, and the avalanche blocked their way back up."

"That alone wouldn't have kept them away," Jo said, resting her hand gently on her barely rounded belly, cradling her baby. "Any ma and pa would have clawed their way back up the mountain to get to their children."

"I remember Grandpa coming back upset about the trail and saying they might not be able to get back up, so he'd have to find them. Then he left for a long time." Ursula glanced up at Ilsa, then Jo, and said, "I used to sneak away from the cabin—Grandma would've skinned me if she'd known what I was doing—and I'd walk to the trailhead. I wanted to go down and help search, and I knew the way Grandpa went down. I'd stand up there and watch and wait. Every day. Days and days, I don't know for sure how long. It seemed like it was all through the spring and into the summer, maybe until winter closed in on us."

"I wonder if Pa Warden ever met Grandpa." Jo ran a finger along the edge of her coffee cup. "I can't quite figure out if they lived there by then. If Grandpa wanted to slip past them, he could've. The trail to get up here starts a good ways away from the Warden cabin. But what about in town? He'd've had to show himself if he was trading. Someone had to know him."

"We'll ask Quill," Ilsa said. "And if he didn't know Grandpa, Quill might know some old-timers in Bucksnort who'd've met him. We could find out more about him from others than from our own memory. I want to hear more from Ursula about what happened when our parents were lost."

"I don't think there is much more. A lot of what I do remember might not be exactly right." She thought, too, of the second Bible. Was it possible that wasn't exactly right, either?

Jo nodded. "I asked Grandpa if I could help find them, too."

"Maybe we asked together." Ursula couldn't remember doing it, but it sounded right. "But I remember asking in front of Grandma, and she shouted at me that I was never, never, ever to go to the lowlands."

"I remember that." Jo looked through the table into the past. She sat at the head of the table. Ilsa on her right. Ursula on her left.

It struck Ursula that this really was Jo's house. She had thought of it as the Wardens', but Dave had sat at one end of the table and Jo at the other.

Jo reached over and took Ursula's hand, then Ilsa's.

Ursula reached across the table, and Ilsa reached for her. She was glad they were holding hands and forming a circle, because it helped her tell a deeply painful story.

"Back then, when I looked down that trail, I'd hear Grandma's warnings in my head saying to stay up. I'd hear Ma and Pa telling us goodbye, saying they'd be back and wanted to take us down. The two voices nearly tore me in half. At first the tug was equal, and it was hard to stay at the top of the trail, even young as I was. The trail looked normal, and I was so tempted to just walk down it and start hunting. But as time passed Ma and Pa's voices grew faint while of course Grandma's voice was strong and full of warnings every day.

"I started to see shadows on that trail, and they grew and stretched in a way that wasn't true. Fear overcame what was real. I'd look at every shadow in that trail and see danger lurking in the darkness. The day came when that trail looked pure black. I'd stand at the trailhead, looking down, and I knew it could only go one place. To go down was to sin. I-I believed Ma and Pa had broken a commandment—Grandma's commandment. I didn't understand she couldn't make them. And then I forgot she had made that one and believed it came straight from God. All I was left with was the notion that Ma and Pa went down that trail, and it led them straight to hell."

Ilsa gasped.

"And if I followed after them, I would, too." Ursula tried to shrug as if it didn't matter. But it did. It had formed her whole life.

"You were eight. Little more than a baby. What a terrible thing for you." Jo's hand tightened on Ursula's.

"I finally quit going to the trailhead. Long before Grandpa gave up on ever finding them, I had given up and adopted all Grandma's worst fears. When she'd talk of the dangers off the mountain, I was in complete agreement with her. I believed every word and did my best to protect you and Jo from those dangers. I suppose, much like Grandma, I've become next thing to furiously mad."

"Are you going to be able to go down now?" Jo's hand tightened even more, drawing her out of the painful memories.

"You can stay up here with Jo," Ilsa said. "Mitch has to go down and see if he can get a posse of US Marshals to help him oust Pike. I'm going along to help protect him. I'd like for you to come with us, but Jo and Dave are staying up."

"I want to go," Ursula said with grim determination. "Please, let me go. I need to do this."

Mitch's plan was all set. They weren't about to just abandon the ranch.

Someone from the family had to stay up here in case Pike's gunslingers came up, and they'd need all the cow-hands to fight with them. Mitch had to go down to identify Canton, and he hoped to have the law with him in the fight down there. Ilsa refused to stay behind. Wax said he'd climb down and ride to Bucksnort with Mitch, stand as witness to Smiling Bob's crimes and fight if it came to that. The three of them would be coming from two directions when they attacked, and Ursula, well, Ursula would decide for herself.

"We've got a little time, don't we?" Ursula looked at her hands, held by her sisters. She was oldest, but they'd grown up first.

Jo squeezed her hand again. "Yes, we'll spend it letting you get used to the idea of going down, and in the end, you'll decide. You can do as you please."

Ursula had a lifetime of training she now knew she hadn't understood correctly. Of course, there was a difference between Grandma's commandments and God's. Knowing that in her head was one thing. Feeling it was another.

It was a failure to stay up here and terrifying to go down.

Yes, she could do as she pleased. The trouble with that was nothing pleased her.

14

Ursula wanted a long visit with her sisters, so they decided to go over to their old home together while Mrs. Warden worked on frying chicken and Quill oversaw the handling of a new calf. Ursula looked forward to the visit, but she hadn't counted on the menfolk coming along.

Dave came because he was overly protective, which was strange because he should know by now that his wife was about the most competent woman in the woods Ursula could imagine. Jo probably ended up protecting Dave most of the time. But Dave, a protector by nature, seemed to think Jo might be in need of extra help now that there was a baby on the way.

That pest Mitch came, of course. He talked too fast. He walked too fast, and he tried to boss everyone around. And he was with five people who had lived out here without his help all their lives, so why did they suddenly need a boss?

And Wax came along. A quiet man who moved with the silent grace that made Ursula think of a mountain lion.

A dangerous man. Wasn't that exactly who Grandma had warned her might exist down the mountain?

Ursula led the way with her sisters only a pace behind. They ran on foot because that's how they'd always gotten around. Jo with her bow and arrow. Ilsa with her knife, and today she carried her medicine bag. Ursula with her hatchet.

"When did you start carrying a hatchet with you all the time?" Ilsa came up beside her.

"I recognize it." Jo came close on her other side, so Ursula had both her sisters. The men weren't running, which left them a distance behind, allowing Ursula to pretend they weren't there.

Slowing to a walk, with a move she'd practiced a thousand times this winter, she whipped the hatchet off her belt and hurled it at a nearby oak.

The hatchet hit hard and stuck. "Right where I aimed." She felt proud of her skill. That was a sin, but before she repented, she enjoyed the shocked expression on her sisters' faces.

"Let me try that." Jo took a step.

Dave caught up and slid an arm around her waist. "You don't need a second deadly weapon."

Ilsa chuckled. "I suppose that applies to me, too. But I am going to try it when I get the chance."

She looked over her shoulder at Mitch. "Honey, can I have my own ax?"

"Probably," Mitch growled and got her moving again toward the Nordegren cabin.

Wax fetched the hatchet and turned it over in his hand before giving it back to Ursula. "Are you that good all the time?"

Nodding, Ursula said, "It's one of the things I did this winter when I was feeling lonely."

Jo looked at the hatchet, then frowned at Ursula and slid an arm across her waist, giving her a one-armed hug. "You must've been really lonely to've gotten that good."

They reached a scattering of boulders and walked around a jumble of them that were twice as high as Ursula's head. Behind the stones—hard to find if you didn't know it was there—a trail led into the canyon where Grandpa had built their home.

Ursula gasped when they stepped into sight of her lifelong home . . . not counting being driven out for the past winter.

"You built more corrals and added another building."

Dave came up beside Jo. "We wanted a couple of men over here with us. I can do most of the chores, but the men like a little space and seemed eager to keep building. I suggested the place needed cowhands. I think they got bored during the long cold winter, and with so many cowhands in one bunkhouse, they got on each other's nerves."

He gave a quiet laugh, and Ursula suspected there was a story there that she probably didn't want to hear. "If the weather was decent, they'd get outside and cut down trees. They did it off and on all winter. Then come spring, this went up as fast as the barn, and four men moved over here. Two were already living in your grandpa's cabin, the one we used as a line shack. So six men are left back in the meadow."

"Aren't half of them moving back down when Pa reclaims his house?" Mitch asked, as if he couldn't abide wasting all that labor for a bunkhouse.

"Then they can spread out even more. Or we can use this as a foreman's cabin. We'll need more hands eventually because our herd has plenty of room up here to grow." Dave sounded confident.

"Let me make sure I have all this straight," Wax said, turning to Ursula. "Your grandparents lived in this cabin with your parents and you three girls. Then your parents went missing, and you were raised by your grandparents. And you've never gone down the mountain."

Ursula nodded her head.

"But you were going down when you found me?"

"Yes. I believe God eased my fears for that one day so I could find you. I learned, though, that I don't want to be completely alone. I'll find contentment even with the Wardens ranching up here." Except, could she be happy while others came and went?

The memory of the courage she found that let her climb down the mountain was still echoing inside her. Yes, she'd turned back when she found Wax. She had no choice. But that courage, that interest in the outside world, was still there.

They walked around the cabin, which sat up against what looked like the back of a small canyon. Ursula followed a well-worn trail around a hidden corner in the canyon to a grassy pasture that spread out behind the cabin. This is where they'd always kept their small herd of cattle.

Ursula stumbled to a halt. "Where are our cows?" There should be several dozen red-spotted cows up here. There were none.

"We turned them in with our longhorns." Jo came up

and patted Ursula's arm. "Our Nordegren herd had enough cows that they were eating down the grass. Remember how many calves we had last spring? Every one of them was growing fast, and the grass wasn't holding out. We even talked about needing to drive them out of this small canyon to find grass."

The Nordegren women rarely ate any of their cows. They milked them, but eating them was too hard when they were more pets than livestock and they could hunt for other food.

"The roast beef Mrs. Warden made for dinner was so delicious. I think we might have made a mistake not eating the cows," Jo said.

Ilsa snickered. "True, but it would have been hard to choose one to eat. They were almost family."

Ursula turned to the Warden brothers. "Dave, you say there was an avalanche of some kind? Do you think that might have had something to do with our parents never coming back?"

"I'd say there almost certainly was a trail at one point," Dave said. "I hadn't thought of it much until I got serious about chiseling my way up here, but I followed a trail up for a time, then it went nearly sheer. I had to scale that by hand, no horse could get past it. When I finally got above that, I found what was the top part of the same trail. But it hadn't been stepped on for years. Scrub trees had grown up, rocks had rolled across it. Only when I started working on it did I realize it was an old trail."

"I remember climbing that," Mitch said. "We used to talk about how that one stretch ruined what would've been a fine trail."

Dave nodded.

"Let's go inside." Ilsa caught Ursula's arm. "I want to hear more stories about our parents. We talked about when they left, but I want to know more. What Ma's voice sounded like. What her hair looked like. Whether Pa liked to kiss her and carry us around. I can't believe we let so many years go by without really talking about them."

"It was Grandma," Ursula said. "Whenever one of us would bring up questions or memories of them, she'd get so upset. I can see now all her anger was really fear and probably grief. But she never cried, never had a soft feeling for any of us. She loved us, but it was a stern and demanding sort of love. Now that I look back on it, I'm sad for her. She wasn't a happy woman."

Troubled by her memories of long ago, she shook her head. Ilsa slung her arm around Ursula's waist. "It's so nice to be home."

"We need to hear more about Chicago, too." Ursula realized she was trying to avoid talking about their parents. But why? Simply because of how badly it had hurt her to lose them?

Or was it another one of Grandma's commandments to remain silent on such a painful subject?

"Yes, my memories are well buried, but I'll try and dig them out."

They headed inside the cabin.

Home.

Ursula could have lived here all winter with Jo and Dave if she hadn't been eaten up with fear . . . and with shame.

And now at the thought of talking about their parents,

her stomach twisted with an unreasonable fear. Being afraid seemed to be her finest talent.

"I think Grandma made talking about our parents forbidden." Ursula looked around her home.

Wax could tell she'd missed it.

"I have the same feeling about that high canyon. I think Grandpa must've told me at some point not to go in there," Jo said.

Wax sat down beside Ursula while Jo and Dave got to work, acting like they belonged here more than the rest of them. And they probably did.

Dave started a fire in the fireplace, and Jo got a pot filled with water and got coffee on to boil. Then Dave found tin cups for them all, and they settled in to talk while the coffee hissed over the fire.

Wax was directly across the table from Dave. Jo across from Ursula. Mitch and Ilsa sat side by side, squeezed in at one narrow end. The sisters seemed to need to huddle together, but the two married sisters wanted their husbands close, too. While Wax could have moved to the foot of the table, he felt a need to be near Ursula. He sensed her pain in dragging these memories out.

Wax wondered at all these women had never said. He had some experience of his own with losing track of long-ago memories.

He saw Ursula hesitate as if saying the first word was beyond her. He remembered something from after his pa died that might make what Ursula had to say easier.

"My ma would never talk about my pa after he died. I

was about the same age you were when your parents died. I had four little brothers and sisters, and at first they were always asking for Pa. Me too, I reckon." He frowned to think of how they'd badgered their grieving mother. "We were young enough we just didn't understand it. But it didn't take long until we all stopped."

"Can you remember why?" Ursula asked. "Did your ma scold or start crying or thrash you?"

Wax rubbed his hand over his mouth, thinking of the things his ma had said. "It wasn't like that. My two little sisters, most of all, kept asking when Pa was coming back. Ma would try and explain what dying meant. Then later they'd start up asking again."

A long stretch of quiet blanketed the room.

"It was her pain. Not tears, though I heard her crying sometimes in the night." Shaking his head, he said, "I've never felt so helpless. I had no way to bring him back. Nothing I could do but try and help run things. Feed the family. I quit asking about Pa, and when the little ones would ask, I could see her flinch and get quiet. My two little brothers followed pretty fast. We were all so young. Stairsteps. The girls little more than toddlers. Besides missing Pa so much, I think Ma was terrified of keeping us all alive. I'll bet you girls could just see it was a terrible thing for your grandma to speak of, and soon enough, your questions ended."

Wax rubbed his mouth again. "I still wonder if I'd've waited a year or so, then asked about Pa again, told stories about him, or spoke of how well I could hunt because of him, if Ma would have welcomed the talk. Maybe my little brothers would have been more comfortable at home, and they wouldn't have run off at such young ages. Maybe if they'd've stayed around, Ma and the girls wouldn't have been home alone when those marauders came through. Maybe the three of them would still be alive."

Mitch said quietly, "That's a lot of weight to take on a young boy's shoulders."

"Hard not to pick up every weight you can when you're trying to take care of your family. We were all in such a habit of not mentioning Pa that it was like a solid wall we couldn't get through. I'd bet it was that way for your grandma, only worse because of her dread of traveling off the mountain. She'd've had no trouble acting in such a way that you'd've quit asking questions. Maybe without her even saying a word."

Ursula looked sideways at Wax. "Your ma and sisters died. And you found them?"

Nodding, Wax said, "And I hunted down the men who did it and killed them." He raised his eyes from hers and looked around the room. "I'd always been a crack shot, but I used the skill for hunting, to feed my family. When Pa died it fell to me to fetch meat. I was out there with a rifle long before it was good sense to let me go. Bullets were costly, so I learned to hit what I aimed at, but I never considered shooting a man."

He rested his big hand on Ursula's shoulder and squeezed gently. "But when I found my ma and sisters dead—murdered—I wanted to kill. I wanted revenge. I used all my animal-hunting skills to track those two men down, and I shot them dead. Then I took their bodies in to the sheriff, planning to explain what had happened and confess to my part in it. I figured I'd end up being hung, and I was so heartbroken for my family I didn't care what happened to me.

"Instead, I found out those men had wanted posters on them. Wanted dead or alive. I earned a reward, and it was a goodly amount. I'd found a career for myself, and I still had enough rage in my heart for those killers that I wanted every murderer dead and buried. I started bounty hunting. Then I got offered a job earning fighting wages from a rancher who had trouble with rustlers. They were just another criminal that needed to be stopped. I was too good with a gun to give it up. I've been living off my gun ever since, until the day I rode alongside a man who shot Quill Warden in the back."

Wax looked up. "It was too much. I wanted no part of it. All the way back to Pike's ranch I made sure to never let Bob or Canada or any of Pike's gunmen ride at my back. I knew they were killers. And if they didn't kill me, someone else would—and soon—because that's the kind of life I'd decided to live. That's when I knew I had to quit or die young."

Ursula reached over and patted him on the chest.

Their eyes met. Time stretched out. Wax didn't know how much. Didn't care how much.

They shared a lonely life. He could see that she understood how a skill that made him good money had led in all the wrong directions.

15

I've wanted to look at the section of the Bible with the writing in it," Jo said, "to see what Ma's full name was before she married Pa."

"I brought our Bibles along with me." Ursula looked at the bag she'd brought from her stone house. She had taken the Bibles with her for the winter and then brought them back to this house where she hoped to stay.

She thumbed through the old black Bible until she found those pages.

"I always thought it was a terrible thing that someone had written in the Bible." Jo leaned close to study the writing.

"Here's Ma. It says her name was Susan Domanski. My middle name is Susan. I was named for Ma." Ursula felt a deep trembling. "What if she has parents still living? Or had brothers and sisters? We could have a family somewhere. Aunts and uncles, cousins."

Jo looked up at Dave. "What do you think? Is there a way to track Ma down? Find out if she has family?"

Dave shrugged and looked at Mitch.

"I'll get someone on it right away," Mitch said. "It's not for sure, but there's a good chance she's from around here since I don't think your pa sounds like a man who traveled far and wide. Unless she was traveling through with her family, and she married your pa and got left behind as her family and the wagon train went on west."

Mitch took the Bible and studied the name. "Domanski. I'll bet she's Polish or maybe German."

"Grandpa used to say Ilsa took after her ma. He used the words *black Irish*. Ursula looked lost. "Is Irish different than Polish?"

Mitch nodded, then went on. "The name Domanski isn't an Irish name, but they might've had some Irish heritage. Your grandpa had to get that idea from somewhere. Maybe your ma told him that. The name is unusual. I can try and find out if there are people named Domanski around here. There are tax rolls and census records. If she did have family close, those folks might have come up to visit you or gone searching for you, if they knew your mother had children."

Shaking his head, he continued, "It's worth a try searching for them. If your parents married nearby, there might be a marriage record. There might even be folks who remember it. If there was no parson around, and there might not have been nearly thirty years ago, then I don't know how to find a marriage record. But Ursula is twenty-seven years old. We'll go back about a year before that and search."

"What else do you remember about your parents, Ursula?" Mitch seemed to think the matter was settled for now. But Ursula wanted to go running down the mountain and just search everywhere for someone who was her family. She'd never felt such a longing in her life.

Mitch's question distracted her from the almost frantic need to start hunting.

"I can remember Ma and Grandma talking a lot and laughing. They mostly got along well. I think their scrapping was when Ma insisted on going to town. She said shopping in the spring and fall was proper, and she wasn't going to let Pa and Grandpa go and have all the fun."

Ursula was silent for a moment as she sorted out her jumbled thoughts. "Ma would wheedle Grandma to get her to come along, or say she wanted to bring us along. I think there was a big fight, and Ma said she wasn't going to live in hiding anymore. That's when they left. They wanted to take us along, but Grandma finally convinced them to go, find a life for themselves, and when they came to their senses, they could return. Or if they insisted on such recklessness, they could get a cabin up and get settled, then come and get us."

Ursula reached a hand out to touch Ilsa. "I remember when you were born. Ma did some good-natured fussing because Pa went off to the lowlands that spring with Grandpa. She was almost ready to have you, so they left her behind. She was too far gone with her baby to climb down a mountain."

There were more stories. Small ones that popped into Ursula's head as she shared one memory and it awakened another. Jo added a few tales. Even Ilsa remembered things that had gotten pushed down in her memory. Things Grandpa had told her about Ma and Pa when they'd gone out on their long hunts for herbs and moss and roots to restock their supply of medicines.

The afternoon faded away, and it was time to go back to the Wardens' place for dinner.

"I think I'll stay here." Ursula liked this old cabin. So much more of a home than that stone structure.

"We'll all go eat together." Jo's hand was firm on Ursula's. "Ma will have made enough for everyone. Then Dave and I will come back here with you for the night. Mitch and Ilsa can stay with Ma and Pa Warden. They'll want the travelers close at hand to tell more of their adventures in Chicago."

Nodding, Ursula said, "I-I th-think it's time I went down to the lowlands. The idea that we might have family that we cut off all those years ago makes me feel, well, not excited really." She rested her hand on her jumping belly. "My stomach is too twisted up to call it that. But I'm determined to face it. Yes, I'll go down with you."

Her stomach twisted again. Wax rested a hand on her back as if he was ready to support her . . . or maybe ready to block her if she panicked and changed her mind.

She might need him to do both.

16

Part of Mitch's plan was insisting—well, he'd tried to insist—on taking the women out of the area, his ma included. He wanted to leave them in Bucksnort under the protection of the sheriff while the menfolk fought it out.

All the insisting in the world didn't budge Jo. She'd refused to leave Dave, and Mrs. Warden had vowed she'd stay and fight at her husband's side.

Ilsa had laughed in his face.

There was a standoff between the stubborn Warden men and the stubborn Warden women until the men knew the snow would melt and the trail would open up before the women would stand down.

There was no waiting that long. They had to get out of here and handle Pike before the trail opened between Pike's ranch and the Warden place. Once Pike took control of the house, it'd take a gunfight to get him out. Through a whole lot of wrangling, Wax had his guns back. Mitch was armed. Ilsa had proved she could wield a knife quick as a rattler. And Ursula had that wickedly sharp hatchet at hand. The four of them were, in all ways, ready for trouble. And now they were going down.

Mitch seemed to still believe he could leave these two women in Bucksnort, but Wax saw the fire in Ilsa's eyes and the grim determination in Ursula's. Wax would believe these women would allow themselves to be tucked away in safety when he saw it for himself.

Ilsa and Mitch had come home by way of Bucksnort. While they were there, Mitch had talked to the sheriff about the wanted posters on Pike. The sheriff promised to send word to the US Marshals, and he'd even promised to see if any cavalry divisions might come to their aid.

Now they had to slip past the five men holed up in the Warden cabin, get back to Bucksnort, and hope the marshals had gathered and were willing to ride in and arrest Pike. That would put an end to all of this before it started.

Then they'd come back and clear those five men out of the Wardens' ranch house. A simple plan with no gunfire involved. Even a crew of gunslingers like Pike had hired weren't going to open up on the cavalry. Wax said a heartfelt prayer that there was a willing cavalry unit in the area—because that would be a miracle.

If Pike was arrested, no one would stand and fight for a boss who could no longer pay. The men on his payroll were only as loyal as their monthly earnings. If Pike wasn't around, they'd drift.

It all sounded so easy, painless, safe.

Wax had nothing but grim doubts.

And now here they stood on the rim of the canyon he'd climbed up.

He glared down the mountainside. He had no wish to

climb down. Being shot off a mountain cured a man of climbing.

Ursula was right behind him, so nervous he could feel her vibrating . . . and she was a dozen feet away from him, so that was some serious shakes she had.

It'd been weeks since Wax had climbed up here and ended up shot. He still ached in his ribs and his leg and, oh, just about everywhere. But it was a whole lot better than it had been. Not mountain climbing good, but it seemed he had no choice.

Wax flexed his fingers and tested his ribs and leg. He still had a lot of tender spots.

Were those men down there keeping watch? It'd make sense that they would have an eye on the mountain since they'd seen one man there already.

Wax had sure enough kept an eye on it after he'd seen Mitch.

Climbing down, they would be a long time exposed. But the trail Dave had used to bring up his cattle wasn't passable yet. That was the one they expected Pike to use to come after the Wardens. It was going to shrink away soon—water ran from it like a river. And the trail from Pike's ranch to the Warden place would clear about the same time. Pike was going to open this ball if the Wardens didn't, and the Wardens weren't the type to hide and wait for the trouble to come to them.

Mitch went over the lip of the cliff.

Wax heard Ursula muttering under her breath. "What?"

She was staring at the cliff, frowning. "The lowlands are dangerous, and now I'm going down to start a fight with a crowd of gunmen. What a way to begin."

She kept staring down as if she were looking into the belly of hell.

Mitch went around a curve below and was out of sight.

Wax shook his head. "It's not all that safe up here. There are blizzards and bitter cold. There are wolves and bears and—"

"Bull elk," Ilsa said as she started over the edge. "Remember that bull elk that knocked me over a waterfall?"

"Get moving, Ilsa," Mitch called from below.

Ilsa smiled and vanished around the curved downward path Mitch had taken.

"You stay ahead of me." Wax gestured to Ursula.

"Why not you ahead of me?"

"Because it occurred to me you might change your mind. I'll be behind you to stop you if you want to run back for the mountaintop, and there's someone below to catch you if you fall."

He looked at her britches, not at all the same thing as Ilsa's riding skirt. Disturbing and improper as britches were, Wax was glad she had something sensible to climb in.

Nodding slowly, Ursula said, "It seems you know me pretty well, Wax." She started down, able to walk for a time up here at the top. Even knowing she was terrified, he admired her agile grace.

He approached the curve and took one moment to check the leather thong on his guns, thankful that the Wardens had reluctantly trusted him enough to give them back.

Before he'd gotten around the curve, he heard Ursula singing, and it helped him forget his aches, or at least accept them and keep moving.

Ursula chose her song for once, instead of just letting whatever music moved in her heart become song. She sang softly of courage.

Be strong and of good courage, fear not, nor be afraid of them: for the Lord your God, he goes with thee; he will not fail thee, nor forsake thee.

As she sang, Ursula considered that she was choosing verses from the big Bible and not the small one. She realized she needed courage for more than facing the outside world. She needed it to look at what she believed and accept the challenge to it. If she couldn't defend her faith, then what kind of faith was it?

And did it mean her sisters could no longer get to heaven if they believed in only the one Bible? Mrs. Warden said getting to heaven, sleeping with the angels, wasn't about anything but faith. If a person had faith, if they accepted that Jesus had died for their sins and believed, they were children of God. One Bible, which Mrs. Warden insisted was correct, or two Bibles, as Ursula believed, wasn't enough to separate a believer from God.

Ursula surely hoped that was true. Otherwise her poor sisters were doomed.

And she could easily fear such a thing for her sisters as she climbed down a mountain that in her childhood, Ursula believed towered above hell. To climb down was to choose eternal flames.

Ursula looked at a long stretch of rock ahead of her.

Occasionally it wasn't so sheer. Finding their way down wasn't hard. She remembered how hard it had been coming up with Wax.

Going down, all she saw was grass peeking and trees budding and the beauty of spring coming.

No flames anywhere.

It was at that moment Ursula realized she was just the littlest bit irrational. And she didn't like it.

She sang on, knowing she'd have to stop when they got lower so her voice wouldn't carry and draw attention. But for now, she quietly sang Bible verses about courage. And felt it growing in her soul until she almost believed she was brave.

17

The downward climb wound around the side of the mountain until they could finally see the Warden place. Ursula's beautiful song stopped, and Wax missed it even though he'd've told her to quit if she hadn't.

All four of them picked up the pace without anyone suggesting it. They were exposed until they got below the tree line. But even as they hurried, Wax noticed something strange. All five horses stood in the corral close to the house, which told Wax those men had settled in there. What kind of man hunters were they to not keep moving, hunting? It struck Wax as lazy. He sure hoped they had some weakness because they were crack shots. Hitting him on a mountainside wasn't easy. Aiming up was always a difficult shot to make.

They reached the ledge where Ursula had found him. It was a likely place to stop, and Wax watched to see if Mitch would call for a rest. He would've told Mitch to keep moving, but Mitch did that all on his own. They both knew firsthand a man on the ground could see a man sitting up here.

Wax checked the low ground compulsively. No one stepped out of the house. Mitch descended below the tree-tops and was out of sight. Ilsa disappeared into the green next. Ursula moved steadily until she was gone, then Wax reached first the spindly trees, then the heavier trunks, and was no longer visible from below.

Breathing a sigh of relief, he saw Mitch find a gentler slope and stand up to walk. Ilsa tagged after him, better at climbing than any of the rest of them by the look of her. Ursula rushed along in their wake. Wax had to hurry to keep up. The climb had tested all his tender spots, and they were aching, especially his leg and the back of his head where a gash was closed but jabbed at him enough to remind him he wasn't at full strength.

He checked his guns again, glad he hadn't lost them in the climb. He hadn't expected to, but checking guns was a smart habit in a wild country where good men and bad rode armed.

They were a while reaching the bottom of the cliff. Mitch led them on a winding path well out of sight of the cabin to the back corral, where he'd hidden the four horses he and Ilsa had ridden from the train. Wax could see by the tracks that no one else had found this hidden corral.

Thankfully, Mitch had brought his packhorses home saddled because he wanted to have saddles for them and the easiest way to do that was to bring them on the horses' backs, so they had enough for all of them, which meant even Ursula got her own. Wax regretted that. He sort of liked having her ride with him.

Silently they rode through the woods, a round-about path that gave the Warden spread a wide berth.

Then they set out for Bucksnort, hoping there'd be marshals to help them. They had a war to fight. Everyone hoped they could win it without a lot of bloodshed.

When they were out of earshot of the ranch, Mitch said, "We'll find out if anyone I sent for has shown up in Bucksnort. If no one's there, I'll send a wire and give them a day to gather. I told Pa that's all the longer I'd wait, so he'll be coming. With or without help, we grab Pike the day after tomorrow, get him back to the sheriff, then tell all his hired guns they're fired. Then we'll head on over here."

Mitch set his horse to a brisk walk as they fell in line on a narrow stretch of trail single file. Mitch, Ilsa, Ursula, and Wax at the rear. Wax was honored Mitch trusted him to guard their back. They picked up speed, and as the horses began trotting, Ursula slid sideways with a sharp scream.

Wax spurred his horse forward and snagged her before she ended up on the ground. He dragged her onto his lap and managed to catch her horse's reins. No one even lost a stride.

Mitch looked back and saw Wax had her. He frowned, and Wax wondered if he was in for a tug-of-war over Ursula. And he wondered whether he could let her go without a fight. Just how far was Mitch willing to trust him?

Mitch didn't come back to get her. Instead, he picked up the pace.

"Why did the horse jump around like that?" Ursula clung to Wax with her arms around his waist, sitting sideways across his lap.

"It's called trotting," Ilsa called back. "Trotting is so

dangerous, Ursula." Ilsa's horse hadn't trotted. It had gone from a walk to a slow smooth gallop without her doing much to convince it to behave in such a way.

"It is *not* dangerous." Mitch sounded exasperated. "It's not near as dangerous as believing there are two Bibles."

Wax saw Ursula's mouth open, no doubt to say something very strange to Mitch. At that moment, the rest of the horses broke into a gallop. Ursula shrieked again and buried her face in Wax's chest. He had trouble even believing how nice it felt to hold her close.

He looked down at the top of her head, white blond hair of a color he'd rarely seen. It was thick and smooth as silk. Wax had seen silk once so he knew. Her eyes were a color of blue as pure as the Colorado sky.

And she wasn't a tiny, delicate woman like Ilsa. She was tall, and that suited Wax because he was a tall man. She was slender but not skinny and had the strength of a warrior. He thought of how she'd guided his hands and feet up a cliff, then borne so much of his weight until she practically carried him to her house. And she could wield that wickedly sharp ax.

Mixed-up notions or not, Ursula was a beautiful, tough, lively woman, with a singing voice that could melt a heart of stone. Yes, even a heart as hard as Wax's.

Wax noticed both Mitch and Ilsa were paying attention strictly to the ride.

"I think you could hold on, riding alone, while the horse goes at this smooth gait," Wax said quietly to Ursula, speaking nearly into her ear. "But I don't know how to get you onto a galloping horse, and if we stop, the horse has to—" He thought of Ilsa's mount going from a walk to a gallop. "Well, most horses have to go through the trotting again to pick up speed."

Ursula looked up at him as they galloped along, and he looked back at her solemnly, wondering that she'd even let him touch her after the things she'd learned about him.

Their gazes locked, and that kiss was there between them.

A lot more was between them, though. Gunfire and danger. Wax's reputation and Ursula's fears.

As he held her, so alive and warm in his arms, it struck him that if he married her and took her back up that mountain and avoided everyone forever—a life that would probably suit her—his reputation wouldn't matter. No one would think much about Wax Mosby if they never saw him. They could have a good, if somewhat restricted, life.

Of course, before that happened, Wax had to convince Ursula to ignore some ugly things in his past.

Bludgeon Pike called his men in. He'd had a man come back from checking the trail late last night to say it was passable—probably. He hadn't fought through the fast-melting drifts, but he thought they could get through soon. The melting had gone on all night and every hour shrunk the drifts.

Pike decided they'd give it two more days.

"Day after tomorrow we ride." He didn't mean *we* precisely. Bludge wasn't going. Last year Wax had done the leading, this year it'd be Clip.

"You'll finally earn those fighting wages I've been paying through the winter." He had ten hired guns and another ten men riding herd. None of those second ten had come in for this meeting. They were there as cowpokes and were none too happy with the meager help they got from Pike's security guards, who earned fifty dollars a month to their thirty.

But the cowhands kept their mouths shut, or if they grumbled, they didn't face Pike with it. Now it was time for his guards to earn their pay.

"Wax spent the winter in the Wardens' cabin. I hope we'll get there and find out we can just drive our cattle right in. If the Wardens are back, we'll have a fight on our hands, and we'll win it. We watched him last fall, and Warden has only six cowhands."

Clip eased his gun in and out of his holster in a move he made all the time. Keeping it loose, keeping it from getting hung up. Keeping everyone on edge in case it wasn't just a nervous movement but the beginning of Norton's deadly fast draw.

"A nester with six cowhands?" Clip smirked, clear as day calling Bludge a liar. But Bludge didn't make an issue of it. It made him mad, though. He was the boss. And he paid well for men to take his orders. He made a clear note of it that Clip wasn't a man to trust.

Bludge knew, if Clip didn't, that after this was all settled, the man would turn his back at some point, and that's when Bludge would shut his mouth with a six-gun. Bludge had no problem with killing, but he liked better than even odds.

"Day after tomorrow we finish this."

18

There were no marshals. Not a single one.

Wax fumed over it. How many men might Pike have found over the winter?

"The marshals have been in touch," Sheriff Hale said. "Rance Cosgrove, the marshal from this area, said he's riding over. He will be here tomorrow, probably, unless he runs into trouble. And he's got men on the way. But it will be a while. A few days, a few weeks. He wants you to wait, Warden."

"I can't." Mitch slashed his hand and paced back and forth the length of the jailhouse. Wax knew a few men like Mitch. Never stopped moving, talking, thinking. They were usually very successful but always hard to be around.

"It's not that I don't want to wait, Sheriff. I can't. Pike's men will come pouring down on my family's ranch as soon as the trail opens, and we're pushing it as it is. There are people in my pa's cabin right now. And any day now, Pike will be back."

"Marshal Cosgrove wants Morris Canton alive. He crossed some powerful men back east who want the money back he stole. If he's dead and the money is lost, those men will be asking hard questions about whether we even tried to bring him in alive."

"I know Canton, and I know he left New York City a step ahead of the law. And he was always in on some underhanded deal or other. He made a big strike right before he left. That's how he's afforded all these gunfighters on his payroll."

Mitch paced back and forth in the small front area of the jail. "What about the cavalry?"

"I've sent word to Fort Union over three hundred miles away. They replied to my wire that they have men out fighting in the Indian Wars. They range widely, and if they can get word to them and if they are in the area—two real big *ifs*—they'll come over and see what can be done to keep the peace. But they've got their hands full settling down restless native folks. That's going to be their first priority."

Wax looked at Mitch, then Ilsa and Ursula. Ursula had a strange expression on her face. Her eyes were wide open, and she seemed to be paying strict attention to every word that was spoken, but at the same time, her eyes slid from one object to another.

He suspected she had no idea what a jail even was.

Or certainly not what one looked like.

Everything was brand-new to her.

Something came to Wax then like a lightning strike. Mitch, Ilsa, and Ursula were mostly unknown in the area. It gave him an idea that he didn't want to tell Hale until he'd talked it over with Mitch. If they tried it, they risked their own lives and all of Mitch's family, but if it worked, they increased their chances of settling this without firing a bullet.

Two real different outcomes.

"Any more questions, Mitch?" Wax wanted to get up and join Mitch's pacing, but he kept his backside leaned against the jailhouse door, refusing to move in a way that made him look other than calm and cool.

Wax could teach Mitch a few things.

Mitch did have more questions, but he was only haranguing the sheriff with the same things over and over.

"What about you, Wax?" The sheriff seemed to focus on Wax's still-bruised but clean-shaven face. The nickname *Wax* seemed pretty foolish now.

"You were on Pike's payroll last season. Still are as far as I know. How are you in here talking on the side of the Wardens?"

"I have a good gun arm, but I don't hire it out to a man who's breaking the law. I'm no outlaw, and if you ignored gossip and just listened to the facts, you'd know that."

"I've never heard of you riding the hoot owl trail, Mosby. That's a fact."

Wax tilted his chin. *Hoot owl trail* was another name for the hidden hills and mountain passes ridden by outlaws in the area, and Wax steered clear of them.

He explained himself to the sheriff as he had to the Wardens.

Hale nodded, satisfied as a man could be who was suspicious for a living. "I'll arrest and charge Smilin' Bob if you bring him in. You know I don't have any real legal authority outside of town."

Wax saw Mitch nod tightly. It didn't suit him that a

lawman could see lawbreaking at a distance and not jump in, but that's the way it was and no sense kicking against it.

"Mitch, we need to make some plans while we wait for the marshals."

Mitch turned on Wax, furious and impatient. "I'm not waiting for a bunch of men who might not show up. Not while my family's in danger."

Wax grabbed Mitch by the arm and yanked him outside.

As soon as they were outside, under his breath, Wax hissed, "Shut up and come along." Wax braced himself to take a fist in the face.

Mitch was curious enough to keep walking, though he glanced back. That's when Wax did, too, hoping the women had followed. He'd been so intent on getting Mitch out of there, he'd sort of forgotten about the women.

They were coming.

Jo turned to Dave, Quill, and Ma as she settled into her noon meal. "Are you sure we shouldn't get going right now? I don't want to miss the fight."

Dave tapped on the table impatiently. "We need to open that trail."

"It'd take all of us doing backbreaking work from morning till night to shovel that trail open," Quill said. "It's melting fast. I thought to give it a bit more time. Let the sun do the work for us."

"Not sure I can sit patiently waiting on the sun. Not for much longer." Dave took a bite out of a biscuit as if he were taking a bite out of his enemy. Or maybe his big brother, who'd decided Dave should stay behind.

Jo jabbed one finger right at her husband's nose. "Don't you think for one minute I'm staying safely up here while my sisters might be coming under the guns of my enemies."

"I never thought it. I know you well enough not to waste my time thinking it," Dave said. "Let's go right now and break a path through that mountain trail."

"Not yet," Quill said. "It'll take them all day today to get to Bucksnort. Mitch said they'd give the US Marshals one day to show up, and if they don't, he'll go without them. He knows when we're coming down. He won't wait one day longer. We need at least a day to dig out the worst of that trail. It's melting fast, but I went down as far as I could get through earlier today."

"So did I." Dave sounded grim.

"Me too." Jo tugged on her bow.

With a firm nod, Quill said, "Then you can see we won't get past the bad spots without hours spent shoveling. Tomorrow we scoop snow. Then we go down and get into this fight the day after tomorrow."

As soon as they were down the street a piece, Wax whispered, "We need to make some plans, and Hale can't hear them. Nobody can hear them."

Wax guided them into the middle of the quiet Bucksnort street that cut in front of the hotel and the saloon. Away from every door and every possible ear. All four of them stood in a tight circle. "You know about Pike's land grab. I only now fully realize I was being sent to nesters where Pike's land claim was good, and he had other men going to folks who shouldn't have been pushed off."

175

Wax frowned over the memory. "When he first went after your pa's place, he called in all his men except me. There was some noise about some of Pike's men heading out, but I didn't know the details. I still trusted Pike and figured it was more trouble with nesters. So when he sent me off on some errand that morning, I went. I couldn't get done what needed doing that day, so I threw in with Smilin' Bob and Canada Phelps, heading for your place. Later, I found out Pike had sent every gunfighter he had, and they were coming at the Circle Dash from different directions."

Mitch listened with a grim expression on his face and arms crossed. Ilsa came to his side and rested one hand on his tense arms. He glanced down, met Ilsa's gaze, and relaxed. He patted her hand. Wax saw love shining out of grouchy Mitch Warden's eyes, and it stirred something in Wax that warmed him. Love was tempting and confusing.

He wanted to look at Ursula, but he didn't. He was afraid of what might shine in his eyes, and he didn't want anyone noticing that.

"Listen," Wax continued. "Except for me, Pike sent every gunman he had after your family. But he didn't go himself." There was a silence so profound, Wax might've heard crickets chirping in the shadows under the board-walks.

Mitch's arms slowly dropped. His chin lifted. Something mean was shining in his eyes now. "You're telling me that Pike sent his men out to gun down the Wardens, and he stayed home alone?"

Wax shrugged one shoulder. "Not alone. He's got regular cowhands. But they're not the most likely bunch because Pike doesn't know what a good cowhand is. And on a normal day, most of them are out riding the range. Far as they know, I still work for Pike. If I ride in there, the few men around the place won't think a thing of it. And every one of them is just enough scared of me to lay back and let me do as I please, and that'll include walking right into Pike's house. They might make a fuss when I drag him out bound and gagged, then go riding out with him draped over a saddle, but I think I can say flat out Pike's wanted by the law and those honest cowhands will let me take him without any shooting. And if you three are with me, well, none of those cowhands knows Mitch Warden from a fence post. I saw you and Ilsa last fall with the Wardens, but none of Pike's men were in town. Whatever word reached Pike, there won't be anyone who saw you and can recognize you. And it's sure as certain no one's seen Ursula."

"If we wait until his gunhands ride off," Mitch said with cold satisfaction, "and let you take the lead, we can ride right onto his place, arrest him, and ride out with him. No one will say a word."

"And if we bring a US Marshal along, he can do the arresting. Pike's cowhands are none too fond of him. They ride for the brand, but I doubt they'd fight me, and not a one of them will fight a US Marshal. For sure not to save that lazy, arrogant coward."

"And once Pike's gunmen know there's no one around to pay them, the fight is over." Mitch sounded deeply satisfied with this plan.

"Having the marshal around will make it all easier to do.

It gives it all the shine of the law without anyone looking to us if they want to get even."

"I'll give the marshal one more day. We'll ride out there, keep watch, and wait for Pike's men to head for our place. We'll arrest Pike, then ride along the trail Pike's men are taking to our place, and look for a chance to give them the bad news that they're all fired. Maybe if we hang back a bit, Pike's men will even drive those five men hunting me away. Fact is, those five men might just quit, too, since Lewis is dead and they won't get paid."

"You make it sound easy, and I doubt it will be, but we can hope." Wax jerked his chin in agreement as he looked around the quiet little town, wondering what they could do for a day. "I reckon we should get rooms in the hotel."

Mitch turned so he was back-to-back with Wax. Between them they could see most of the town. A line of businesses facing each other. Most of the ramshackle, unpainted wooden buildings were empty. A saloon, a barber shop, a land office, a livery stable, a general store, and the hotel were the main businesses in operation. They stood near a side street that ran so it was a dead end at the hotel.

Between them, Wax felt like he and Mitch were braced to take on the whole town. Into this standoff came a quiet, shy sounding voice.

"I have never seen so many people in my life."

Wax counted exactly eight. Not including his group here. So twelve in total.

"And what is a hotel?"

Wax turned to look at Ursula, who was staring in fascination at the little hotel right down the street from them. It was painted white with glass windows on the downstairs and up. Two full stories. It really was a grand building by Bucksnort standards. And it sure as certain looked grand by Ursula Nordegren's Hope Mountain standards.

"It's time for a noon meal." Wax looked at Mitch, who nodded.

"Let's take the ladies out to eat." Mitch offered his arm rather grandly to Ilsa, who took it as if she'd done it a thousand times before.

Smiling at Ursula, Wax offered her his arm. At the same time, he tried to keep an eye on the other men on the street, who were looking with open curiosity at the strangers in town. He'd seen two of them before, but they weren't Pike's men. They didn't seem to recognize Wax without his beard and moustache.

But what if they did recognize him? There was nothing unusual about a Pike hand coming into town.

Ursula looked from Wax's bent elbow to the way Mitch and Ilsa walked ahead, smiled uncertainly, and took his arm. They strolled like grand ladies and gentlemen to the hotel to let someone else serve them a fine meal.

"Let me explain what a hotel is." Wax was delighted to realize he was with someone he could tell plenty of things to like it was fresh news. It made him feel smart, and that wasn't a feeling he got all that often.

Ursula pointed at whatever caught her eye, and Wax explained as they walked the short distance to the hotel. Mitch got rooms for the night. One for the women, one for himself, and one for Wax. Mitch and Ilsa told a funny story—it seemed funny now at least—about their being trapped into marriage due to unfortunate sleeping arrangements and Mitch's mother snoring.

Ursula promised sincerely to stay in the room with Ilsa. Hearing that gave Wax the smallest twinge of regret.

No marshal the rest of that day. Mitch, not a patient man at the best of times—and this wasn't even close to the best of times—was driving Ursula out of her mind with his fretting and pacing.

Ilsa seemed not only to be fine with the fretting but also she said things that made it worse and seemed to like it being worse.

Ursula did not understand people at all. And she was afraid to say most anything because she tended to start singing. She'd drawn some confused looks.

There was no denying that living with only her sisters, and more recently, completely alone, had made her strange.

They got through the day with food being brought to them, which made her nervous. Who could say what the cook had put in some of these things?

People milled all around. What if one of them had a fever or started shooting?

And she had a thousand questions.

Wax answered the endless questions Ursula asked, with Ilsa and Mitch adding things about Chicago, which had to be exaggerations, though Ilsa was an honest soul.

The night was unbearable. Ursula couldn't sleep. The few times she dozed off a voice or footstep or horse outside in the livery corral startled her awake.

She felt as if the walls were breathing, alive with masses of people pressing against them.

Ilsa had warned her not to leave the room. Ursula didn't understand why exactly, something about rules and no one could help but break them. It didn't matter. Ursula wouldn't have left this room if a herd of stampeding long-horn cattle were chasing her.

It was a mercy when the night ended at last.

The next day was a Sunday.

"Let's go to church," Wax said at the breakfast table.

Ursula was busy marveling at people just bringing food to the table and not showing any sign of wanting help cooking or cleaning up. "Shouldn't we offer to help wash the dishes?"

Ilsa shook her head. "It makes no sense, but these folks seem to want to do it."

"We pay them to do it," Mitch said. "It's how they make their living. If we do it for them, they're out of a job. You don't want them to be out of a job, do you?"

Ursula's brows arched. "Out of a job washing dishes? I'd think they'd welcome it."

As for church, it was a concept Ursula understood but had never paid much mind to. "We worship God all day every day. Why should we go to a building to worship today?"

"Because it's Sunday. Because God commanded us to remember the Sabbath day and keep it holy. And because we're here." Wax wiped his mouth on a snowy white cloth. There was one for each of them, and Ursula didn't touch it. She didn't like to think of it getting dirty and making someone wash up a mess she'd made.

With a quick, hard shake of his head, Mitch said, "We Wardens rarely go to church out here because we're too far from town. And I never went back east because I was too busy making money. I should have known I was headed down the wrong path once I didn't feel right about going."

Ursula wondered at her sister's husband.

"But we went in Chicago." Ilsa grabbed Ursula's hand. "The music is so beautiful. Many people all singing together. You would have loved it, Ursula."

Ursula thought of what she'd heard of the crowds of people in Chicago and felt very skeptical of whether she'd love it.

"I didn't go to church much growing up, either," Wax said. "Our farm was too far from a church. But we honored the commandment without a church building. We spent Sunday morning in Bible reading and prayer. Me and my ma and my brothers and sisters."

"What about since then?" Ursula asked.

Wax jerked one shoulder. "A man who hires out his gun arm isn't a good fit for church. I reckon I should've known I was headed down the wrong path once I didn't feel right about going."

Wax echoed Mitch's words, and the two looked at each other with solemn eyes.

A bell rang outside. "That's the church bell summoning us to services. I'd like to go." Wax laid the white cloth on the table and stood. Everyone else followed him outside.

Standing in front of the hotel, they looked at the small building straight across from the saloon. It was made of bare wood, but the word *Church* was painted above the door in tidy letters and above that word a white cross had been painted.

A horde of people were gathering out front. The biggest crowd Ursula had seen yet. She quickly counted and lost track when she got to twenty.

Wax and Mitch looked at each other again.

"The parson is the one who married Ilsa and me."

"You think he'll be happy to see us?" Ilsa sounded friendly and hopeful.

"I think he'll remember us, but that's not the same thing."

The folks gathered in front of the church filed in. The bell quit ringing.

"Let's go." Wax led the way.

19

Inside, Wax chose a bench, Ursula followed, and Ilsa came behind her. Ursula was glad to be surrounded by people she trusted. She was even glad Mitch filled up their bench so no one else could sit in their row. Of course, that didn't begin to handle the folks in front of them and behind them. Ursula kept her eyes on her clenched hands and listened, then to her surprise everyone stood up and began to sing. It was startling to recognize the song. One of Grandma's favorites.

"'A mighty fortress is our God, a bulwark never failing.'" Ursula's voice lifted in praise as it always did when she sang.

Heads turned. Eyes fastened on her.

She clapped her mouth shut.

Heads whirled away. Eyes straight to the front. They continued with the song, as if they were sorry they'd been caught staring.

"Stop please. Everyone please." The parson broke into the song.

The church fell silent as the parson left the front of the room and came the few paces from where he'd stood behind a wooden stand, straight for Ursula. Mitch was nearest him on the aisle. The parson noticed Mitch, lowered his brows, and frowned for a second.

Ursula wondered what Mitch had done to earn that expression. It was one she was sure was on her face a lot concerning Mitch.

Then he reached past Mitch and Ilsa to take Ursula's hand.

She really hoped he didn't have a fever.

"I'm Parson Graham. You have a beautiful singing voice. I could tell it surprised you when everyone turned to look. I hope you know it's because we all thought it was so lovely."

Then Parson Graham shook his head and let Ursula go, which she was glad of.

He turned to look at the crowd of people gathered in the church. "Isn't that so? None of you wanted to embarrass her."

A woman came forward and rested a hand on the parson's arm. "My husband is exactly right. Please don't stop. I can feel God's gift coming from you when you sing. No one intended to make you feel awkward on your first visit here. It was just so lovely, we wanted to see who had joined us. Thank you so much for coming to worship with us this morning."

The expectant look on the woman's face seemed to invite Ursula to tell her whole life story. How she'd come to be in Bucksnort, at this church, with Wax, Ilsa, and Mitch. But to talk in front of all these people was beyond her.

Several people murmured similar kind things.

Ursula barely managed to say, "Th-thank you. Yes, I love to sing, I shouldn't have been so loud. I—I—" It jumped into her head what Mitch and Wax had both said. "I live too far out to get to services, but we h-happened to come to town and—and it's Sunday, so—"

She was exhausted from all the words.

The parson reached again, patted her on the arm, then left her alone. His wife beamed a smile at Ursula, then returned to sit beside two young children.

Ursula wanted to run outside, but Wax was on her right and Ilsa was on her left and beyond that Mitch. People in front of her, people behind her . . . there was no escape.

Parson Graham stood in front and began singing again, nodding his head, smiling at Ursula to encourage her.

Wax started singing, then Ilsa, and even Mitch, who had stood quietly during the song before, now sang.

Ursula forced herself to continue, though at a much lower volume. But it was still a beautiful song, and Ursula felt her spirits lift even as she sang more quietly. It really was nice to sing in a group. It made her wonder at Ilsa's stories of attending church in Chicago with a large group of beautiful singers. Maybe she *would* like it.

When the singing ended, the parson preached on worry and what a sin it was. Ursula took that sermon like it was an arrow straight to the chest. Because it was her most besetting sin. Worry. The parson had the right of it. God called His followers to stop worrying. Ursula planned to do that right now.

Then she caught herself worrying that she might not be able to.

"Ursula, hold up." Wax rested his hand on her arm, and she turned to see what he wanted.

Mitch and Ilsa were slipping out of the bench seats and mixing with the folks walking toward the back door. Ursula was close enough to all these strangers as it was. She was glad for an excuse to hang back.

The parson and his wife had walked out before everyone else. She noticed them standing at the door talking as the people lined up to shake their hands.

"What is it?" She couldn't manage a smile. Between the crowd and the strange attention she'd gotten for her singing, it was all she could do not to push past Wax and stand with him directly in front of her.

"Did you notice Parson Graham reading from the Bible?"

"Yes, of course. He picked verses deliberately to make me feel bad. To remind me I'm a sinner. That wasn't very nice of him."

Wax smiled. She hardly noticed his faded bruises anymore. They were still there and the gash along the left side of his face might leave a permanent scar, though it wasn't going to be disfiguring, maybe a mottled white rash he'd always wear.

"I figured the parson was talking straight to me, too," he said. "All that warning about worry. Right while we're worrying about how to get—" Wax glanced left and right, then leaned close enough she could feel his breath on her ear when he whispered—"How to get Pike."

That narrowed her eyes, and her chin came up. "You

thought he was preaching at you, and I thought he was preaching at me?"

"I reckon if a parson has God guiding his words, most sermons carry a message that touches everyone. And most folks probably struggle with worry."

"That must be it. I was feeling like he was scolding me, and I was wondering how he knew so much about the worries I tote along with me like a heavy satchel."

"I'm sure you should lay your burdens down. So should I. So should we all." Wax smiled wider.

Ursula smiled back. "I think if I did, I might just float away, because I'm carrying a heavy load of worries."

"Miss Nordegren?" The parson's voice turned her to face him. The church had thinned out. Mitch and Ilsa stood talking with the parson's wife by the door, and voices came from outside.

But Ursula couldn't see those outside, and that gave her some comfort.

"Yes, that's my name. Ursula Nordegren."

"I heard what you said about worries." The parson was a soft-spoken man. He was slender and an inch or so shorter than Ursula. "I apologize if you felt like I was preaching straight at you. I honestly felt like I was giving myself a lecture. I can always find something to worry about. It's a sin, but I think God understands that the lives He's given us come with burdens. He wants us to trust Him, and He forgives us when we fail. That's one of the great beauties of our faith."

Nodding, Ursula said, "It was a fine sermon. I am glad we came to church."

Wax said from behind her, "Tell us again which verses

you preached on today, Parson. Where they are in the Bible?"

The parson's eyes lit up. Someone wanting to talk about his sermon must be a thing to get excited about.

"Let me show you." Parson Graham rushed to the front of the small building and picked up the big Bible.

Ursula had to wonder where the smaller of the two Bibles was. Surely a preacher would have both.

Parson Graham came back, thumbing through the pages in a way that seemed as if the parson cherished his Bible deeply. As if just being near it gave him encouragement and strength.

"Where's the other one?" Ursula felt a trembling deep inside herself. Soul deep.

The parson stopped leafing through pages to look up at her. "What other one?"

"The other Bible."

A look of genuine regret crossed his face. "You want one to look at while I talk with you about it? I'm sorry, but this is the only one I have. We could both look at the pages while I point out the text. And . . . uh . . ." The parson looked toward the ceiling as if something were up there. Then he snapped his fingers. "I know. Mr. Poston has one. Several of the families do, most in fact. Believers, if they can possibly afford it, often have the Bible. Sometimes it's the only book in their home. But the Postons live only a block away. They were the young family with the redheaded children, two little boys? We could get theirs if you would prefer not to share."

Ursula dug around in her head to find the right question. Parson Graham seemed so good-hearted and kind, she wanted to trust him.

"Have you heard the Bible story of 'The Grasshopper and the Ant'?"

The parson hesitated. "The ant is used in many verses. And most often as an example of hard work. Usually there is a challenge, a sluggard is called to accounts."

He thumbed quickly to the middle of the Bible. "Here it is in Proverbs. That's the one that comes first to mind."

Go to the ant, thou sluggard; consider her ways, and be wise: Which having no guide, overseer, or ruler, Provideth her meat in the summer, and gathereth her food in the harvest. How long wilt thou sleep, O sluggard? when wilt thou arise out of thy sleep?

Parson Graham looked up. "This is very much the Bible story behind the fable 'The Grasshopper and the Ant.'"

"The Bible story behind it?" Ursula felt her head twist a bit, like her brain wasn't quite sitting straight inside.

"Yes, many wonderful fables are based on Bible verses and stories. They are written in such a way as to bring out the moral of the story. 'The Boy Who Cried Wolf,' for example, is about trust. A boy is untrustworthy and his townsfolk stop listening to him. Then when he really needs help no one answers his call. The Bible is full of stories of honesty and trust."

Ursula wanted to escape the parson's words. In fact, she made a move to do just that, and Wax stopped her from going backward. The parson blocked her way forward.

191

Wax's hand moved up and down her spine, almost reaching the chill, the soul-deep confusion.

"Parson," Wax said in an easy voice, "why don't you and your wife and children join us for the noon meal. I understand you performed the wedding ceremony for Ursula's sister Ilsa and her husband, Mitch Warden. It would be a pleasure for us to have you as our guests."

The same look came over the parson's face he'd had when he first noticed Mitch. "Their marriage was blessed under . . . irregular circumstances."

"It all worked out," Wax said, still caressing Ursula's backbone. It distracted her enough she forgot she had, for one second, considered making a run for it. "They're expecting their first child and are happy with their life together. I know they'd like to visit with you."

Wax knew no such thing, and Ursula almost jabbed him with her elbow for his falsehood.

The parson lit up. "That's very nice of you . . . uh . . ."

"It's Jacob Mosby. Call me Jake." Wax's hand reached past Ursula, and the two men shook each other's hand. Ursula had a memory of Grandpa doing that sometimes with her. He'd say, "A handshake is as good as swearing an oath."

"I appreciate the invitation. I do know my wife has a meal roasting. Chicken, I believe."

"Is it something that could be put up and kept for your evening meal? We'd love to visit more with you."

Ursula tried to be very subtle when she kicked Wax in the shins using her heel. Then she shifted and stood on his toe as hard as sneakiness allowed.

The parson glanced at the door to see it was empty. "I'll go ask my wife."

"We'll head on over to the hotel. We're staying there, and I know they're expecting us for Sunday dinner. I'll warn the cook we might need a bigger table. A few more will be welcome."

"I believe my wife has an old family Bible tucked away." The parson narrowed his eyes as if trying to remember where it might be. "Would you like me to bring it? It's a special book, precious to her. Mine is newer. Wait, instead of hers, I'll give you mine as a gift if you want the Holy Scriptures. I'd consider it a privilege."

"Her Bible is like this one?" Ursula gestured at the black leather-bound volume.

"Oh no."

Ursula's heart lifted. At last she'd met someone with both Bibles.

Of course, she'd only met the Wardens and Wax. And since she'd come to town about three more people. This wasn't that big of a group. Someone somewhere had to have both Bibles besides her.

"My wife's Bible is very old. It came with her family from England before the Revolution, and it stretches back long before they came here. It's got all the family records written in it. I'll use that one to study for my sermons, and you can have mine. Age doesn't change the eternal Word of God."

Ursula's shoulders drooped. "There's no reason to give me a Bible, Parson. I have one at home."

"Would you like to borrow this to read once dinner is over or in the evening?"

He really was a kind man. She could imagine a more-than-one-hundred-year-old Bible and how fragile it might be. That's why it had been so carefully stored that he wasn't quite sure where it was. To offer his Bible and say it was not a problem for him to use such an old one, well, he didn't show by so much as a lowered brow that he would be risking damage to something very precious.

"I appreciate your generosity, but we're leaving town, possibly as soon as tomorrow morning. I'll get back to my own Bibles . . . uh, that is my own Bible very soon."

20

"You invited Parson Graham to lunch?" Mitch's brow rose. "He struck me as a scolding kind of man."

Wax suspected that meant Mitch worried, too, and thought the sermon had been aimed at him. Or no, maybe this was about his wedding.

Wax rolled his eyes. "That's only because he caught you breaking one of the most basic rules of decency."

"It wasn't just him," Ilsa said. "We got caught by about fifteen people."

There were three other tables with diners at them. An empty table nearby would be convenient to pull up when the Graham family joined them.

Ursula said to Ilsa, keeping her voice low, "The parson and I talked about Bibles, though I didn't exactly mention about there being two. But by the way he talked, it's clear the Bible he held is, in his view, the one and only Bible."

"At last you figured out there's only one. Hallelujah!" Mitch raised both hands heavenward.

"Mitch, hush." Ilsa slapped his shoulder.

"I didn't figure out anything," Ursula snapped. "I'm just saying the man is as confused as the rest of you heretics."

Mitch's hands came down. "I'm not surprised. You seem like the stubborn type. Clear evidence everywhere you turn, and you aren't interested in be—"

"Mitch." Wax cut him off.

"No!" Mitch jabbed a finger right in Wax's face but kept his voice fairly low. "She needs to figure it out. It's not right that she believes what she does."

Wax hesitated to break in. Mitch was being unkind no doubt about it, the half-wit. But he was also right. And a woman who'd cut herself off from her family for the winter did have a stubborn streak. Maybe she needed plain speaking.

Or maybe she'd use that little hatchet on Mitch.

"Mitch, stop." Ilsa held up a hand and next thing to jammed it in Mitch's face. "We know there is only one Bible," Ilsa said in more of a hiss than a whisper. "But it is a lot to ask for someone to turn away from something that's been held closely, in faith, all her life. Ursula needs time. And no matter how long she takes, she is a woman of faith. She's made her peace with God. If she never believes exactly as we do, she's still my sister and in many ways my mother. I love her, and I won't let you badger her."

Mitch reached up and pulled Ilsa's hand down from where she still held it in his face.

Wax saw something flash in his eyes, and after knowing Mitch for a very few days, he'd bet no one told Mitch what to say or how to say it.

Then he watched Mitch draw Ilsa's hand closer and kiss that flat palm. The flash in his eyes wasn't anger, it was something far warmer, far more intimate.

"You're right." He turned to Ursula. "And I apologize. I

was rude, which is far too easy for me. I hope you'll forgive me."

Silence fell over the table as Mitch looked at Ursula, and she looked back, then her eyes shifted to Ilsa.

"You really do believe this. That there's only one?"

Wax looked around and saw several people watching them. And why not? Mitch and Ilsa had a knack for putting on quite a show. He'd bet there were plenty of sparks between them. It was no wonder they'd ended up having a fast wedding.

A commotion at the door drew Wax's attention. Parson and Mrs. Graham entered with their two young daughters. Mitch rose to his feet and went to shake the parson's hand. "We're glad you came."

Wax stood and went to the empty table. With the least fuss possible, he moved it and a few chairs beside theirs to make one bigger place for them all to sit.

The waiter hurried over. "I'll do that for you."

"It's done." Wax gave the young man an easy slap on the shoulder.

"Are you ready to order now?" The boy seemed nervous. Wax had to wonder if his reputation preceded him.

Or maybe the boy was a big old sinner, and he was uncomfortable in the presence of the parson. Didn't matter as long as the food came.

Mitch led the Grahams over. He was deft about it. Used some polished manners that made Wax think about Mitch being a big success back east. He probably knew a whole lot of manners most of them had never heard of.

Wax saw him maneuver the parson into the seat to Ursula's right before pulling Ilsa around to sit by him.

21

Ursula watched her little sister, so relaxed and confident with these strangers.

It was all she could do to meet their eyes, mutter hello, and stare at her hands twisted in her lap.

She'd seen more people in the last day than she'd ever imagined. So many people it seemed inevitable that God would think the world was all getting too close.

God had promised there wouldn't be another Great Flood, but a new Tower of Babel incident had to be right on the horizon.

These people were here to challenge her deeply held beliefs. The upside-down notions that were being pushed at her shook her faith. And that was Satan's work. Surely it was. Knowing that steadied her. Whatever came of this meal, Satan would not win. Even if this strange belief they all had about only one Bible was true . . . and she felt herself sliding toward believing it . . . she was still a woman of faith. One Bible or two, God was in His heaven. Jesus died and rose and saved her from her sins.

Mrs. Graham sat on the other side of her husband with

the two little girls squeezed on one end of the table, as if they'd rather be uncomfortable than be too close to a stranger. Ursula knew how they felt.

Ilsa sat across from Mrs. Graham with Mitch across from the parson, and Wax sat at the head of the table.

The menu was short. Roast beef or fried chicken. Both came with biscuits and scalloped corn. The only difference in the meals besides the meat was the kind of gravy you got on your mashed potatoes.

There'd be pie for dessert, and despite her nerves, Ursula was looking forward to that.

The parson launched immediately into talking about worry. Ursula's brow furrowed as she listened to him talk of his Bible. Clearly only referencing one.

Sin or not, she was worried, and that was that.

When the parson took a breath, Mitch said, "Parson, Ilsa and I will always fondly remember that you performed our wedding ceremony."

The parson and Mitch, Ilsa, and Mrs. Graham, too, talked about the wedding in such overly polite details Ursula wondered what exactly had happened. They were all being vague. Ilsa and Mitch had told her and Wax the story earlier, but this little conversation sounded like they'd just come to the church and all was in order from the beginning.

Most certainly no one mentioned Mitch's bedroom.

Ursula was more used to plain speaking. Her eyes met Ilsa's and her sister's flashed with silent laughter. It was clear Ilsa was amused by everyone's careful way of speaking.

They didn't return to the subject of the Bibles. Instead,

Mitch found out the Grahams had served in a church in Denver for a time, until they felt called to a mission field farther into the wilderness.

Mitch knew a lot about Denver. Of course, Mitch seemed to know everything about everything—or at least he thought he did—so Ursula wasn't overly surprised.

She concentrated on her food while everyone else chattered. When she was done, she folded her hands tightly in her lap. It occurred to her that she was still lonely, even in the midst of all these people.

Had her isolation on that mountaintop really been that different from being in town? Was this loneliness something that she carried inside her? Had she been lonely with her sisters when they were the only ones on top of Hope Mountain?

Something must be wrong inside her. No matter where she lived, she'd be alone all her life. A crushing sadness gripped her heart. She couldn't have joined the conversation even if someone wanted to talk to her.

A strong, steady hand rested on hers.

He'd kept his hand beneath the tablecloth so no one could see. But she felt Wax's touch.

She looked up into his eyes. It was then she realized that not everyone else was chattering. Wax had nothing to say. The touch made her feel less alone in the middle of a crowd.

Wanting so much to be connected to someone pitched her heart into an impossible emotion. It couldn't be love. How did a woman even know what love felt like?

Especially a lonely woman like her.

He had to be a bad man. The Wardens seemed to think

ill of him. Even he had called himself dangerous. And yet all she knew was good.

Falling in love with him was a foolish thing, and yet she wondered if she might be doing that right now. She was able to relax her tightly gripped hands, open them to hold his. He saw her nerves, her worries, the pain of the confusion about her faith.

Finding Wax on the mountainside had been a terrible burden and a wonderful joy. He had needed her. And being needed had overcome her isolation.

Now, here, again, he reminded her she wasn't alone.

As their gazes held, Ursula wondered at the warmth she felt inside. It was all so confusing, and so wonderful.

"Ursula, isn't that right?" Mitch's voice broke into the moment she shared with Wax. With a tiny shake of her head, she turned to see Mitch looking at her in his usual annoying way. He didn't need her to answer a question. He'd just noticed her looking into Wax's eyes, and he didn't like Wax.

Well, she could hardly start snarling at Mitch in front of the parson. Something she was sure Mitch knew full well.

"Isn't what right?"

Mitch was very willing to repeat himself.

Ursula tried again to join in with these people. But a secret kept her steady. Secretly holding Wax's hand. And he held on to hers just as tightly.

She wasn't a friendly person on the best of days, but right now, all she wanted was to be alone. Or maybe, what she really wanted was to be alone with Wax.

---oOo---

Wax came away from the meal not sure if it had helped or made Ursula feel worse.

He worried about that. And, as he'd just been reminded, worrying was a sin. While he was in a sinning mood, he wanted to add an even bigger sin. He wanted to drive a fist right into Mitch Warden's mouth.

The man thought he had some right to be Ursula's guardian. Considering how he'd ended up married, he didn't have much business telling anyone else how to behave. And Wax was in the mood to explain that to him with a few short, sharp jabs to the face.

Add to that, from what Wax understood of how things had gone on last fall, Mitch had been in Chicago for the whole winter. Wax decided he'd known Ursula longer than Mitch. And he knew her *better* than Mitch. Wax had more right to decide who Ursula paid attention to.

Of course, there was another choice.

Ursula was a woman full grown who'd taken care of herself along with two little sisters for years. They ought to both just shut up and let Ursula run her own life, make her own decisions and hold hands and gaze into the eyes of whomever she chose.

Wax decided it was time to explain all this to Mitch. If fists got involved, so be it. He waited until they'd waved the parson and his nice family off. No sense inviting a crowd to watch Wax pound some sense into Mitch's stubborn head.

They stepped out of the hotel, Wax leading the way because anger was pushing him to move faster than the rest of them. Mitch was right behind him.

"Warden, I'm tired of—"

"It's the marshal," Mitch said, cutting him off. He caught Ilsa's hand and pushed past Wax. "He's finally made it to town. That's Marshal Cosgrove, the one we talked to last fall, Ilsa. C'mon."

Wax turned toward the jail to see a man dismounting. He hitched his horse and walked toward the door with his boots clumping on the wooden sidewalk and spurs jingling.

Mitch, with Ilsa in tow, jogged down the hotel steps to the street and strode toward the jail.

Wax grabbed Ursula's hand just to make sure she stayed close. Well, not just.

Then they followed hard on Mitch's heels.

Finally, they could get on with their plan. Rance Cosgrove, the US Marshal for the region, was a short, stocky man who looked as tough as the rugged trails he rode. Older than Wax but still with plenty of youth left. He had dark hair long overdue to be trimmed and dark eyes that looked out of a face coated with trail dust. Eyes sharp enough they seemed able to look right inside a man's head.

Wax didn't like it because, even having lived a life he wasn't ashamed of—much—and even quitting Pike and confessing everything to the Wardens and the sheriff, there were a few things he didn't want anyone to know. Most especially this lawman.

Cosgrove listened to Mitch recite all he knew, and Mitch's desire to ride to Pike's without delay.

"We need to wait," Cosgrove said. "There are marshals coming, but they'll be a while. I want to give them a week to turn up. The three of us can't brace this Morris character and ten gunslingers."

"There are five of us," Mitch said. "My wife is an uncommonly dangerous woman."

Ilsa waggled her fingers at the marshal in a way so unthreatening Wax almost closed his eyes in pain.

"My wife has saved my life—" Mitch turned to Ilsa. "Is it five times now?"

Ilsa smiled and tilted her head sideways in a charming little shrug. "I quit counting."

Mitch smiled, then said to the marshal, "Ursula is also dangerous with her hatchet."

Wax thought Mitch was just guessing about that, since they probably couldn't convince Ursula to stay behind.

"And Wax," Mitch continued without delay, "is fast as lightning and knows the layout of Pike's—"

"I know more than the layout," Wax interrupted. "I know the man. Morris Canton, who goes by the name of Bludgeon Pike out here, is a low-down, no-good coward. He's been planning all winter to claim the Wardens' house and land as his own. He's swallowed up a lot of homestead claims, but the Warden ranch, the Circle Dash, is a prime piece of land with good grazing and plenty of water. And Pike figured he could get his cattle on it, too. He's been planning to go racing in there as soon as possible this spring and take over. Set plenty of men up there and dig them in. He figures the Wardens will come back, and he wants to be in position to hold that land. He should be sending his men to attack any day. If we wait until the trails are passable, Pike will send his men to the ranch and stay safely behind at his own place."

The marshal's eyes narrowed as he considered this. "Will he keep a few men home to guard his own place?"

"I heard the talk last fall," Wax said. "He wants to go in there with guns blazing. Send so many men no one wants to stand against him. He never talked about holding men back."

"We hope to end this without it coming down to a shootout." Mitch took up the telling of their plan. "We don't want to kill and die to hold our land. More than that, we don't want to ask others to die for us. But we will fight if we have to. Not a single one of us is going to let Pike's land grab stand. But if we follow our plan, we might end this without it turning into a turkey shoot."

"It's a solid plan." The marshal tugged on a small beard that made Wax long for his own. "One problem. At least a couple of names Wax has mentioned are wanted men. I can't just let them ride off, and they won't come along peacefully."

Cosgrove drew his gun to inspect the load, careful to keep it aimed at the ground. "There's no way the five of us can bring in ten men without shooting trouble."

"Let's play it this way." Mitch stepped closer to Ilsa as if to guard her. "Let's get Pike. Bring him in. Lock him up." Mitch quickly told the marshal about the five men who'd wintered in the Warden cabin.

"So now we're talking about fifteen fighting men?" The marshal's brows arched high enough it lifted his hat. "And if those five men took money for killing, they all need to be brought in, too. We're waiting for more marshals."

"It's possible there'll be a gunfight there between Pike's men and the five in our cabin, and that will bring down the number of gunmen on both sides. Maybe to a number we can manage. And my pa is going to be watching for that trail to open up. If he can, he'll come down from Hope Mountain with my brother and our hired hands. And that adds fourteen tough men to this fight. This could end without a shooting war, Cosgrove. But it all gets real ugly if my family comes down without us. That mountain trail will be open any day. We'll come from one direction with the news Pike is gone. Pa will come from another direction with all our cowhands. We'll have all these varmints under our guns. I'm hoping they'll realize they've got no choice but to surrender."

"You've been back east too long, Warden. Not a one of those men is going to raise his hands and surrender. Run away, maybe, but if they're trapped, they'll fight."

Mitch's jaw tightened. The two men glared at each other.

Wax broke the staring contest. "We're heading out tomorrow, Cosgrove. We have to. To delay puts Mitch's family in too much danger. We hope you'll ride with us."

The marshal's eyes shifted between Wax and Mitch. He wasn't happy about it. But Wax could tell he didn't feel right letting them go alone.

The sheriff picked that moment to join the conversation. "I'll ride along. My deputy, too. I could try and form a posse. I might be able to gather men who'd fight. Some likely hands in this town, lots of Civil War veterans."

"There's still only seven of us, and two of the seven are women." The marshal held up a hand before anyone could speak. "Mighty tough women, I'm sure."

Mitch scowled at him but stayed silent.

Truth was Wax wasn't all the way excited about Ursula

coming. Yes, she was a tough woman. Strong and brave. Fast and accurate with that ax. But he still hated the thought of bullets flying with her in the middle of it.

He didn't speak, though. He figured Mitch would just scowl at him, too. And anyway, he'd already accepted that Ursula and Ilsa were coming.

"I can handle a shovel as well as any man." Jo jerked the shovel out of Dave's hands.

He leaned down close until his forehead rested on hers.

The noonday meal was over, and the men had gone to the trail with Quill. Jo had followed Dave out of the cabin just a minute or two behind the men.

She was glad the men had left them to their small disagreement. She wouldn't call it a fight exactly. That was too serious. They simply disagreed, and she was only reminding Dave that he was being a stubborn oaf with his ridiculous order that she not help.

He probably wanted her to go bake another pie or something.

"Why don't you help Ma get supper? She's cooking for everyone today, the hired hands included because our bunkhouse cook is helping clear the trail of snow."

"That trail will be open much faster if we all work together."

Dave picked her up, shovel and all, and kissed her. "We're going to be getting in each other's way as it is. The trail is narrow. And we don't have enough shovels for everyone."

"Your pa brought all of his up. You have a good supply."

"A man living on a mountain peak better be prepared to shovel snow."

"You're using both of our shovels. You should use me, too. It's not some quick job easily accomplished. It's long hours of hard work. Every hand helps. I'm fast and tireless when it comes to snow."

Dave kissed her soundly.

"Don't try and distract me." But she dropped the shovel, and her arms curled around his neck. She knew she was acting for all the world as if she'd been distracted.

When the kiss had gone on entirely too long, the cabin door opened behind Jo.

"I'm going to be working long hours in here to feed all of us, Jo."

Jo whirled around to face Ma. She felt the heat climb into her cheeks that said she was blushing.

Ma just smiled as she held the door open. "I know you want to get into this fight, and right now it seems like shoveling is the way to do it."

"It is. I don't like being tucked into the house, left behind, while Dave and Quill and all the hands work so hard."

Ma blinked. "You don't think feeding all these men is part of this fight? You don't think making a meal for twelve hands, plus Quill and Dave and the two of us, will be a lot of work and a huge help? It's a big enough part of the effort to keep two women busy all afternoon."

Jo jerked one shoulder and gave Ma a sheepish look. "You're right. Part of the reason I didn't think of that is you make it seem like you can just whip up a meal for sixteen people in a wink, Ma."

"I can make a meal for twelve people in thirty minutes." She winked. "Oh, forget that. If I need to, I can make a meal for thirty people in twelve minutes."

Then Ma grinned. "But some help would be welcome."

Jo smiled back. "All right. I know everyone works better on a full belly. I'll stay behind and cook."

She rested one hand on her belly. "I know I need to make some changes. Be more careful while I'm expecting this little one." She turned and slid her arms around Dave's waist. "It's hard, though, when I feel this fight for the Circle Dash is in part for any children we have. But at least for right now, I'll stay out of trouble."

"Thank you." Dave patted her on the shoulder like she was an obedient horse. Jo fought the urge to roll her eyes.

"You won't get through the snow on the trail and go on down without me, will you?" She had a strange compulsion to keep an eye on him. When this fight started, she wanted to be right in the middle of it. Her fingers tightened around the strap of her quiver, and she vowed that she'd be there. If they left her behind, she'd hunt them down and join the fight.

"No. We'll be all day getting through that trail and even then, it'll be barely passable. We hope we can clear it enough to set out tomorrow." He held both her shoulders in his two strong hands. "We're taking you and Ma. I promise you, Jo. I give you my word."

Nodding, Jo said, "Then I trust you."

She picked the shovel up from where she'd dropped it, thrust it into his hands, then turned to work with Ma on food and tried to look at it as part of the battle they had ahead of them.

22

They met at the sheriff's office long before dawn.

Her second night in town and pure exhaustion helped Ursula get a few hours of sleep. Maybe she was getting used to this wild, noisy place.

It was even beginning to seem normal that someone brought her food. They had strange ways down here, but in a crowd like this, they probably had all sorts of unusual customs. There were ten people in the dining room with her and her group. Plus the woman who asked them what they wanted and brought it. And Mitch said there was at least one person cooking in the kitchen, which was a separate room all to itself. Ursula would've liked to have seen it.

But not today. They had to arrest Bludgeon Pike. She'd save looking around at the oddities and wonders of town for another day—if she ever came back.

Marshal Cosgrove was in the livery saddling his horse. The sheriff led his up from one direction, the deputy, Lenny Keats, from another.

"I had answers to some of my wires last night," Cosgrove

said. "I hope three, maybe four, other marshals will be here within the week. Once I told them some of the outlaws we have a chance of rounding up, they got real interested. Are you sure you're not willing to wait?"

Mitch shook his head. "I'd like to have them along, Cosgrove, but we've got to keep an eye on Pike. As soon as his men ride off, we need to arrest him. If we miss our chance this could turn bloody. We're going. You can come along or be left behind."

"I'm coming. We'll bring Pike in, and then we'll see." Cosgrove acted grouchy, but he never quit tightening his saddle.

"I tucked a note in the belly drawer of my desk telling them where to find us," Sheriff Hale said from on horseback.

"I told them in the telegraph you would. They might make it ahead of time."

"And don't forget," Mitch added, "we might end up having to draw back and keep watch for days waiting until Bludge's gunslingers ride for the Warden ranch."

They saddled up and were leaving town before the sun rose.

Sheriff Hale and Deputy Keats rode along, bringing up the rear. Wax had to admit he was glad for the company. The Pike ranch was east of town, while the Wardens' was a long way north. Bucksnort made a corner in a triangle to the two places.

They rode at a steady pace. The trail twisted some, and there were rises to climb, but it was a generally downward slope along curving trails, winding around the foothills of the mountains.

Pike's ranch was nowhere near as far from Bucksnort as the Warden ranch. Only a few minutes after the sun had fully risen, Wax pulled his horse to a stop. "We leave the main trail here." He reined his horse to follow an almost invisible trail that led to high ground to the west of Pike's property.

When he reached a boulder-strewn stretch, he pulled his horse up. "We can watch from here." He dismounted and saw the others following suit. There was grass to be found for grazing to keep the horses content. And a stand of scrub oaks could be used to hitch their mounts.

Then, on foot, Wax led them to an overlook not overly far from the ranch yard.

"We can get down that trail, but it'll be all we're worth." Quill swung up onto his horse as the dark gave way to the first blush of dawn.

The men had shoveled all day yesterday, and still the trail was treacherous. The horses might have been able to break through without the cowpokes needing to shovel. But it was a rattlesnake of a trail on the best days of full summer. It wasn't even close to that now. The shoveling gave them the best chance to get into this fight. Falling off an icy cliff wouldn't help anyone.

Late last night, Dave had ridden down just to see if they could get a horse through. Quill would have done it if Dave hadn't been ready with his horse and too fast for his pa to catch. Jo had watched the two strong men fight for who would take the chance, and who would be the first to risk his life for this family. She loved them both for it. And Dave had made it down and back. Now the rest of them got a turn.

They set out. This time with Quill in the lead. There was one stretch in the middle where Dave had literally chiseled a trail out of the side of a sheer cliff last fall. That was where he suspected there'd been an avalanche.

The trail was so narrow a horse would be wise to stay on tiptoes. The wall of the cliff rubbed on the rider's shoulder on one side, and on the other, a stirrup dangled over a forty-foot drop.

Adding ice and snow made it a foolish thing for a man to attempt. They were all going. A gang of fools.

The plan was to all gather at the bottom, then slip up close enough to see if those five men were still in the cabin and clear them out before heading to Pike's ranch.

One by one they headed down. One by one they passed the most treacherous stretch. Jo's heart beat so hard it reminded her of how she liked to sneak up on animals to test herself against them. She was conscious of her heart beating faster when she was having fun, and she'd wondered if an animal's ears were sharp enough to hear that. Because of that question in her mind, she tried to control every emotion and was good at it.

Today she'd use all of her skill. She knew how to slip around in the woods, silent as smoke. She knew how to track as if the animals had left behind hand-painted signs telling her they'd been this way.

The menfolk were determined that this was their job, but Jo knew better. No man would best her in a silent attack, and that was just what they needed.

214

She touched the spot where her bow and quiver criss-crossed.

She was ready to fight, and she was planning to win.

"Look there." Wax jabbed a finger at a line of men riding away in the direction that would take them to the Circle Dash Ranch.

"Those are his gunmen. I recognize Smilin' Bob and Canada Phelps." Wax stared intently and continued naming off every one of Pike's men but one. He'd named them last night, too, but today there was a new face. From this distance, he couldn't say who it was, only who it wasn't. There was one man who hadn't been part of Pike's gun-fighting crew last fall.

"Almost every one of them has a wanted poster on him. Pike hired a nasty bunch." Cosgrove's jaw got tight. "And you didn't mention Clip Norton."

"Is that Clip Norton? I know his reputation, and it's a bloody one. But I've never seen him before. So Pike's already replaced me. And with a mean one at that."

Cosgrove whirled toward his horse.

Wax snaked out a hand and caught Cosgrove's arm. "You don't dare go after them."

Cosgrove's head snapped around to glare at Wax, then shook his head as if he had to force himself not to tear down the hill and arrest every one of those ten men. "I know. You're right. We would never survive to bring them in."

Wax went on. "Even with seven of us, you're right, we can't bring them in today. We have to get Pike out of there and locked up. He wasn't among the riders."

"Stayed behind like the worst kind of low-down coward," Mitch said. "Sounds like the man I knew in New York City. He always hired his dirty work done."

"I want every one of Pike's gunmen arrested. We'd wipe out a good chunk of the crime in this corner of the West if we had them. I hope a few marshals are riding hard to Bucksnort."

"And there go the cowhands." Wax watched another group head out. "All ten of them. Of course, he could have hired more. We always add men in the spring. But even if a few are left around the place, the resistance will be mighty thin."

"Let's give Pike's men time to get a few miles down the road." The marshal swung up onto horseback and patted his mount as he watched the second group disappear around a hill. "Sometimes someone forgets something."

"Think they rode off without any bullets?" Wax said acidly. "It's not likely those men, setting off to fight, forgot much."

"I know, but a horse can come up lame or throw a shoe. I've seen a lot. And the ride to the Warden place is at least a couple of hours."

"I'd say if they set a good pace, they could beat two hours by a few minutes." Wax had made the ride. "Unless the trail is drifted with snow or bogged with mud. I reckon there'll be some of both."

They all mounted up and sat atop their horses, watching the ranch. Time inched past. Mitch in particular twitched like grease on a hot skillet, but Wax was ready to finish this, too. They should have waited a full hour, but it hadn't been near long enough when Mitch's patience broke.

"It'll take us a while to ride down to the ranch. And there's a closer spot where we can have a lookout if we need to wait any longer." Mitch pointed at a rise where they could have one last check of the place.

Wax exchanged a look with the marshal, the sheriff, and the deputy. All three men gave firm jerks of their chins.

Marshal Cosgrove said, "Let's go."

Bludgeon rubbed his hands together in glee. Today was it. Today he'd take over the Circle Dash Ranch. He'd be a powerful man in an area without much law.

It still burned that he got driven out of New York City. He had considered hiring someone to kill Mitch Pierce, but he had to get his place out here set up first. He needed to get everything firmly in his hands.

He went to the window to gaze out on his kingdom, and the shock knocked him backward. He barely stayed on his feet. Seven horsemen were riding down the trail toward his cabin.

One of them Mitch Pierce. Pierce. Here. It was impossible. But he believed his own eyes.

Near panic, he could think of nothing but to run and hide. He grabbed a gun and the purse full of gold coins he kept in his desk drawer. He ran to the back door, thinking frantically of where to hide. He'd never found a handy bolt-hole like he'd had in New York City.

They'd be here before he could get a horse saddled.

Then his newest hired man came riding out of the barn.

"Over here!" He waved frantically.

The cowboy was only a skinny kid, a barely grown

boy. He rode his horse over. It was all Pike could do not to shout at him to hurry. When his drover got close, Pike reached up, grabbed the front of the kid's shirt and yanked him to the ground. He took the kid by such surprise he fell with a yelp. To keep him quiet, Pike gave him a vicious slash with the butt of his pistol. In his fury, he aimed the gun and only the need for quiet kept him from shooting.

Instead, he tried to holster the gun but fumbled it, then scrambled for it on the ground until he got it in his sweaty grip and shoved it properly into the holster. His breath was ragged. His hands shook. None of his plotting and planning had included his trouble from the East finding him out here.

He clawed his way onto the horse's back. Pike didn't ride much. He preferred a buggy, but he knew enough to mount up.

He turned to gallop straight east. Run. He'd head straight for the train and set up somewhere else.

He gritted his teeth so hard they hurt.

Sure, he'd run from New York City, but he'd had some warning. He got out of New York with his money. This time he'd ride away with nothing but the gold coins in one purse, the clothes on his back, and a horse.

He knew how to make money. He could ride to San Francisco. Set up his protection scheme again.

But he'd be starting from the bottom, and to take charge of a gang and a neighborhood took a long, hard fight, especially in San Francisco, where crime was already a big business.

No.

He jerked on the horse's reins so hard the animal reared up high.

Pike cursed aloud, then clamped his mouth shut.

He wasn't giving it all up.

It went against his good sense to fight. But he had to do it. He was angry enough to do it. He was ready to do it.

And there was only one place he needed to be. He wheeled his horse and rode for the trail all his high-priced gunhands had taken. He took off after his gunslingers, riding as fast as he could, keeping the ranch house between him and Pierce and whoever else was with him. Pike had counted six men riding with Pierce, and Pike lived by the rule that he could only see half of an attacking army, so he figured more than that.

If he could catch up with his men, he might get out of this with his skin and his money.

This time he was a man of the West. A strong, wealthy rancher and that type didn't run.

This time, instead of running, he'd get to his hired guns, and with them on his side, he'd face Pierce and win.

23

He's getting away." Wax knew the layout of the ranch, and he had eyes like nine eagles. He saw that kid look toward the back of the house and ride over. Then he heard galloping hooves and knew it was Pike.

Pike had seen them. But what had made him run? The marshal didn't even have a badge in sight.

Wax spurred his horse toward the retreating rider. He looked back. "Stay with the women, Mitch. Ursula at least can't ride fast."

Wax rode like the skilled horseman he was. It twisted his gut to abandon Ursula, but he couldn't bring Pike and his gunmen down on her or any of the Wardens when he owed them for being with the man who'd shot Quill.

If he rode like blue blazes, he could catch Pike before he joined his gunmen, and he could do it alone.

Then he heard a horse coming behind and knew the marshal was following. Two against Pike was a winning hand. Two against Pike and ten hired killers was death.

He'd chosen a life that led to death. And this might be his time. But at least he'd face it knowing he fought for right. He fought with God on his side. As he raced along, hoping to end this without gunfire, he prayed as he'd never prayed before.

He reached the ranch yard and, without even slowing, raced around the house to see the young man sprawled out unconscious on the ground. If Pike had killed that boy, Wax swore he'd find a way to hang him twice.

He knew the land well enough to know exactly where his slimy boss would run to. His high-priced killers. To hide behind them and let them take the bullets—and give them.

Blast it, they should have waited longer. Let the men get farther down the trail.

Leaning low on his horse, Wax urged the stallion to dig deep. He was a powerful runner with good stamina. The horse Pike had wouldn't be able to stay ahead for long. But he only had to stay ahead long enough.

Ilsa was hard on Wax's heels. Ursula pounded along behind her little sister.

Ilsa kicked her long-legged brown horse, and it sprang into a flat-out gallop. Ursula knew the difference between a walk, trot, and gallop now. And she could hang on through a gallop—or she sure hoped she could. She clung to the saddle horn and didn't try to do anything else. When Ilsa's horse went directly into the smooth run, Ursula's did, too.

She heard Mitch pounding along behind her. When he caught up, he gave her a strange look—probably surprised she hadn't fallen off—then in a wide spot in the trail, goaded his horse to pass her. Once ahead, he leaned low over his horse's neck. Ursula saw in every line of his body his determination to catch Ilsa.

He wanted to protect his wife, but he couldn't do it if he couldn't keep up with her.

Ilsa rode on, leaning low over her horse, too.

Ursula imitated Mitch and Ilsa and tried to match their speed. Her horse was a black mare, a perfect match for Wax's stallion. Mitch and Ilsa rode a matching pair of brown horses that were also a stallion and a mare.

Wax had mentioned what good horses they were. Mitch had brought them back from the East and tucked them into that hidden corral with plans to breed a line of champions.

Ursula almost smiled. They'd all have to ride hard to catch Ilsa. Ursula marveled at her skill on that horse. Horse and rider moved together like one creature.

Ilsa, with her strong horse under her, was apparently intent on catching and passing Wax. That must mean she intended to catch Pike herself. Ursula wouldn't bet against her little sister.

The marshal was coming, as were the sheriff and deputy. Ursula could hear their pounding hooves behind her, but she didn't risk taking a look.

All Ursula knew was Wax had hollered, "He's getting away!" And the race was on.

Jo was being a good, obedient little wife. She didn't plan to remain one long, but she wanted everyone to reach the bottom safely before she went hunting.

She'd cast off her dress, overriding Ma's insistence that her hunting clothes with britches and small bits of fabric sewn on to help her hide weren't proper.

Probably hunting men wasn't proper, either, and Ma was determined to help with that. Jo just waited until everyone was outside saddling up, and she emerged with her old clothes on.

Ma was still calling out dire protests when Jo swung up onto her horse.

"It's a safer way to ride down the mountain, Dave." Jo appealed to her husband rather than trying to talk sense into his ma. And while she talked, she rode toward the top of the trail.

She heard Ma muttering behind her, but that only made Jo smile. Ma loved her, and Jo delighted in it. A mother's love at last. And a baby on the way.

Her life was perfect.

Except they were headed for a gunfight. That put a stop to her smiling.

She ran her fingers along the strap of her quiver. She could change this fight a lot if she could take a few bad men out of it before it began. In complete silence, she could cause a lot of trouble.

What she'd heard about the five gunmen at the Warden house was grim. Mitch's enemy back east had paid for skilled assassins to hunt Mitch. He'd sent one, then two, now five. And all were dangerous men.

These five men would be very good.

If they could be taken by surprise by a few silent arrows throwing them into confusion, this fight might be over before it began.

At the base of this twisting, slippery trail was a stand of woods with a trail beaten into it by the Wardens driving their cattle. Snow had covered the trail all winter, but it should be visible now, or at least very soon. The heavy woods would stay more deeply in snow than sunlit areas.

Jo had a little bit of time.

This trail wasn't visible from the cabin. The Wardens planned to ease up close. See what they were up against before they went swarming out to take back their cabin.

During that time, she could thin the herd—or maybe stampede them.

But first they had to get down this mountain, and every step was gut-wrenching.

She fell into line. Ma Warden ahead of her, Dave behind. Dave had drawn the line at letting her bring up the rear, but he'd wanted her back as far as possible, save for being last. So he'd taken that position to watch out for her.

The trail was decent up high. Steep but not dangerously so. It was wide and easily traveled. Up here it was mostly blown clear of snow. The trail wound around a curve ahead, but it wound back, and Jo could see below them the worst stretch.

Quill led. He was visible again in the trail's curves, dozens of feet below where Jo rode. His twelve cowhands came along behind him. She could see all the way to the bottom and knew they had a long, slow ride ahead. She touched her bow and quiver where they crisscrossed over her heart and pondered that she might be in a fight for life and death today. She had never considered killing a person, and she didn't want to do it. But they faced men who needed to be stopped from what sounded like a lifetime of evil.

Would she kill to save her husband's life?

To save her own life and with it the life of her baby?

With an abiding prayer in her heart for God to protect them all, she followed Ma ever downward.

Hooves pounding, wind whipping in his eyes, Wax closed the gap between him and Pike. His horse was breathing hard, but the stallion was game. Pike, just ahead, glanced back. His eyes bugged out as he saw who was following him. Fear and anger fought for control of his expression. He went for his gun.

Swinging his arm backward, Pike fired behind him while galloping forward. That was no way to shoot a man, and Wax didn't even slow down as he charged on.

The bullets went wide off the side of the trail. If he'd gotten even close, Wax would have pulled his own six-shooter and ended this, but he ignored the bullets and plunged on.

Wax was close enough he heard the gun click on an empty chamber. Pike faced forward. He fumbled at his gun belt. Wax saw it was full of extra bullets. But it was hard reloading at a dead run. The gun wobbled in his hands as Wax closed the gap, and Pike had to feel hot breath down his neck.

The nose of Wax's black stallion passed the flank of Pike's young chestnut gelding. Wax heard the young horse breathing hard, nearing the end of his speed.

Wax's mount reached even with Pike's saddle. Wax

leaned farther forward to try to grab Pike and drag him off his horse.

Pike glanced back and saw Wax on his left. Pike lashed his gun at Wax's head. The gun struck Wax's shoulder and bounced off hard enough it went flying, the empty gun tumbling uselessly to the side of the trail.

Pike leaned down, urging every ounce of speed out of his horse. Wax considered drawing his gun, shouting at Pike to stop. But Pike wouldn't, and this didn't have to end in a shootout. Wax didn't want it that way.

Wax gained another foot and grabbed for Pike's collar. Pike jerked the reins on his horse to veer sideways and put space between them. Pike's horse whinnied and tossed its head, protesting the hard hand on its reins.

Furious that the man didn't admit when he was licked, Wax pulled his feet free of his stirrups, dove across the galloping horses and plowed Pike down to the ground. They hit and rolled. Sharp rocks slashed Wax's back. He skidded across scrub juniper and pebbles, fighting to hold on to Pike. Every still-tender bone in Wax's body howled with pain. Then he slammed up against a man-sized boulder. Pike flew forward, and Wax lost his grip.

The polecat tumbled head over heels, then staggered to his feet. Wax looked up from where he lay facedown on the ground and saw his quarry escaping. He launched himself at Pike and caught a boot. Pike staggered and fell. Wax clawed his way forward, ignoring the stones and thistles scraping the skin off his hands, ripping his jeans. He caught Pike and grappled with the squirming, howling fool. Wax got a fist around and slammed it into Pike's mouth.

Like the coyote he was, instead of fighting back when

the hard knock separated him from Wax, Pike leapt to his feet and ran. Wax flung himself after Pike and tackled him. They landed hard on the merciless ground.

Pike clawed for one of Wax's guns. Wax grabbed for it before bullets ended up flying after all.

Then suddenly Pike jerked himself loose.

Wax jumped for him, and someone grabbed him by the back of his shirt.

"Whoa, we've got him. Settle down." The marshal's voice. The marshal held Wax. It took a second or two for Wax's head to clear enough that he realized Mitch had Pike. Pike hadn't jerked himself loose. Mitch had torn Pike away from Wax's grip.

The marshal was restraining Wax while the sheriff clapped shackles on Pike's wrists.

"Let's get out of here in case any of his men heard that gunfire." Sheriff Hale dragged Pike off in the direction of the horses.

"You and the deputy take Pike in," Wax said.

"And watch him," Mitch added. "Like all cowards he's a backstabber and a sneak."

Pike, his lip bleeding, both eyes swelling shut, and his clothes torn nearly to ribbons, wrenched against the sheriff's hold and snarled at Mitch. "How'd you get out here, Pierce?"

"That's why he ran," Ilsa said as she led Pike's horse up. She'd caught it somehow. "He recognized you, Mitch. He saw you riding toward him and knew all his plans were in ruins."

Nodding, Mitch said, "I never thought of him catching sight of me. Stupid mistake."

Ilsa patted him on the arm. "I'm sure it's one you won't make again. Let's hope there's no need to become even more skilled at fighting."

"We've got to go after Pike's gunmen. There's a good chance my family is coming down off that mountain. I have to be there to fight with them. We'll tell Pike's men he's gone, arrested, and they won't earn another penny from him. Maybe we can still head off bloodshed."

"I need to arrest every man jack of them. I can't just tip my hat and let them ride off." The marshal looked grim as he watched the sheriff and deputy prepare to leave their little war party. They were outnumbered even before they lost the two lawmen.

"Don't forget to check on that man Pike knocked cold on his ranch, and make sure he's all right." Wax was impressed with Ilsa's good memory in the midst of mayhem.

The sheriff nodded. "If any help shows up in Bucksnort, I'll send 'em hard down the trail to help you."

"Send them straight for the Circle Dash," Mitch said. "Pike's ranch is out of the way."

Wax mounted up as did Ilsa, Ursula, Mitch, and Marshal Cosgrove.

When the sheriff was out of earshot, Wax muttered, "I reckon, like most things, we've got this to do on our own."

The marshal reined his horse to lead them down the trail those ten gunmen had taken. None of them had shown up with guns blazing yet, so Wax hoped they hadn't heard Pike emptying his gun at Wax.

Mitch fell in beside Ilsa. "Why did you take off ahead of me like that?"

Ilsa gave him a pert smile and didn't answer.

Wax rode alongside Ursula, breathing hard, bringing up the rear. Battered half to death, bleeding, and scraped up, he was back to feeling almost as puny as he had when he'd been shot off a mountainside.

She turned to him. Those blue eyes shining fit to put sunlight to shame. "That was the bravest thing I've ever seen."

All his aches melted away.

She handed him a kerchief. "Your lip is bleeding. And you've got dust and grit in your hair and on your face. But considering you seemed to fly through the air to capture that horrible man, you're in very good shape."

His chest swelled. His shoulders squared. His chin came up as he took the kerchief. He dabbed at the swollen spot on his lip, then swiped his face and hair and watched gravel rain off of him. None of it mattered. None of it even hurt.

Not when he had a woman as beautiful as Ursula Nordegren treating him like he was a hero.

Slowly a smile bloomed on his face. He leaned close enough to Ursula that Mitch and Ilsa couldn't hear them.

"When I turned around and saw you coming at a full gallop after me, I just fell all the way in love with you, Ursula."

Her head came up like a startled deer. She looked at him, and for a moment he wondered if, like a startled deer, she'd turn and run. Hard to do on horseback when she couldn't steer the horse, but he braced himself for how badly that would hurt.

When she didn't run, he forged onward. "I don't want to let another minute go by without me telling you. I

wonder if you would consider me as a man who is . . . is
. . ." Wax was no poet, and he fumbled what he wanted
to say just because it was so important, and he wanted it
to be so perfectly right.

"Would you consider joining your life to mine, Ursula?"

Her bright blue eyes widened. "Y-you m-mean . . ."

"I mean you should think of me when your thoughts
turn to a man. A man you want to spend the rest of your
life with. I would consider it a blessing straight from God
to have such a wonderful woman think of joining her life
with mine."

Her eyes blinked furiously. Maybe it was the dust still
hanging in the air after Wax's fight with Pike. Or maybe
she was on the verge of tears. But she was sure enough
paying close attention. And she wasn't kicking her horse
so she could go ride between Mitch and Ilsa.

"I can hardly believe I'd be so lucky as to have such a
wonderful man be interested in me."

With that, Wax leaned across the small bit of space
between their horses and kissed her.

Mitch didn't even notice how enthusiastically Ursula
kissed him back.

But Wax sure did.

24

Ursula pulled back from the kiss. The wonder of being wanted by someone cracked something open in her heart. As if she'd had a coating of ice around it, and now, with the ice gone, feelings flooded free and scalded her—in the best way possible.

"You do me a great honor." He reached his hand across and took hers. He had to pry it off the saddle horn. She didn't mean to fight him . . . exactly. She was beginning to feel like an old hand at riding. Instead of holding the saddle horn so tight, her hand gripped his.

As long as the horses were at a walk, there didn't seem to be a risk of her tumbling off, so she let him take possession of her hand, and they rode along like that for a quiet stretch.

It couldn't last.

The marshal wheeled his horse around. "We've gotta be coming up on them. How much farther to the Warden place?"

The marshal looked at Mitch, who said, "I don't know.

I've never been down this trail. Pike's place wasn't here when I was a youngster."

"I know the trail," Wax broke in. "We're most of the way to the Wardens'. We're coming to a low rise, heavily wooded. We'll ride over it and down, then on to a higher hill. At the top of that second hill, we can look down on the Warden place. I expect those gunmen of Pike's will leave their horses tucked back up in here soon, then spread out rather than all go right along the same trail."

"Let's get our horses hidden." The marshal turned off the trail, dismounted, and led his horse deeper into the rugged rocks and underbrush. There was a stand of trees not too far away, and he led his horse behind it. A good place to hide them.

Mitch, Ilsa, and Wax, with Ursula tagging along behind, soon had their own horses staked out to graze.

"I know these men," Wax said, "all but Norton. And I know this land. I know about where they'll set up."

They set out walking together for a time, then Mitch said, "I can recognize where we are now. We're coming up on the east side of our property. I know a spot that'd be a likely overlook from this direction."

Nodding, Wax said, "There's a good spot straight ahead. Another to the north of this trail and one to the south. There are ten gunmen. It figures they split up three, three, and four. We need to do the same."

"And you're thinking when we see them, we need to just call out to them that they're fired? You think they'll ride off on our word?" The marshal looked mighty skeptical of that plan.

"What about letting them fight with the men in your pa's cabin?" Ilsa asked, testing the edge of her knife.

Ursula rested her hand on the hatchet attached to her waist. "I think we can take them."

All four of these tough, dangerous people turned to look at her. It was as bad as when she'd been stared at for singing in church.

"Hold up." Jo's voice must've snapped because instantly, every single cowhand and all three Wardens turned to look at her. "I'm going ahead."

"Now, Jo, honey."

Jo held up a hand, and Dave fell silent. "You know there is no one better at slipping around in the woods. Let me go in there, get close, check on where these men are."

Ma rubbed her mouth. Jo could tell it was to keep herself from talking.

"Dave"—Jo gave him a narrow-eyed look—"you know I can do this better than anyone else."

He gave her a look so stubborn she didn't know if he'd admit it or not.

As if it caused him physical pain, he said, "No one better. No one I've ever heard of is better."

"Ilsa is." Jo had to be honest. "And Ursula is mighty good. It wouldn't surprise me if I found my sisters coming from the east while we come from the west."

She looked from Ma to Pa to Dave. "I will be careful. I've got everything to live for. You know how careful I can be. I used to make a game out of easing up close to a deer and slapping her on the back before she'd see me coming."

"You did?" Jimmy Joe, one of the Wardens' hired hands, sounded skeptical but real impressed.

"And grizzlies too."

Dave flinched at that.

"All wild critters. I'm good at this. I can vanish like a ghost. I can waft through the woods as silent as fog. I know how dangerous five hardened gunmen will be. I'll be careful, and I'll be back quick to let you know where they all are. We need to know that before we try and take the ranch back."

She touched the bow and quiver crossing her chest. "If someone is out alone, I might thin the herd, but only if I can do it silently so no one is alerted."

"As long as you remember these men might be nearly as wary as a deer." Dave took her reins, unhappy but willing to let her go. "Use all your skill. Don't let up for one brief moment."

"No man is more alert and wary than a deer, but I'll go in with that on my mind and be very careful. Give me a chance."

Disgruntled, Dave said, "You've been planning this from the first, haven't you?"

"Yep, didn't see any need to start arguing about it ahead of time."

Dave glowered at her, but she saw that he also knew she was right.

"I'd take you with me, but you're a sight noisier than I am in your boots." She gestured to the moccasins she wore along with her hunting clothes.

It looked like he had to almost break his jaw to move it, but he managed to say, "Holler if there's trouble."

Then in an unexpected move, he stepped close, snaked an arm around her waist, and kissed her soundly. "You and that baby are the most important things in the world to me. So be careful. I love you."

He let go, his hand sliding briefly across her still-mostly-flat belly, then stepped back.

She loved him so much, she found it impossible to speak. With a curt nod of her chin, she turned and rushed into the woods.

The plan was simple. They'd split up the land and the outlaws, then pick them off one by one.

The marshal went straight forward, but he didn't take the trail clearly traveled by Pike's gunmen just a short time ago. He stepped off the trail and almost melted into the woods. Wax was impressed.

Mitch and Ilsa went north.

Wax went south of the trail with Ursula. The minute they were out of sight of the others, Ursula caught Wax's arm in a grip so tight he winced.

"Let me go first."

Wax whipped his head around. "I will not."

She leaned close. "Living up on that mountaintop alone made me good at moving silently in the woods. It was a game I played with Ilsa and Jo. I can vanish like a wisp of smoke. They're better than me, but the three of us are better than anyone else."

Wax glowered at her. "You don't know anyone else. You have no idea if you're even good at all. You might tramp around out there like a herd of stampeding buffalo."

Ursula frowned. "What's a buffalo?"

Wax sighed. "It's a big wild cow and mighty noisy."

Ursula patted him on the arm. "I'll bet anything right now, Jo is having this talk with Dave, and Ilsa's having it with Mitch. Of the three of you, I'd say you're the smartest."

"I'm also really good in the woods. At reading signs, following a trail, and keeping quiet."

"I believe you, but you aren't as good as me. And that's only because I spent my whole life playing at different ways to be silent. Let me find them, then I'll be back for you. I'm not going to start a fight. Just locate them."

He had no intention of doing it. He looked down at his feet, gathering his arguments to keep the woman he loved from taking a terrible risk.

When he'd prepared what to say—and it didn't take long—he looked up.

She was gone.

Vanished like a wisp of smoke.

Well, all right. She was good. But figuring the ten men split up in thirds, she was going in after three or four armed men. He was insulted. How did she know how good he was?

"Ilsa, you go first. Scout them out. I'll wait for you here." Mitch grinned at her, and Ilsa kissed him soundly.

"Thank you. I won't be long." She whipped her knife out of the scabbard she always wore and clamped it in her teeth, then leapt for the lowest branch of a towering oak.

He called up in a loud whisper, "Don't kill anyone if you can help it."

She looked down and grinned around her blade, then went on scampering upward.

Climbing came as naturally to her as walking. Of course, she hadn't had time to weave long vines and sturdy roots into ropes. She had them all over the top of the mountain. Swinging through the air felt like flying. She loved birds, and since God hadn't seen fit to give her wings, she'd figured out the next best thing.

Now, in these dense woods, she picked the tallest tree and raced up with a skill only a bird could best.

She reached the top in complete silence. Up high, the wind buffeted her, and it cooled her from the exertion of the climb.

She scanned the area to the west, picking out likely overlooks. The land below her treetop swooped down, then right back up to a wooded rise that must look down on the Warden ranch. Her family's ranch. She wasn't about to let it go without a fight.

One man was easy. He wore a red kerchief around his neck. As if he wanted to be found. She expected to find three or four, and two more were easily spotted. But a fourth? She dared not start this until she'd found all four or was sure there were only three.

These outlaws had the instincts of prowling wolves who were looking down on prey. They didn't know it yet, but there were predators in these woods more dangerous than they were.

The Nordegren sisters.

25

Jo found the cabin in time to watch two men walk toward the barn. They came back out almost instantly, carrying ropes. They lassoed two horses out of a corral and led them into the barn.

Getting ready to ride off somewhere? Should she rush to get the Wardens to stop these two before they left? Or let them go and only deal with three? There were three more horses grazing on spring grass in the corral, so she suspected the other three men were around here somewhere.

The Wardens' cabin was beautiful. A long log cabin with glass windows, and a pretty porch built with split railings made from saplings.

Through the glass windows, Jo saw someone moving. So at least one of the men was in there. Stumped because she couldn't sneak in closer with those two men likely to come out of the barn any minute, she eased behind a pile of windfall oaks. Bushes had grown up through the jumble of trees until they formed a solid wall. There she waited on the west side of the clearing around the Warden ranch yard.

She knew all about patience and possessed it in great measure. But she also feared Dave didn't have enough of it and would come dashing in here to save her any minute.

Easing southward, she tried to get a better view through the windows, nearly a hundred feet away. As she moved, she knew her clothes made her nearly invisible, and she was silent enough she could be mistaken for the bending grass and twigs of the woods.

The two men rode out of the barn and split in separate directions. Maybe they had chores to do or maybe they were going to stand guard? Maybe they'd ride out and two more would ride in. If that was true, then there were possibly two men hiding in the direction these men rode. They might have spare horses, though Wax had said he'd seen five riders come in on five horses. He'd seen no extra critters.

Then she realized one of the men was riding straight toward her.

Ursula heard Wax coming and stopped, annoyed that he was going to make her watch over him as well as hunt for these outlaws.

She slid back out of his path. He walked right past her.

"Wax!" she hissed, making sure it was loud enough he could recognize her voice, but soft enough not to tell the whole forest there was a woman running loose. They were still a fair distance from the closest man, so she could talk, but very quietly.

He skidded to a stop. He tried to look unsurprised, but she'd startled him and that was that.

To give the man credit, he didn't come even close to shooting her. That risk had occurred to her when she'd hissed.

Under his breath, he scolded, "What are you doing back there?" He scowled as if she'd done something wrong.

She rolled her eyes heavenward and prayed for patience. Coming up to him, she patted him on the arm. "I can see you don't trust me."

That wiped the scowl off his face. He looked sincerely hurt. "I do trust you, Ursula. This isn't about trust. It's about letting you march off into danger while I stand idly by."

"It *is* about trust. But then how could you know how well I move through the woods? You've never seen me hunting. I accept that you want to protect me. You don't trust me to be so skilled I can handle hunting these men up in such a way they'll never know I'm near. And you were very quiet when you came after me. I heard you, but most wouldn't. Come along. We'll hunt these men together."

"I had planned to convince you to go back and let me hunt them alone." He sounded the littlest bit hopeless when he said it.

"Let's go." Ursula pulled her hatchet from her belt and examined the edge. It was sharp. She kept it that way. But a woman checked her tools.

They walked through a heavily wooded area and skirted around open stretches broken with jumbles of boulders and a few clusters of scrawny woods. The hills rolled ever upward. Then they reached a broken canyon that was wide open. They could see clearly all the way to the top of the next rise.

Ursula reached out a hand to stop Wax just as he reached out for her.

She turned and smiled at him. They were thinking alike. That struck her as a good sign.

"They'll be up there." Wax's voice was so quiet someone ten feet away would think it was the wind.

She gestured with her hatchet toward one man out in the open from this direction, but he was hunkered down behind a stand of aspen that lined the crest of the hill.

A second man was a fair distance to the south of him. Wax pointed before she could, so she nodded. A third man almost caught them by surprise, because he was too low to watch the ranch. What was he doing down low? Was he supposed to be keeping a watch to the back? He seemed to be intent on his saddle partners above him, but maybe he could see more of the men spread along to the north. The ones the marshal and Ilsa were after. Mitch, too, Ursula admitted. She hoped he didn't slow Ilsa down too much.

All three outlaws had their attention firmly fixed forward, not looking behind them at all. Poor woodsmen, every one of them. Ursula wondered with some disgust if she could just walk up there and whack them over the head with the butt of her hatchet and be done with her share of this.

With a nudge, Wax urged her farther south, where the land wasn't broken by this open space, so they could stay hidden. Much wiser than her reckless plan—but she'd've never actually just marched out in the open, it was just fun to imagine it.

She slipped along in the woods in the direction Wax had chosen. He was very quiet, and she checked back to make sure he was there.

He had a cheerful expression on his face. She might call it satisfied, smug even. Probably because she was following his orders.

She didn't mind following orders if a person ordered her to do something she was planning to do anyway. It was when she disagreed with him that there'd be trouble.

Then she thought of the way he'd talked. Of the two of them together forever. She seemed to remember something in the Bible—and yes, she was now thinking there was probably only one, though it made her nervous to accept that—there was something in there about wives obeying their husbands.

She'd have to see if that was a hard and fast rule or more of a suggestion to be ignored if the husband asked his wife to obey some really foolish order.

Maybe she needed to talk to the parson again.

They rounded the open area and slipped up on the man closest to them. This villain was farthest south. When they got close, Wax tugged her to a stop, then pointed to himself and the man ahead. He had a pleading look in his eyes.

He wanted to do it himself.

Ursula shrugged and ducked back mostly behind a tree. With a graceful sweep of her hand, she sent Wax on without her. She saw him draw his gun and braced herself, afraid she was about to see something awful. And loud.

Wait, if Wax fired a shot, he'd alert the whole hill.

What was he thinking?

She had to stop him.

Ilsa saw a fourth man. She hadn't been looking high enough. He was right at the top of the far rise. In fact, if her sharp eyes were reading it right, he was slightly over the crest, crouched low and dressed to blend in with the undergrowth of the woods.

Smarter than the one with the red bandanna. She made a note to be extra cautious with this one.

Climbing down from the treetops, she saw a pathway up in the branches that would lead her straight to the red-bandanna gunman.

She was tempted to take him out of this fight right now.

But she'd told Mitch she was just going to find them, then come back to him. And she was no woman who cried wolf. She'd said she'd come back, and she wanted her husband to know he could trust her.

Scampering the rest of the way down, she found Mitch checking his gun while sitting comfortably behind a rock. He wasn't even worried she'd go off on her own. The man did trust her. It made her glad she'd decided not to go hunting on her own. Of course, she'd never seriously considered going after an outlaw on her own.

Not without telling him.

She removed her knife from her teeth. "I found four."

Mitch snorted. "Of course, we'd get the group with four."

"But that leaves the marshal to handle three by himself. It's Ursula and Wax who only have three for the two of them. Anyway, however many we have, we can handle it." She smiled and felt a reckless desire to single-handedly sort those men out at the tip of her knife.

"You're right about that. We most certainly can."

"I can get one by climbing along toward him." She pointed to the treetops. "I'll drop down on him and get him out of the fight silently. Then we get the next two at the same time."

She explained where the second and third man were hidden and her special concerns about the fourth man. Mitch had a few ideas that had merit, and she changed her plan slightly.

Climbing back to the level where those branches entwined like a floor in the treetops, Ilsa wondered just how good Ursula was with her hatchet. And where in the world was Jo?

Dave would want her to keep low, let the man go past, then come to him for help.

He'd want her to, but he knew her better than that.

She eased deeper into the woods along the trail the man would take into the woods. Jo saw the tracks on her way to the cabin, but she'd stayed off to the side of them. Now she knew exactly where he'd go.

Thinking through ideas, one after the other, Jo knew the main thing she needed now was absolute silence. Yes, she could get him with her bow and arrow. But it was silent only if she killed him. An arrow in the shoulder might make him shout in pain or call out a warning. She had no interest in killing a man. To save her husband, her child, her sisters, yes, she'd fight with lethal force if she had to. But this was none of those things. She'd be killing just to even the odds, and she'd have to shoot him from cover.

That was the way of a coward.

Instead, because he was riding at a slow walk, she had time to plan her attack. She stalked him like he was a rummaging grizzly. She slid closer to the trail. Picked her spot with care. Closed in even more.

He rode past.

His horse looked into the bushes right at her, but it didn't flinch. Its ears pricked back, then forward. The man must have felt safe. He wasn't paying attention to his knowing horse.

She took a second to feel bad that she hadn't been quiet enough to fool the horse, but then there hadn't been a whole lot of time to calm herself. She was downwind of the critter, but maybe the horse could hear her rapid heartbeat. Jo never underestimated an animal.

She reached for a nice sturdy rock about the size of her fist, then, using a knee-high stone as a step, she launched herself upward, using a slender tree to help her vault high enough. She landed on the horse's back right behind the man and brought the rock down on his head with a sickening thud.

Wrapping her arm around the man's waist to balance him, she made sure he'd been knocked into a sound sleep before she dropped her handy rock. Then she took the reins and rode the horse straight for the Wardens' place.

Smiling, she took her prisoner to meet his fate and waited for Dave to be proud of her.

26

Ursula couldn't yell at Wax to be quiet. That'd be stupid. As stupid as shooting someone when they were trying to silently sneak up on three men, each one separately.

Before she could rush out and stop him, he shifted his grip on his revolver so he held it by the muzzle. He moved an inch at a time in complete silence. When there were no longer trees between him and his quarry, he dropped to his belly. If she hadn't known just where he was, she'd've never spotted him.

With a slight catch in her throat, she realized just how skilled he was in the woods. Someone had said something about a gray ghost. Mosby the Gray Ghost. She wasn't sure who'd said that. But it was when she'd first met the Wardens, and they'd talked so much, remembering it all had been overwhelming.

She felt pride in his skill, which, she might say, was as good as hers, maybe as good as Jo's. In a sudden silent surge, Wax came up off the ground and slammed the gun butt down.

The man dropped to the ground with a crunch of leaves and twigs. Beyond that sound when he fell, the whole thing had been silent.

She watched Wax tie the man's hands and feet with moves so fast she couldn't follow what he was doing.

Wanting a closer look, Ursula almost left her concealed spot. But she decided to wait. She'd already disobeyed him once by fading back into the woods while he was still trying to talk her into staying behind.

No sense making a habit of it.

While she waited, she considered that Wax seemed to her like a nice, mild-mannered man. He'd been nothing but kind and gentle with her.

But he was supposed to be a known gunman. A dangerous man. And he'd just knocked a man cold without a moment's hesitation.

It crossed her mind that she might, right now, be falling in love with a wolf in sheep's clothing.

Ilsa had the first man unconscious and tied like a hog. Or no, not tied like a hog . . . hog-tied, that was what Mitch had called it. She had no idea what a hog had to do with tying up a prisoner. But Mitch's one attempt at explaining what the saying meant had only confused her.

Then Mitch was beside her. He checked the bonds, then used a handkerchief to gag the man so he couldn't wake up and warn the others. Lately he'd taken to carrying an extra kerchief or two and a couple of spare neckties. They'd come in so handy through their troubles in Chicago.

Truly, they'd taken far too many prisoners in their short married life.

Now, he pointed to his man, then jabbed himself in the chest with his thumb. She pointed at hers. They'd be near the crest of the hill when they reached their next intended victims.

Ilsa set off in one direction, Mitch in another. She scanned the hills to her left, the area the marshal needed to clear out. Her eyes landed for a second on the marshal, who was moving with impressive skill. She watched for a bit, not wanting to move when he was in sight and distract him. The intense expression on his face told her he was coming up on one of the men he wanted to take out of the fight.

Then the marshal was out of sight. She waited, listened, and from a good distance, she saw a rustling of tree limbs, then nothing. Then the marshal moved again into her sight. She worried because if she could see him, so could others, but most of the men were facing away from the group sneaking up on them.

All of them, she hoped. A rear attack hadn't occurred to them.

Which made them fools.

The marshal vanished into a thicket, and she turned back to the man she was after, not wanting Mitch to get ahead of her. The plan was to take both men out of the fight at near the same moment because they were even with each other on the hill crest, and if one of them was struck down, the other might be in a position to notice.

She eased along, staying low, picturing herself like a snake slithering along on its belly. A snake about to strike. Studying the area around her, including her back trail, she finally found Mitch from the grass waving as he moved. He really was very good. Not great, but good enough for today.

It was strange that she felt such love for a brusque, bossy man as Mitch. He suited her right down to the ground. That's the only way she could explain it.

Taking a moment, she searched where the fourth gunman, the one she'd been most wary of, was hidden. He wasn't there. Alarmed that he might have seen her or, more likely, Mitch, and be coming, she froze, watching for any movement.

Finally, she spotted him. He'd come in her direction but far off to the side. And he would move past her before she could reach him. This one highly skilled man was closing the space between himself and his gang, and if they got together they'd be harder to take.

Should she drop back until the man stopped moving? Or move faster so whatever that man was after, he wouldn't have any help with it?

Then the second man, the one Mitch was intent on, started following after the fourth outlaw.

Ilsa figured all of them, for some reason, were joining up. The end of their chance to divide and conquer. It was now or never, and neither man was paying attention to what was happening around them. The man she was supposed to handle lagged far enough behind that she could get to the path he was walking before he was past her. He went into a heavy stand of oaks, and she had her chance to move on him unnoticed.

She hoped.

Like an angry rattler, she struck.

One wickedly sharp blow from the hilt of her knife.

He crumpled soundlessly to the ground. She tied him up and gagged him. She carried extra kerchiefs, too. Though this time she'd also wrapped lengths of rope around her waist. A woman carrying neckties seemed foolish somehow.

Mitch materialized beside her. She hadn't heard him coming, and she was impressed.

"Did you get your man?" she asked.

Mitch nodded. "Did you see that other outlaw moving south?"

Ilsa quickly told him what she'd seen the marshal do. "What do you think made them start moving?"

"I don't know, but I think we'd better find out."

Ilsa and Mitch set out to get their last man. If they took care of four men, and Ursula and Wax and the marshal wrapped up with the other six, that just left the men in the Wardens' cabin, and she assumed Jo was over there with Dave and his family and all the Warden hands. And with only five men to subdue. Men who'd come here to kill Mitch, the lousy varmints. It bothered her that she didn't get to fight them herself.

At least, with all those Wardens and their cowhands, Jo didn't have to handle all five of those men alone.

"You weren't supposed to capture them yourself." Dave hadn't said he was proud of her, and it hurt her feelings. But he looked down the trail as if he expected her to be dragging all five men in the Wardens' cabin and the ten gunmen Pike had hired behind her, so Jo decided to take that as an unspoken compliment instead.

The big half-wit.

Jimmy Joe and Parson Fred, two of the Wardens' cow-hands, stepped forward to catch the man she'd ridden in with and drag him off the horse. She appreciated the help because her arm was getting tired.

Jimmy Joe was a youngster given to being overly talkative. Parson Fred really was a parson. Jo had figured it for a nickname until Dave had proposed. Parson Fred spent the spring roundup, fall cattle drive, and winter with the Wardens and went to his mission field during the summer months.

Parson Fred had performed Jo and Dave's wedding. Now she had a special fondness for the man.

She liked him even better when he said, "You are a woman to ride the river with, Mrs. Warden. I've half a mind to talk your sister into marrying me. You're a likely family."

That thought threw Jo for a moment. "Ursula's a shy type, as I'm sure you've noticed."

Parson Fred nodded, then with Jimmy Joe asking questions everyone knew the answers to, they bound and gagged the outlaw.

Dave caught Jo by the waist and lifted her off the horse. She flung her arms around his neck and grinned.

"I didn't choose to attack him. He rode straight past me. I couldn't let him get away."

Ma gasped with quiet horror. Quill patted his wife on the shoulder.

"Now we know where everyone is, and we have to hurry back." She quickly told the Warden crew about the man riding off in the opposite direction while this one delivered himself straight into her hands. The other three men were, she was almost certain, in the house.

After some discussion, they all headed into the woods on foot. Jo in the lead.

Not all of the Warden hands were woodsmen, so the noisier ones hung back while Jo and Dave, and around five others who proved themselves able to be reasonably quiet, slipped up close to the tree line to consider how to charge the cabin without getting shot.

27

Wax had the man he was aiming for knocked cold, tied up, and dragged behind a boulder, out of sight of his gang members.

He hoped Ursula was impressed. He'd been fast and silent. He'd seen her vanish. And in their search, he'd seen her moving around silently, carefully. She was good, and he admitted it. But he was better.

When his prisoner was well hidden, Ursula joined him. They had two men left.

"We should get them both at the same time," Ursula whispered.

Wax didn't like it, but she had a point. "I'm worried about the marshal. We left him to tangle with at least three of these gunmen single-handedly. He's a tough man, no doubt about it. But that's a lot of dodging around."

"So in order to hurry, we should split up?" Ursula smiled.

Wax narrowed his eyes. "Stop acting happy about this."

She wiped the smile off her face.

"You take the one nearest. That's Canada Phelps. The

one on past is Smilin' Bob. He's the one who shot Quill Warden. He's mine." Wax pointed at the man closest. "Canada is lazier. Look at him sitting by that boulder. He's not even looking down at the cabin. He's just waiting for Bob to signal him to go. That's his way. The two of them are saddle partners and Bob's the leader. See how Bob is crouched as if ready to.spring?"

It made Wax sick to send Ursula after a man alone. "Give me time to get close to Bob, then watch for my signal. We'll both move at once."

She drew her hatchet from her belt.

Swallowing hard, he said, "Y-you're not gonna chop on him, are you?"

That really wiped all her amusement away. "Oh, for heaven's sake. Of course not."

She flipped the hatchet so the blade was at the bottom. He hoped she didn't accidentally chop herself. Well, they had to do this, and he could take Bob down then come and save her if necessary.

They moved together until Ursula was about twenty paces behind Phelps, then Wax went on. When he was in position, he moved until he could see Ursula. She was watching intently in his direction and some of the tension he could see, even from fifty feet away, eased out of her shoulders when she spotted him. She nodded once with a firm jerk of her chin, then turned to go after her outlaw.

Wax moved faster. He wanted Bob down and out of the fight before Ursula got herself into trouble.

Wax was within striking distance when he heard gunfire. The bullet slammed into Bob, who fell backward. As Wax dropped to the ground, Bob pulled the trigger, firing his gun over and over, wildly, into the air from flat on his back.

Wax hit the ground as bullets sprayed a nearby oak tree and ricocheted.

Bob's gun clicked on empty chambers, and Wax moved to disarm him before he had time to reload.

He got there in time to see Bob in the final throes of death. Then gunfire sounded from his right again—the same direction the bullet that killed Bob had come from. Near where the marshal should be. Whirling to his left, Wax looked desperately for Ursula. He saw her still a few steps away from the boulder where Phelps had been leaning.

Phelps was on his feet. His gun drawn, aiming straight for Wax. His eyes flickered to Bob, and a killing rage came into his eyes.

Ursula stepped out from behind that boulder, with Phelps facing away from her, and she brought that hatchet butt down hard on Phelps's head.

His eyes went blank. His gun fell free. Phelps sank to his knees and wavered there for a few seconds, then fell facedown on the ground.

Wax heard more gunfire from his right.

The marshal must be in trouble. Wax sprinted for Phelps and helped Ursula bind and gag him and drag him out of sight in just a few seconds.

He caught Ursula's hand and said, "We've got to go help."

They dashed toward the shooting. Wax was dragging the woman he loved into a gunfight.

But he couldn't leave her behind, could he?

Praying God would watch over His foolish servant, Wax ran toward the sound of raining death.

Mitch tackled Ilsa to the ground as soon as the first shot went off.

She looked up to see the man they were closing in on, the last one, turn and charge right toward where the shooting had started. Right to where the marshal was.

A gun went off far to their left, in the area where Ursula and Wax were.

A gun went off again and again as if being unloaded desperately. Then it fell silent.

Dread swept over her to think of Ursula in the middle of a gunfight. Desperately she nudged Mitch. "Get off me. Those shots came from where Ursula was headed. We've got to protect her."

There was a stretch of seconds while she felt Mitch struggling with the obvious truth. Now two guns fired.

Fighting to stay calm, Ilsa hoped the silence didn't mean her sister was now dead or dying. Ilsa's heart pounded as she thought of quiet, lonely Ursula dying from the dangers that stalked the land at the bottom of Hope Mountain, just as Grandma had always predicted.

"All right." He slid off of Ilsa. "But stay down. We crawl toward the gunfire. Don't stand up and sprint toward it. We can't help Ursula if we're dead."

Ilsa crawled fast, using all her woodland skills. Listening for running and shouting. Anything that would give her some idea of where all these villains were.

"The first gunfire would've been near Ursula. Now the shooting is centered ahead of the marshal." She crawled toward the fight as she judged the direction of the guns.

Honestly, figuring out where gunfire was coming from wasn't her greatest skill. "At least based on where the marshal was when I last saw him. And he was moving slow. I don't think they're shooting at him or my sister or Wax. At least not anymore."

"Then what?" Mitch kept up with her on his belly. "Are they shooting at each other?"

Ilsa studied their surroundings. The gunfire was too far up the hill in the direction of the Warden ranch for that. "I think one of the men at your pa's ranch walked into this mess, and someone opened fire on him."

"The fight does seem to be ahead of us." Then a third gun started firing. "And now someone else is in it—I think that sounds like the man who we were after."

"Let's head for where we think the marshal is. If Pike's gunmen are fighting those assassins who came after you, we should just keep our heads down, then deal with the last one standing."

They changed directions. Mitch said, "There should be more men shooting by now."

Happier with their crawling now that it wasn't straight for a shootout, Ilsa asked, "Why aren't there more guns? Our outlaw rushed to get into the fight."

She paused with her crawling when what it all meant came to her. She looked at Mitch, who'd stopped beside her. "I think it means the rest of them are out of the fight. We were after ten men, and only two from this direction are shooting and one from the direction of your ranch, which should mean it's not all of your family and your cowhands—that'd be a lot of guns. Between us, Ursula and Wax, and the marshal, we've taken eight men prisoner."

Mitch smiled. "That's a good success rate."

A howl of pain from ahead accompanied a frenzy of shooting. Judging by the direction, Ilsa thought it was the last man the marshal had needed to capture.

Now two men were firing at each other.

Thundering hooves announced new arrivals to the fight from the direction of the Warden ranch. One of the two gunfighters quit just as new guns joined the fight. Ilsa knew it was more than two riders, and there were supposed to be five men at the Wardens' place. If one was over here getting shot at, then there could be four more gunmen entering this fray.

Ilsa said, "Let's get to the marshal, then go make sure Ursula is all right. We can always go hunting for whoever survives that gunfight later."

"There's shooting over that rise." Quill Warden pointed to a trail that led east of his house.

"Is that gunfire from Pike's men?" Jo asked. "That's the direction I saw the other man ride."

Dave knew his way around down here. Jo didn't. She crouched in the woods beside him. They hadn't launched an attack on the ranch house yet.

"Possibly, probably." Dave's jaw was so tight it was a wonder he could talk. "Unless it's Mitch and your sisters."

Those were two far, far different choices when it came to getting into the fight.

Three men came sprinting out of the cabin and raced toward the corral. They had their horses roped and saddled within minutes.

"Hold up until those men ride out." Quill didn't sound happy about his decision. "Then we'll follow."

As soon as they thundered out of the yard to the east and were swallowed up by the forest, all the Warden crew were in the saddle and riding after them.

"Be mindful," Jo said, thinking of how to trail a wary animal. "Don't let them hear us, or they might duck off the trail and hide in the forest, lie in wait for us." No animal would do that, except maybe a wounded cougar. But these weren't animals, they were something worse.

The Wardens reached the shelter of the forest trail. There were fresh hoof marks cut into the muddy trail from the three riders ahead of them.

They followed along. Jo found herself pushed toward the back of the line. She looked over to see Ma was beside her on her right. The two of them protected, sheltered by the big strong men.

"They do it because they love us," Ma said, sliding her hand over the pistol she wore on her hip. "And right now Dave has a powerful need to protect you and the baby."

Jo nodded. "But it's hard knowing I'm the best tracker of the bunch. I understand it. I do. It's kind and loving and annoying. Mighty strange." Then a sudden move to her right whipped her head around even as she drew her bow and aimed. She let an arrow flash past Ma's face, then another went behind her back.

"Hold up," Ma hissed loud enough to stop everyone.

Jo was off her horse, running for her prey. This was no hunting expedition. She hadn't seen an elk in the woods, but a man.

She reached him as he dragged himself toward his rifle,

thrown aside when her arrows landed within an inch of each other in his shoulder. Before she could pounce, Ma grabbed the man's rifle that had flown to the side. Dave landed on the man with both knees and slammed a fist into his face.

The man collapsed backward, unconscious.

Jo was aware that all around her Warden hands swarmed off the trail, their horses in hand. If one man realized someone was coming on their back trail, then the two other men knew, too. They might've left just one man behind because they were in a rush to reach the shooting ahead, which was still going on, but the Warden crew could no longer ride down this trail. They had to proceed cautiously.

Parson Fred tended the wounded man while the rest of the Wardens dealt with the horses. From here on they'd be on foot.

Jo took advantage of everyone's distraction to hurry forward, wanting to get into the lead and make sure no one else lingered in the woods, waiting for a chance to kill someone she loved—both here and ahead if her sisters were mixed up in this gun battle.

28

Wax caught Ursula by the arm and dragged her straight to a gun battle.

It all hit her at once. This was the deadly danger Grandma had feared. Yes, she'd feared sickness, too. And she'd lost loved ones to sickness. But she'd also feared guns and dangerous men.

It hit so hard, Ursula froze. That pulled her arm free of Wax's, and she dodged behind a tree. As determined to hide from him as everyone else.

She was stung by the realization that she'd tasted complete loneliness last winter and decided to join the world. Now she was finding dangerous people everywhere.

She wanted her stone house. She wanted solitude and safety. From deep inside a warning bell rang, reminding her that she'd come so far from where she'd been last fall when the Wardens invaded.

She'd grown in her faith and her courage. She'd found a strong man she could love. She wanted to spend her life with him. But how could she when he brought the whole outside world with him?

Yes, he was a dangerous man, but he was also a re-deemed man. But she couldn't pick him, then shut the two of them off forever. Wax wouldn't be able to live like that.

Then he was there, crouching near where she had hidden herself. His face a mask of concern for her. He reached out a hand for her, and she flinched away.

That must've caused him pain, and the guilt of hurting him added to her fears.

Another reason to shut herself away: she couldn't hurt anyone else.

"Ursula, I have to go. I have to get into this fight and make sure Marshal Cosgrove and your sister and Mitch are all right. But you should stay right here. If I'd thought you'd obey me, I'd've ordered you to stay behind right from the first."

She saw a flash of humor in his eyes. As if thoughts of an obedient wife were on his mind.

"I'll come back for you." He reached again, and this time she didn't move away. In fact, she reached back. Touched his hand. Then he gave her a hard nod as if the situation suited him.

Then he was gone. And she was left feeling like a failure, a coward, a betrayer. Just how she'd felt all last winter when she'd run from the sickness that had caught hold of Ilsa. When she should have stood bravely, risked her life to help care for her precious little sister.

Now, hiding like this, she was doing it again.

And she couldn't stand herself. She was alone now. But she was going to help her family. Her friends. Her man. With no idea where Wax had gone, or even how long ago because she'd been so busy wallowing in her cowardice that she didn't know if he'd been gone one minute or ten, she set out. She would have to be careful because now she didn't know where anyone was and no one knew where she was. She could find herself with every gun in the place blazing right at her.

Her little sister's head came up, and Jo spoke before she got a knife thrown at her. Not that Ilsa would be that careless.

"Ilsa, it's me." Jo's voice brought Ilsa's head around. A grin bloomed on her face even as she lowered the knife she'd been about to throw at whoever was sneaking up behind her.

"Jo, you're safe."

"And I snuck up on you." Jo grinned back. "Not an easy thing to do."

Ilsa launched herself into Jo's arms. "I admit I was distracted by the gunfire."

Mitch came up beside Ilsa just as Jo let loose. "Is my family in this mess? Is that some of our group in that shootout?"

"They're behind me. We got to your ranch house ready to take it back by force. Before we could, one of the five killers fell right into our hands, and we took him prisoner." Jo considered herself being modest for saying "our" hands. "Another of them set out alone in a direction away from us and rode up here. When the shooting started the other three tore out. We caught one of them that hung back."

Jo looked over her shoulder, figuring Dave would be coming soon. "And now I found you sitting here as if you were watching a bird's nest in the spring."

Ilsa smiled again. Then her smile faded. "Based on the gunfire, we think eight of Pike's ten hired gunmen are out of the fight. Mitch and I only know for sure what we've done, and we have three of them tied up and gagged." Ilsa told the story from this side of the hills, including Pike's capture. "We are here with a US Marshal. The remaining gunmen from Pike's are fighting with the men who were in the Wardens' cabin."

Ilsa's voice went grim. "We heard gunfire from the spot Ursula should be, and we're heading over there to check on her."

As she finished talking, Dave emerged from the woods, glowering at Jo. This time Mitch told Dave what had been going on, and he said it a lot faster.

"The rest of our bunch is behind me, spread out in the woods, trying to get a look at the fight without getting themselves shot. I'll be right back." He looked at Mitch. "Can you try and get my wife to wait for me?"

"We'll be here for about two more minutes," Mitch snapped. "We're worried about Ursula, and we aren't waiting long."

Dave gave him a narrow-eyed look, then ran.

He was back in under two minutes, but then, no one had whipped out a pocket watch. Jo figured they'd've given him longer if he needed it.

They headed straight south, hoping they'd find the marshal and see how many men he'd caught.

They found him sitting behind a tree with a bloody

bandage tied around his arm, sipping from his canteen. Far from the fight.

When they told him they were worried about Ursula and Wax, he gave a fast report.

"I got one of mine, got him tied up back yonder. Before I could get to the next one, here comes a stranger riding from the Warden ranch. The men I was after opened fire. Just opened up with no idea who the man was." Shaking his head in disgust, the marshal said, "I got clipped by a wild bullet, but I haven't fired a shot. I got out of the line of fire, but they've moved on forward, away from me, and no bullets have come my way. I'm waiting to see who survives this, then I plan to go arrest them."

"We're going to check on Ursula," Jo said. "Are you all right? Is your arm badly hurt? Do you want anyone here with you?"

They listened to the gunfire. It sounded like maybe three men shooting it out. "Nope, it's just a scratch. Hurts like fire, but it's not going to slow me down much. I'm just going to sit here until they all run out of bullets. Durnedest gunfight I've ever been in."

The four of them headed on for Ursula and Wax, alarmed by the complete silence from this part of the forest when there'd been so much shooting only minutes earlier.

Wax found a spot where he could watch the fighting. Clip Norton had found good cover, and two men Wax had seen once before were trying to kill him. These two were among the men who'd shot him off a mountainside. He recognized them and wondered where the other three were.

There were two dead men visible, but they were face-down, and Wax couldn't identify them. Only three guns, from what he could see, were firing. Wax didn't let down his guard, but he hoped very much these three men were the only ones left.

All three of these varmints were skilled men, deadly shots.

The two from the Wardens' weren't just firing blind. They were covering for each other as one slipped closer, changed positions, trying to find an angle on Clip. One would move and draw his gunfire, then, while Clip was distracted, the other would move.

Clip had a strong position. He'd found a stack of windfall trees that'd been swept into a pile probably by an avalanche.

Judging by the number of trees and how tightly they'd packed against each other, Wax guessed the original avalanche had been a barrier that'd caught every new tree that'd come tumbling down for decades. It was the next thing to a fort wall, and with a curve to it, he was covered on three sides.

Clip was dug in there, with an impenetrable shelter. There seemed to be open slits in a few spots he could aim through. Every bullet came close to getting the two strangers when they moved.

Wax had a chance as one of the men moved in his direction. This one was so intent on watching Clip, he wasn't looking anywhere else.

The gunman faded back from Clip's withering fire until he was out of range. Clip had to know he only had minutes before one of these two men could get the drop on him and end this. But that was only true if Clip didn't get them first.

Back where Wax hid, he could move just a bit, and the gunman coming his way would pass within a few feet of him. Then the two packs of outlaws would be down to one against one, and the whole group Wax had come with could finish this.

He chose a spot to lie in wait.

29

Ursula only took seconds to see Wax get in position to waylay a man coming for him. Riveted on the risk Wax was about to take, a movement to her left didn't gain her attention until too late.

Almost too late.

A bleeding man she'd thought dead sat up, saw Wax, and moved unsteadily but without hesitation. He clawed through the forest floor. It took Ursula a second to see the gun he searched for. He saw it at the same moment.

It struck Ursula hard, the memory of a time she'd killed a rattlesnake that slithered out of a rock toward a still toddling Ilsa. She'd reacted with lightning speed to kill the snake.

That same urgent action struck her now.

He dove for it as she rushed straight for him.

Silently.

So much of her childhood had been spent silently in the trees. The games she and her sisters had played were second nature to her. The risks were there in nature, but she knew how to take care of herself.

And this outlaw was as much rattlesnake as man.

Drawing out her hatchet, she rushed soundlessly forward. The bleeding man caught up his pistol.

The butt of her hatchet came down hard. She aimed for his head but missed. She hit his shoulder. A shout of pain ended any chance of defeating the man silently.

Wax whirled around.

The man still ahead drew his gun ready to fire. Ursula slammed herself flat on the ground.

Someone shot the bleeding man in the belly three times, cutting off the shouting.

"No!" the nearby man roared in rage. Ursula could only believe this man had been his partner. The shooter's eyes landed on Ursula. His gun turned.

Wax opened up. His bullets struck home. The second man fell within feet of the first, both now bleeding, dying.

"Wax, get down!" Ursula knew being quiet was useless at this point.

Wax rushed for her, caught her arm, and dragged her behind a low pile of boulders as a new shooter aimed at them. Then two guns aimed for them.

Bullets pinged off the stone, and Wax threw himself over Ursula, flattening both of them to the ground.

Another higher boulder behind them got hit with the gunfire and the bullets ricocheted back toward them.

Two gunmen. Two left. Ursula had lost count of how many they'd started out with, but it sounded to her like they were down to two fighting men. And both of them were aiming right at her and Wax.

Did that mean they were the only ones left to fight? Could her sisters be dead?

She opened her eyes to see Wax, his weight fully on her, his eyes intent as if he was right now planning some way to give his life to save hers.

Her hand was trembling when she touched his face. She left bloody fingerprints. Was it her own blood? She had no memory of being shot, but it was possible she hadn't noticed in all this madness.

When her hand rested on his face, he turned to her, focused on her, paying attention as no one ever had before.

"If we aren't going to make it out of here—"

"I won't let them get past me, Ursula."

Which only confirmed his willingness to die for her.

Whatever else was true in her confused training about the Bible, she was sure no one disagreed with the verse "Greater love hath no man than this, that he lay down his life for his friend." And that's what Wax was offering her right now. Love. The greatest possible love a man could give.

She whispered, "I want you to know I love you."

A bullet caromed. Shattered bits of rock slashed at both of them. A scratch appeared on Wax's cheek. A stone that would have hit her if he wasn't shielding her with his body.

The intent expression eased, though it didn't go away. He leaned down and kissed her.

"I love you, too, Ursula. When we get out of this mess, I want you to marry me. We'll go live on top of that mountain together, though I think we should build our own house. You and I and our children can find a quiet, secluded life free from this kind of ugly violence."

The gunfire rained past them. Rocks exploded.

Then a look of grief crossed his face. "I never wanted to fire my gun again, certainly not at a man. But I've killed a man after telling God I was done with all that."

Something struck one of her moccasins, but it didn't hit her foot. A bullet maybe. She was going to die in the arms of the man she loved.

"The most beautiful thing about God is His forgiveness. Yes, you failed. You shot someone because you were fighting to save others. God must be heartbroken when an evil man dies in his sins."

Closing his eyes, Wax said, "I sent a man to hell today."

The gunfire continued, cutting closer it seemed with every shot.

"No, his choices, his decisions to live a disbelieving life, sent him there. Of course, we're not to judge, but considering he was a killer for hire, it's hard to expect that he'd made his peace with God."

Her voice dropped but still eased in beneath the blazing explosions over their heads. "But my point is, if you ask for it, you'll find forgiveness. So ask, then start again today, right now. Tell God you're done with all of that again, and do your best. That's all any of us can do."

One of the shooters shouted. His gun fell silent.

The other gun cut off.

In the silence of the terrible morning, Wax and Ursula looked at each other. Then he smiled, kissed her, and said, "I think someone just saved our lives."

Then he rested his forehead against hers. Their breath mingled. Their fear turned to hope.

It seemed like a long time before he inched his head up past the boulder.

She shoved herself up to look over the rock to see Ilsa pulling her dagger out of one gunman while Mitch tied him up. Dave was binding the other shooter where he lay facedown on the ground with an arrow in his backside.

"Be careful when you take the arrow out," Jo said. "They're a nuisance to make, so I try not to break them."

Wardens came out of the woods in all directions. Some of them had men with them, bound and gagged.

Ilsa came and looked over the edge of the boulder at Ursula and Wax. "Have you been shot?" Grandpa's little medicine woman.

Shaking her head, Ursula said, "We got hit by flying rocks mostly. And I think they shot a hole in my moccasin."

With a tight gasp, Wax stood, studied her moccasin, then grabbed Ursula's shoulders and hoisted her to her uninjured feet. He had blood running down his face from the scratch across his cheekbone.

She reached up to touch the shallow wound, frowning. "Is this the worst of it, or did you get hit when you shielded me?"

"There should be fifteen prisoners." Mitch started talking before Wax could answer. "Let's get a head count. And don't forget there are wanted posters on most if not all of them. We're going to get rich off reward money."

"You should both sit down and let me look you over." Ilsa jabbed a finger at the rock that Ursula had feared might be the place where she and Wax would lose their lives.

Marshal Cosgrove emerged from the woods, his arm bleeding.

"We're fine," Wax said, still giving Ursula's foot a worried look. "Maybe you should check on the marshal, Ilsa."

She hesitated, but finally Ilsa turned to the only one in their company who had a bullet wound.

Jo found the horses hidden by Pike's men. Dave and a few of his hands rounded up the horses that had gotten loose from the three killers riding over from the Circle Dash.

There were thirteen outlaws here. Two were left behind where Jo had captured them earlier.

Cosgrove tried to take charge, but Ursula noticed that there were a whole lot of other people trying to take charge, too, so he had to scramble to try to be the leader. Mitch mostly gave orders. Dave and Quill had their own ideas about running things. Ma and Jo were decent generals on this battlefield, too.

Ursula felt Wax's tension as he fought down the need to get everyone lined up and in order. Another person who wanted to run things.

But rather than do that, he stayed beside her when everyone else got busy. Ursula finally calmed down enough to collapse.

Wax caught her and hoisted her into his arms. The low boulder was close at hand so Wax sat down with her in his lap. She shook hard. Wax's hold was so tight she was afraid he might raise blisters.

Even so, she didn't want him to let loose.

They sat together quietly. Ursula's shaking eased enough that she realized he was shaking, too.

Everyone else scurried around throwing outlaws over their saddles.

"Say the word," Wax whispered, "and I'll take you back to the mountaintop. We don't need to go to town. If you'll marry me, we'll wait until everything calms down and ask Parson Fred to bless our union. You don't ever have to see another person as long as you live . . . except me."

"That's a big promise. Not one I'd ask you to make and more than likely not one you can keep."

He just held her tighter.

"We'll go to town when we take the prisoners in and have Parson Graham speak our vows," she said, holding on just as tight. "Then, I think I'd like to just ride off a ways. Stay off the mountain for a little while. But with no gunfights."

He kissed her hair. Then he managed a weak laugh. "That sounds just fine. You can look around at the world when it's calm, then when you've had enough, we'll go back up to your home and your sisters. I'll find another meadow up on that mountain, and we'll just settle in to a quiet life."

"I'm not sure where my home is. Can we move into the house I grew up in, or is some Warden taking it over? I think the Wardens bought the whole mountaintop, although how a man can buy part of God's creation is a mystery to me. I may not have a home to go back to."

"We'll figure it all out soon enough."

Ilsa came up to where they sat, her blue eyes shining with worry. "Are you ready? Are you coming with us to turn these men in?"

"Ursula and I are discussing it," Wax said.

Mitch came up beside Ilsa, walking fast, talking fast. "We all have to go. You shot one of them, Wax. It was self-defense, and there were plenty of witnesses. Even so, we all have to go so we can make it clear what happened out here from where everyone was standing. And you've got a share of the reward money, including a reward for Pike. There's a price on his head."

"We're going." Ursula stood. Wax rose with her, still supporting her. But the shaking had eased enough that she could stand without an arm around her, if she wanted to, which she didn't.

"We can buy you a new pair of shoes." Wax turned her toward where they'd left their horses.

"We brought your horses up." Jo jerked her thumb to the tidy row of horses all ready to go.

Ursula stood straighter. Her sisters were right here. Mitch was at hand, and Dave came walking over. Now was as good a time as any to make the announcement. "Wax and I are getting married."

"You can't marry Wax Mosby." Mitch, as usual, thought he ought to run everything.

Ursula thought a moment. "No, actually I'm not."

She felt Wax stiffen beside her.

"I'm marrying Jake Mosby. He's a new man with a new name." Ursula had honestly never enjoyed being bold quite so much as right now. "And I'm living in my own home—the one I grew up in—on top of Hope Mountain, so any Wardens who are living there right now can just get out."

Ilsa shrugged one shoulder and said rather weakly, "Honestly, Mitch and I thought we might live—"

"We're living there. Mitch is always boasting about how rich he is. Build your own house."

"We're going to." Mitch didn't sound all that bossy right now. "We thought until the house is up, we might—"

"Just move in with Dave and Jo. I don't want to live with anyone but Jake."

She glanced at the man she loved and caught him grinning. She slapped him in the belly with the back of her hand. He just grinned bigger.

She really couldn't wait to marry him.

"And if you Wardens bought every acre of land on *my* mountaintop, well that's just greedy. You're going to have to let loose of it so we can have some."

"I don't think Wax Mosby—"

"His name is Jake." Ursula cut Mitch off. "I'm not speaking to a single person who calls him anything else."

She had a good mind not to speak to any of them no matter what they said. She looked at Jake, who took her hand and weaved his fingers between hers.

"Let's go to town and get married," he said, "then wander awhile."

"You're not going back up to the mountain straightaway?" Jo asked. Her expression lightened. "You're going to travel?"

Ursula nodded.

Jo flung herself into Ursula's arms. "I'm so happy for you."

Ilsa hit them with her light, yet sturdy weight. "I'm so happy for all of us."

They clung to each other and laughed, and maybe cried a bit.

30

They rode to town in the middle of a crowd.

Wax—no, he'd better start thinking of himself as Jake. Jake Mosby. And what if Ursula included *him* in her promise to not speak to anyone who called him Wax?

Anyway, he wasn't proud of that name.

He might never shake his reputation. But up on that mountaintop, with only one trail that wasn't mountain climbing, he wouldn't have too many people happen by to pester him.

Ursula rode beside him with more riders behind and a string of horses bearing their ridiculous number of prisoners stretched out for a long way behind them. Most of the prisoners were alive, which was a real wonder.

Ilsa was just ahead. She looked back and talked, full of the story of her and Mitch catching three men and the fourth running off when the shooting started.

Jo was ahead of Ilsa, and she had plenty to say over her shoulder, too. It seemed she'd caught one of the five assassins single-handedly and one almost alone, though

Ma and Dave had helped. Dave looked deeply aggrieved when she told that part of the story.

And Ursula, well, Jake didn't think she'd ever be a real talkative woman, but she listened and smiled and added some of the story of their hunt. She wasn't nervous or acting like she was hemmed in or overwhelmed. Not at all.

The marshal led the way. Right behind him were Quill and Isabelle Warden. A few Warden hands rode next.

The sun was set by the time they reached Bucksnort. Two more marshals had arrived in town only a few minutes ahead of them.

The Bucksnort jail had never seen a load like that. But Marshal Cosgrove was annoyed at all the trouble these outlaws had caused, so he just kept stuffing them in the small cell with Pike. Then he sent wires to ask for more men to escort his gang.

They were packed in so tight Jake didn't think any of them could even sit down. Well, one sleepless night wouldn't hurt them.

He studied the cell full of cranky men, most of them with bad headaches. A few men went to the undertaker. Five had died in all. Mostly they'd shot each other, but Jake had to tell about the one he'd shot.

The sheriff said it was Kid Booth. Jake hadn't recognized him. And in the woods, Jake hadn't been sure if he was with the men at the Wardens' cabin or with the Pike riders. He just knew the man was aiming at Ursula.

Booth had a hefty price on his head. Jake was going to get that one for himself. Sickening though it was, Jake knew these men were bad for the West. It would be a better land for having so many villains under lock and key.

It was late at night before everything got settled down and those on the right side of the bars could leave the sheriff's office and head for the hotel.

Ursula had gone with the women to get rooms and see about food at the hotel. By the time the men came in, the women had cleaned up and combed their hair.

Mrs. Warden had rushed down to the general store, wakened the owners, and came back with an armload of dresses. Ill-fitting and used, but she was horrified that Jo and Ursula intended to traipse around town in britches.

She did let Ilsa stay in her riding skirt.

Jake walked through the dining room door, and his eyes went right to Ursula.

Her heart did something odd. It felt light and fluttery, like maybe it had sprouted wings and taken flight. It was like nothing she'd ever felt before, and Ursula looked back at him as she pressed her hand over her heart.

Even though it was a completely new feeling, she knew she'd have to get used to it. It was love, and it would last a lifetime. Something she'd never considered for herself.

Their gazes locked. Jake walked toward her. Ursula was vaguely aware that other men came in behind Jake. Warden hands.

They filled up the hotel and all the tables. Even this late at night, the hotel owner and his wife had been thrilled with all the business and made them feel very welcome. Now the couple began hustling in and out of the kitchen carrying plates piled with ham, pancakes, and scrambled eggs.

All of this went on as Jake came near and sat beside her. Reached for her hand. He announced, not loudly, as if he didn't care if anyone heard but the two of them, "I think we should wake the parson and get married right now."

Ursula nodded.

"Absolutely not." Mrs. Warden took charge.

Ursula wasn't sure why she got to make this decision.

Mitch said to the room, "We're going to make several thousand dollars in reward money tonight. Pa, Dave, and I have discussed it, and we are going to divide it among the hands, all except the money Wax gets for shooting Booth."

"His name is Jake." Ursula said it with a louder voice than Mitch had.

"Um . . . uh, sorry. Right, Jake." Mitch raised his eyes as if he were looking to God on high for strength. He'd better use his prayer time to ask for safety, because Ursula was about to kick him hard in the shins.

Which reminded her one of her moccasins was almost torn off after being shot. It was near to hanging from her ankle.

"Let's just have Parson Fred bless our vows." Jake was only talking to Ursula now. So, he wasn't about to let Mrs. Warden make this decision, either. "We can do it right here, as soon as we're done eating."

"Agreed." Ursula spoke firmly before Mrs. Warden got a word in.

Mrs. Warden's brows lowered. "A woman shouldn't be married in such a helter-skelter fashion. It's not proper."

"What's proper," Jake said, "is for two people who love

286

each other to promise to be together, to swear it before God and man. Then keep those promises for the rest of their lives. When and where we take those vows changes neither her vows nor mine."

Jake looked across the room. "Which one of you is Parson Fred?"

Ursula couldn't keep track of them, either. There were a dozen men, besides the Wardens and Jake and the man and woman serving them dinner. Her mind was overflowing with names, and she'd quit even trying to remember them.

She studied the men and could see a bit of pink color rise on one man's face as he ate, staring strictly at his plate. If that wasn't clue enough, a couple of the men glanced at him.

"I figured it out," Jake said. "It'd be sinful of you to be asked to perform a wedding and refuse."

"If you lead them to speak their vows, you're fired," Mrs. Warden said. "Ursula needs a bath and a good night's rest. And I need some time with a needle to make her dress fit better."

That brought Parson Fred's head up. His eyes flashed, almost like a man who didn't think Mrs. Warden got to make this decision, either. "Well, ma'am, I was only riding back to that mountaintop to help with spring branding. If you want me to go before, I reckon you've got plenty of hired hands. It's close enough to my time to spend with the native folks while they move to their summer hunting grounds. If I'm fired, I'll leave. But that'll be after the wedding."

Ursula suspected Parson Fred didn't like being given

orders by Mrs. Warden any more than she did, leastways not when it was none of her business.

"Mrs. Warden, Quill, I will come back around next fall, and if you've a mind to have me help with the fall cattle drive, I'll throw in. I'm a top hand. I can get a job anywhere. But first and foremost, I'm a parson. No one tells me how to do my job." He glared at Mrs. Warden, and he transformed in Ursula's eyes from the quiet cowpoke to a man of God.

Then he said to Ursula and Jake, "Finish your meal, and let's get on with a wedding."

Ursula was suddenly struck by what was ahead of her. Tying herself to a man for life. She wished now she'd let Mrs. Warden bully her into waiting a day or two.

Mrs. Warden did manage to get Ursula to wash her face and hands. Jake too. And she begrudgingly assured Parson Fred that he wouldn't lose his job after all.

Ilsa rushed out of the room and returned a moment later with a handful of wildflowers that were dripping water. She thrust them into Ursula's hands. Ursula thought they might have been the flowers she had noticed earlier in a vase by the front door.

"What are these for?"

Ilsa shrugged. "I saw a painting in Chicago of a wedding. The bride had flowers."

Ursula used the edge of her too-short, too-baggy black skirt to dry them off, then stood holding them, her arms dangling at her side. Jake came up beside her.

Ilsa lifted Ursula's arm. "Hold the flowers in front of you with both hands."

"You've got some strange notions, little sister." But Ursula held them as Ilsa told her to. It seemed to make Ilsa happy.

"Now we're ready." Parson Fred dragged his hat off his head. He'd worn it through the meal, as had most of the men. There was no better place than your head to store a hat in such a crowded room.

"Dearly beloved."

Ursula had never been to a wedding before. She could have gone to Jo's wedding, but she'd refused. Parson Fred had spoken those vows, too.

The parson kept talking, and Ursula tried to listen, but her ears were buzzing with some kind of . . . well, shock probably. She forced herself to concentrate, it was her wedding for heaven's sake. She had to make vows. She'd better listen to see what she was promising.

"Do you, Wax—"

"It's Jake."

The parson flinched as she snapped at him.

Beside her Jake stood holding her hand—the one not occupied with flowers. He squeezed it, she hoped it was in gratitude, rather than asking her to hush up.

"My correct name is Jake Mosby, Parson."

Ursula didn't listen for a bit. This part of the wedding was for Jake. No reason she needed to stop worrying.

Then she remembered the one and only church service she'd ever been to. It was about how sinful it was to worry.

And she worried about that.

The vows were spoken, and Parson Fred pronounced them man and wife.

Ursula was embarrassed to find Jake got to kiss her right

in front of everyone, but she was a little too nervous to dodge his lips.

Then he was smiling at her as they faced each other, holding hands. The flowers were definitely in the way, but that didn't stop Ursula from smiling back.

Jake took the key Mitch gave him for their own room.

As Mitch handed it over, he gave Jake a few gruff words of advice about brides. Including the fact, Mitch told him rather mournfully, that brides could be shy and delicate things. Even wives that wielded knives, or hatchets. Mitch cautioned that he'd been married a long time before wifely things occurred in his marriage. Jake appreciated the warning. He thought he could learn to like Mitch Warden, if he had to . . . and it looked like he did.

The Wardens and their cowhands filled the hotel. Several of them offered to set up camp outside town, but no one had so much as a bedroll to make the camp comfortable. In the end, several went along with Alberto, the Wardens' foreman, to sleep at his brother's house. Alberto's brother had the bad luck of having a welcoming nature and a good-sized house in Bucksnort—which meant a nice-sized space on the floor in front of the fireplace. He was getting a flood of guests tonight.

Most of the Warden hands would head home early tomorrow morning. It was a plumb fool thing to leave the ranch completely unmanned like this.

Ma and Pa Warden were eager to move down from the mountain and see how their house had weathered a winter without them. They had to get their cattle down out of the highlands, and as soon as time permitted, they'd commence with spring branding.

Dave thought he should go along to help with the hard sorting job, since his cows were staying on the mountaintop. And Mitch was eager to be home without having to fight for his life. Of course, their wives would accompany them.

Jake and Ursula were going to stay down here awhile.

But first Jake had to manage this wedding night. He let Ursula go ahead of him into their room. Worrying—sin that it was—about how to spend the night with his wife, Jake went in, closed the door, then stood still as Ursula turned to him. He wondered if she'd tell him to get out.

As he braced himself to be agreeable, even if it meant sleeping at Alberto's brother's house, Ursula's face lit up.

"I'm finally alone." She threw herself into his arms. Kissed him long and deep. When she came up for air, she added, "Alone with you."

No sign of a shy and delicate wife anywhere.

And one didn't show up at all to interfere with his much-anticipated wedding night.

It turned out Mitch didn't know what he was talking about.

Epilogue

Three little girls ran wild atop Hope Mountain.

"Mama, watch me!" A little blond girl ducked behind a bush, showing how she could vanish like a ghost. Except she was completely visible in her pretty pink calico dress, which was in bright contrast to the sage grass of summer. But Bonnie Jo Warden was only three. She would improve her woodland skills with practice.

Jo had told Ilsa and Ursula she was planning to make a very small bow and arrow for Bonnie for her fourth birthday.

Dave didn't approve, but Jo thought she knew best.

A little dark-haired girl, her head wild with corkscrew curls, came swinging across the yard. Her hands slipped on the rope, and she plunked to the ground, landing on her bottom. Greta Isabelle Warden started to cry.

She'd been swinging very slowly, as she was only allowed to climb a short stump and the rope was on a limb about five feet off the ground. So she only had a slightly tender backside. Ilsa rushed to her little girl and swept her up in her arms, kissing her hair. Ilsa didn't let her daughter run wild outside every day. It was doubtful her little one would ever get to swinging through the treetops with her ma's skill.

Ilsa herself wasn't doing much swinging these days, either. She was a few months from having a new baby.

Ursula's daughter, Susie, toddled toward Jake. When he picked her up and hoisted her high, she sang an adorable song about loving her papa. Ursula, sitting in a rocking chair Jake had made, smiled and rested her hand on her belly. Her sisters had gotten a head start on her with children, but she'd temporarily pass them when this next one was born any day.

Jo was only mother to one. But her turn would come.

They were all gathered outside the old Nordegren cabin Jake and Ursula lived in, surrounded by a ranch Jake had carved out of rugged woodlands. He had planned well, and they had a prosperous ranch with plenty of water.

Dave and Mitch needed his water, so they shared their grass with Jake. All of them worked well together.

In the midst of the playing children, Ursula's attention was drawn to a rider who emerged from the trail that cut through the forest from Dave and Jo's new cabin to Ursula's old, established one. Mitch and Ilsa lived up here, too, in a fine house they'd built in the high meadow where Grandpa's second cabin had been.

Ursula thought the house was ridiculous, with an outhouse inside and water that ran out of a faucet both hot and cold. There were so many shocking things in that house. But Ursula had to admit it was beautiful and comfortable. For all its outlandish fussiness.

The rider got close enough to where they'd gathered outside of Jake and Ursula's cabin, as they often did, for her to recognize Dave. He'd been spending every spare minute improving the trail from the Warden ranch in the lowlands to the two Warden ranches and one Mosby ranch on top of Hope Mountain. This year, Dave hoped he'd done enough work to keep that sidewinder of a trail from blowing shut with the winter snow.

Ursula smiled in greeting, then her smile shrank at Dave's solemn expression. He was a man with an easy smile. But not today.

Jo turned to watch him. Her brow furrowed. Ilsa hugged her little Greta close. They all sensed his mood.

He didn't keep them waiting for one unnecessary moment.

"We found something today when we were working on the trail." He dismounted and, leaving his horse ground-hitched, stepped to Jo's side.

Bonnie ran out of her hiding place with her arms raised, shouting, "Up, Papa." Dave paused for a moment to smile at her, then sweep her up in his arms and hug her. "Hi, sweet girl."

He propped her on his left hip and slung his right arm around Jo's waist, pulling her close.

"What is it?" Jo frowned up at him.

"I think . . . no, no." He shook his head and then spoke as if he were forcing the words out. "I am sorry, but I don't *think*, rather, I'm *sure* we . . . we . . . I'm sure we found where your . . . your p-parents . . . are. Where they died."

All three Nordegren women faced him. Ursula rose to her feet. The little girls whimpered, sensing the upset.

Jake came to Ursula's side. He urged her back into the rocking chair and rested Susie in her lap. Then he crouched beside her and took her hand.

Jo turned to face Dave. "Go on. You can tell us."

Their eyes met. Ursula saw the regret in Dave's, for bearing this news. "We've talked about how there must have been an avalanche on that trail, since your grandpa had to drive his cattle and horses up here."

"The avalanche must have happened when Ma and Pa were going down, or maybe when they coming home," Ursula said, wishing she could remember more about that time.

"We found their . . . their remains."

"They were killed in that avalanche." Jo leaned harder on Dave. "Grandpa must have at least suspected. He'd've seen there was a landslide cutting out his trail."

"It was a hard place where we found them. No one man could have moved the stones without a lot of work and horses to do the heavy lifting." Dave looked from Ursula to Ilsa, then down into Jo's eyes.

Ursula felt the burn of tears. "It's not like we haven't known they died. There was no other possible explanation."

Jake squeezed her hand. "It's still hard to hear."

"We're building coffins," Dave said. "We'll bury them beside your grandparents."

Ursula looked around at the gathering of family. Jake and Susie with her. Jo with Dave and Bonnie. Ilsa with Greta—Mitch was gone. He had probably been working with Dave, but he should have come back to be with Ilsa when they heard this news. But maybe he'd gone somewhere else. Maybe he didn't know yet.

Ma and Pa Warden were at the bottom of the mountain. Loving parents and grandparents. Even the cowhands were friends. Ursula's and her sisters' lives had grown so much.

"Remember when we lived up here all alone?" Ursula said quietly. "Remember when we thought that was all there was to life, and we were scared of going to the lowlands?"

Jo rested her head on Dave's broad chest. "That was a lifetime ago."

"Life is so much better with other people in it." Ilsa hugged little Greta. "Poor Grandma didn't understand that. She had too many losses. She felt safe up here, and I'm afraid she'd gone just the littlest bit mad."

"I was the worst of us all," Ursula said. "I still struggle some days to face people. I think I know how Grandma felt. But because I really have no choice, because I love all of you too much to cut you off, I can fight that reflex to be a hermit."

Jake's hand tightened on hers, and he smiled at her. "If you run, I'll just come with you. Susie and me."

She smiled back, through the burn of threatening tears.

"You couldn't escape us if you tried, Ursula," Ilsa said with a flash of humor shining through eyes that were etched with a new grief.

"We would hunt you down." Jo stayed encircled in Dave's arms, but she turned to smile at both of her sisters. "And you know if I go hunting, I find what I'm after."

Ursula rested one hand on her belly as the baby inside her kicked. With Susie curled up on her lap, Ursula pulled her hand free of Jake's and slid it around his neck, looking long at his kind eyes. "And I don't want to be alone.

Not anymore. Right now, when we are facing some sad news, I've never in my life been so grateful to not be alone."

"This makes me think of all the stories you've told us of Ma and Pa. Now would be a good time to hear more, Ursula." Ilsa never tired of stories.

Talking about their parents had awakened old forgotten memories. An incident Ursula remembered jumped into her mind. She had opened her mouth to tell another tale when more riders drew her attention.

"Mitch is back." Ilsa turned to watch him ride up with three strangers.

Ursula, always a bit nervous around strangers, rose to her feet, and trying to move casually, she stepped just slightly behind Jake. He knew her so well. He slid his arm across her back and drew her up beside him. He'd never allowed her to be less than his equal in anything and that must include greeting strangers.

When the newcomers, an older couple around Ma and Pa Warden's age, and a younger woman, still a good number of years older than Ursula, reached them, they dismounted. The first thing that struck Ursula was the older woman leading the way. Her dark hair was streaked with gray. And she had lines on her face from a long life. But what she noticed was, the older woman looked so much like Ilsa it was impossible to pretend otherwise.

The younger woman had such a strong resemblance, the older woman must be her mother.

The older woman studied Ilsa, walked near to her as Mitch came to Ilsa's side. With eyes full of pain and love, she faced Ilsa.

The older man and younger woman looked at Ilsa, then at Jo, finally at Ursula.

The older woman said, "The folks in Bucksnort told us how to get to the Warden ranch. Mr. Warden went for Mitch. We found you when Pinkerton agents came to our home and told us they'd been searching for us for years."

Three years. Ursula knew Mitch had been searching. She also was sure their arrival was as much a surprise to Mitch as it was to the rest of them. They must have talked with the Pinkerton agents and set out for Hope Mountain without writing ahead or even sending a telegram. Though how would Mitch know he'd gotten a telegram or a letter until the next time he rode to town?

"Mitch spent the ride up the mountain telling us about the three Nordegren sisters. The daughters of Susan Nordegren. My daughter, Susan Domanski Nordegren."

She reached a trembling hand toward Ilsa. "You're the very image of my daughter. I'm your grandma Domanski. My daughter vanished so long ago. I knew she had children because she wrote to me a few times after she married. But I had no idea where to find you. I . . . I—" Her voice broke.

Ilsa gave Mitch an uncertain look, then, at his encouraging nod, Ilsa drew the woman into her arms.

Anger swept through Ursula to think these people had been out there all this time. Of course, they had *two* grandmothers. How had they grown up, all alone, without even thinking of their mother's family?

But Ursula knew how. Grandma had never said a word about any family off this mountain. Grandpa had taught them to survive up here alone. He had to have known their ma had family, and yet, as he aged and his health failed, he'd never once spoken of them as someone the girls could go to if they needed help. And all because those people lived in the dreaded lowlands.

The older man came up beside Ursula. "I'm your grandfather." He turned to the woman with him. "And this is your aunt Annie."

Annie took Ursula's hand. Her eyes filled, but she breathed deeply, and the tears didn't fall. Through the brimming eyes, Annie smiled. "There are more of us. I have another sister and two brothers. We have, between us, twelve children, and a herd of beautiful grandchildren." She looked at Ursula's little one. "And is this your daughter? What's her name?"

It was hard to speak, and that had nothing to do with being afraid of strangers. Ursula's throat was tight with unshed tears. "Her name is Susan. For my mother. We call her Susie."

A single tear escaped and ran down Aunt Annie's cheek, then a second. But it didn't stop a smile so bright Ursula blinked as if she were staring into the sun.

Grandpa had gone to Jo. Each one of them had someone. And it sounded like there were plenty more.

Ursula asked, "Where do you live?"

Grandpa turned, holding on to Jo. "California. It's a fair distance on horseback but only a few days by train. Years ago, we were passing through the area on a wagon train when Susan met your father. He was smitten, well, they both were, and he convinced her to marry him.

"We were a few years hearing from Susan. We didn't know where your pa really lived, though he spoke of living nearby where he'd met the wagon train.

"But Susan knew where we planned to settle. A few letters were exchanged for a time, but it was too far to come for a visit. We didn't even consider that anything had happened to them for a long time. Letters are undependable. We tried to find her, but we couldn't track down anyone who'd tell us a thing. We knew you were with your grandparents, but we didn't know you lived on this mountain. Susan had tried to tell us where it was but . . ." He shook his head helplessly. "We should have come. We should have found a way."

Grandma let go of Ilsa. "We can talk forever. We want to know you all. You girls, your husbands, and children. Mitch has told us a lot. But there's so much more."

"I love hearing stories of my parents," Ilsa said. "I was around a year old when they left, and we never knew what became of them."

Until today.

So much to talk about. Grief to share. Stories and memories. Ursula felt a song rise to her lips, but she held it inside. Since she'd married Jake, she'd realized her music had largely come out of her loneliness. She still loved to sing. She'd even, at Jake's urging, written a few of the songs down that came over her.

And maybe she'd sing for her grandparents sometime.

But for right now, she was too busy talking. She leaned on Jake's strong shoulder and kept the secret song in her heart.

But it rang through her thoughts. A song about faith and love and finding a family for three girls who'd grown up wild and lonely until they'd become brides on Hope Mountain.

About the Author

Mary Connealy writes romantic comedies about cowboys. She's the author of the HIGH SIERRA SWEETHEARTS, KINCAID BRIDES, TROUBLE IN TEXAS, WILD AT HEART, and CIMARRON LEGACY series, as well as several other acclaimed series. Mary has been nominated for a Christy Award, was a finalist for a RITA Award, and is a two-time winner of the Carol Award. She lives on a ranch in eastern Nebraska with her very own romantic cowboy hero. They have four grown daughters—Joslyn, married to Matt; Wendy; Shelly, married to Aaron; and Katy, married to Max—and six precious grandchildren. Learn more about Mary and her books at:

maryconnealy.com
facebook.com/maryconnealy
seekerville.blogspot.com
petticoatsandpistols.com

Sign Up for Mary's Newsletter

Keep up to date with Mary's latest news on book releases and events by signing up for her email list at maryconnealy.com.

More from Mary Connealy

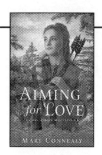

Growing up in Colorado, Josephine Nordegren has been fascinated by, but has shied away from, the outside world—one she's been raised to believe killed her parents. When Dave Warden, a rancher, shows up at their secret home with his wounded father, will Josephine and her sisters risk stepping into the world to help, or remain separated but safe on Hope Mountain?

Aiming for Love
BRIDES OF HOPE MOUNTAIN #1

You May Also Like . . .

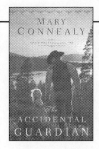

Trace Riley has been self-appointed guardian of the trail ever since his own wagon was attacked. When he finds the ruins of a wagon train, he offers shelter to survivor Deborah Harkness and the children she saved. Trace and Deborah grow close working to bring justice to the trail, but what will happen when the attackers return to silence the only witness?

The Accidental Guardian by Mary Connealy
High Sierra Sweethearts #1
maryconnealy.com

Gabriella Goodhue had put her past as a thief behind her, until a woman in her boardinghouse is unjustly accused and she is caught gathering evidence by Nicholas Quinn, a fellow street urchin against whom she holds a grudge. Nicholas refuses to lose her twice and insists they join forces—but their feelings are tested when danger follows their every step.

To Steal a Heart by Jen Turano
The Bleecker Street Inquiry Agency
jenturano.com

Haunted by painful memories, Olivia Rosetti is singularly focused on running her maternity home for troubled women. Darius Reed is determined to protect his daughter from the prejudice that killed his wife by marrying a society darling. But when he's suddenly drawn to Olivia, they will learn if love can prove stronger than the secrets and hurts of the past.

A Haven for Her Heart by Susan Anne Mason
Redemption's Light #1
susanannemason.net

◈ BethanyHouse

More from Bethany House

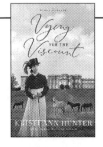

When a strange man appears to be stealing horses at the neighboring estate, Bianca Snowley jumps to their rescue. And when she discovers he's the new owner, she can't help but be intrigued—but romance is unfeasible when he proposes they help secure spouses for each other. Will they see everything they've wanted has been there all along before it's too late?

Vying for the Viscount by Kristi Ann Hunter
HEARTS ON THE HEATH
kristiannhunter.com

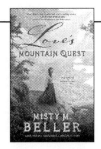

After her son goes missing, Joanna Watson enlists Isaac Bowen—a man she prays has enough experience in the rugged country—to help. As they press on against the elements, they find encouragement in the tentative trust that grows between them, but whether it can withstand the danger and coming confrontation is far from certain in this wild, unpredictable land.

Love's Mountain Quest by Misty M. Beller
HEARTS OF MONTANA #2
mistymbeller.com

Ex-cavalry officer Matthew Hanger leads a band of mercenaries who defend the innocent, but when a rustler's bullet leaves one of them at death's door, they seek out help from Dr. Josephine Burkett. When Josephine's brother is abducted and she is caught in the crossfire, Matthew may have to sacrifice everything—even his team—to save her.

At Love's Command by Karen Witemeyer
HANGER'S HORSEMEN #1
karenwitemeyer.com

◊ BETHANYHOUSE